"I dream of a man who sweeps me away with his passion."

Amelia gazed deeply into Crispin's eyes. "No, Cris, being comfortable is not enough for me."

Crispin pushed to his feet, looking down at Amelia. "Yes Amie, we've both seen passionate love, but was it really so great? Your father willed himself to death . . . he forgot all but the loss of his love. My parents were so engrossed in each other that they ignored me, their only child. If that is love, I'll pass." He sighed, exasperation laced in the sound. "We could have something so much better, Amie. It could be solid, sure, not a seething mass of intense feelings."

Amelia held still, melting beneath the heat of his expression. Here was the man she'd always dreamed of. Gently, softly, he shaped his lips to hers, learning the texture, brushing against the edges. Her lips parted beneath the light touches and she offered all to him. . . .

ENCHANTED

Acclaim for *Portrait of Dreams*

"Victoria Malvey's *Portrait of Dreams* [is] a sensually sweet tale of love found and fought for. The spark that makes a book a bestseller is present on every page of this beautiful story. FIVE STARS."

—*Affaire de Coeur*

Books by Victoria Malvey

Portrait of Dreams
Enchanted

VICTORIA MALVEY

Enchanted

SONNET BOOKS
New York London Toronto Sydney Tokyo Singapore

An *Original* Publication of POCKET BOOKS

A Sonnet Book published by
POCKET BOOKS, a division of Simon & Schuster Inc.
1230 Avenue of the Americas, New York, NY 10020

ISBN: 0-671-02071-4

First Sonnet Books printing March 1999

10 9 8 7 6 5 4 3 2 1

Cover art by Sandra Kaplan

Printed in the U.S.A.

To my beautiful, vibrant niece,
Lindsey Brett Conover

This one is for you—

For all the smiles you gave to me;
For all the times you let me "play mother" to a girl,
brushing your hair and talking about boys;
For all the love you shared so readily;
For all the times you listened to my stories over and over again; and
For the way you lived your life, enjoying it to the fullest.

We all miss you so very much, Linds.

I know that right now you're up in Heaven
pairing angels into great couples,
playing with all the children who were taken too soon,
and showing everyone how very easy it is to be happy.

I love you, angel.

Aunt Vicky

Lindsey Brett Conover
April 14, 1979–March 22, 1998

[illegible]

[illegible]

[illegible]

[illegible]

Daniel [illegible]

Special thanks to Amy Pierpont,
my incredible editor,
for all your encouragement,
your generosity with your time and energy,
and, most of all, for your patience.

You're the best, Amy!

Prologue

Dovedale, England
August 1822

The soft rustling in the trees made Crispin pause. He squinted against the brilliant afternoon sun as he looked up into the branches. "Amie? Are you up there?"

"Come forth, bold knight, and rescue the fair maiden from her peril," a young voice called out.

A huge grin split Crispin's face. "Fair maiden? Surely you aren't referring to yourself, Amelia?"

Her squeak of protest brought a laugh from him. "And just what do you mean by that, my high and mighty Marquess of Tamerly?"

He caught a glimpse of Amelia perched delicately upon a tree limb far above him. His brows drew downward, concern washing away the smile. "You are up far too high, Amie. Climb down now."

Her sigh was loud and dramatic. "From heroic knight to old grump. How is a girl ever supposed to keep up with your abrupt moods?"

His scowl deepened. "I'm not finding this amusing, Amelia. Come down from there at once before you fall and hurt yourself."

"I'm not sure if you are aware of this or not, Cris, but you really are *not* my brother."

"If I were, perhaps you'd listen to me." He took a step closer to the tree. "Now come down before I am forced to climb up and get you."

"You're only my neighbor," she protested again.

"Having put up with your antics for the past few years gives me the right to protect you from yourself."

Amelia couldn't hold back a smile as she gazed down upon Cris's ferocious frown. For some reason she couldn't quite understand, whenever he scolded her and looked so upset with her, it made her feel cared for, loved. His concern was far preferable to the distant, unaware looks she earned from her father.

"Amelia," Cris said warningly. "If I have to fetch you, I will not be happy about it."

"And just what will you do?" she challenged, enjoying their game.

"Paddle you good and well."

"Ha!" she returned. "You have never laid a hand on me."

"Today is the day I'm going to start," he promised.

"I don't believe you." Amelia swung a stocking-encased leg as she awaited his response.

Cris's low mutterings amused her. Her giggles died quickly enough when he called out, "Fine then, Amelia. I will inform my aunt of your transgression."

The smug tone of his voice was well placed for the threat was more effective than any other he could have devised. Since the death of her mother six years ago, Amelia had begun to spend a good deal of time with Cris's Aunt Patricia.

"You wouldn't," Amelia said, trying to sound more assured than she felt.

"I most certainly would," Cris retorted, rocking back on his heels. "And she would undoubtedly give you one of her sighs and a sound lecture on your behavior."

"So?" Yet, even as Amelia responded, she shifted upon the limb.

The corners of Cris's mouth tilted upward. "You know as well as I that you hate to have Aunt Patricia unhappy with you. Why, you never so much as make an improper comment in front of her."

"And what is so wrong with that? I happen to love Aunt Patricia a great deal."

"I know that, Amie," said Cris, his tone gentled, "which is precisely why you will climb down from there before I am forced to involve her."

Amelia shook her head, knowing that she was caught by her own emotions. Even a glance of mild disapproval from Cris's aunt was more than she cared to experience. Nothing mattered more than earning Aunt Patricia's respect. Well, perhaps her friendship with Cris ranked up there too. Oh, and then there were her four younger sisters. And her—

Amelia broke off her thoughts when Cris shouted his final threat.

"So be it, Amelia. I'll be sure to escort you directly to my home as soon as I drag you from this tree." Cris reached for the branches nearest to him.

"Don't climb up," Amelia called out, quickly shifting from her comfortable spot on the branch, gathering her skirts in one hand. "I'm coming down now."

With her movement, Cris settled back on his heels. Amelia could feel his gaze upon her as she made her way down.

By the time she reached the ground, she had forgotten about his threat. "Did you come to find me?"

Cris nodded, his ill humor gone just as quickly. "I stopped by Ralston Hall and Mrs. Burke told me you were wandering about the woods like the little hoyden you are."

"She did not say that!" Amelia protested, her hands fisting on her hips. Mrs. Burke had been her family's housekeeper since Amelia was an infant and certainly loved her far too much to call her a hoyden!

"No," he agreed, his tone cheerful. "I added the last bit."

"How nice of you," Amelia said dryly.

Cris nodded once. "I know. I'm sure Mrs. Burke would have said it if she'd been less polite."

"You tease me horribly." The smile in her voice softened the accusation.

"True," Cris admitted without hesitation. "But you deserve every bit of it."

"Did you come to play?" Her expression brightened.

Cris smiled down at her, reaching out to tug on one of her loosened braids. "I shall miss you following me around, Amie."

Affronted, Amelia drew herself up. "I don't follow you at all. We're friends . . . aren't we?" She didn't like how her voice wavered on the question.

"Of course," he reassured her, "even if I am older and wiser, I've enjoyed knocking about with you."

"You taught me to ride," she reminded him, ignoring his jibe.

"So I did."

"And you showed me the falls here in Dovedale."

"That too," Cris agreed. "We've been stuck here in the country with each other for quite a while, Amie."

"I haven't minded," she returned fiercely.

"Neither have I. Living so close to each other, how could we have been anything but the best of friends?"

Warmth radiated within her at his acknowledgment. "Would you like to go riding?"

"I'm afraid I don't have time. I'm about ready to head off."

"Must you really go away to school? Why can't you keep Mr. Franks as your tutor?"

Cris reached up and plucked out a twig that was caught in her braids. "It's time, Amie. If my aunt hadn't insisted I remain here in Dovedale I would have long since headed off for Eton."

She stayed still beneath his ministrations, comfortable with his care. "Who will I spend time with when you're gone?"

"You will still have your sisters and my aunt, Amie. I'm the only one going away," Cris replied softly.

Amelia faced him again, pulling her tangled braid over one shoulder. "But . . . but . . . my sisters are so much work." As soon as she said it, she felt guilty. "I mean, they are still so young and they look up to me to give them love and comfort and—"

"Hush, Amie, I understand," Cris interrupted, grasping her by the shoulders.

"It's different with you, Cris. I don't have to worry about doing the right thing or watching out for your safety. I can just be me."

"I know, I know," he murmured, enfolding her close, hugging her into him.

Amelia snuggled inward, wrapping her arms around the friend she secretly thought of as her own storybook hero. How often had Cris held her like this, offering her a safe haven from the sadness of her own home? After her mother's death, her father had begun to withdraw, leaving her feeling as if she'd lost both parents. Then Cris and his aunt had come to pay their condolences.

She'd never forget the night Cris had come upon her as she sat crying for her mother. He'd soon enticed her from her curled-up position beneath the stairs. The silly imaginings of an eleven-year-old boy had pulled her from her overwhelming grief, making her see a glimpse of hope for the future. Over the years, he and his aunt had come to be more than neighbors and Cris was more than her friend. He was everything—her savior, her hero, her knight in shining armor.

And now he, too, was leaving her.

"When will you be back?"

Cris stiffened. The action made Amelia grow cold. She couldn't bear to lose Cris too.

"The thing is, Amie, I'm not quite sure," he replied, his voice gentle. "My parents have suddenly decided to take a break from their travels. It seems they've remembered I exist. They have informed me that during breaks from school, they will introduce me to London society." A rush of harsh laughter rumbled through him. "I suppose at ten and seven, they've decided I'm not too much of a bother, and they can finally bear to have me around."

Amelia didn't know how to ease the pain she heard in Cris's words, so she simply hugged him tighter.

It seemed to work for, when he began to speak again, his tone was lighter. "In any case, I shall probably remain in town during my breaks."

"And what of Aunt Patricia? What shall she do without you?" She knew Cris and his aunt were more like mother and son, than aunt and nephew.

"She has said she will travel to London to spend time with me there." Cris looked down at Amelia.

"I know she'll be lonely when I'm gone, so it comforts me to know you'll be here for her."

"You know I love her," Amelia said, nodding.

"I count on that." Cris took a step backward, bending down to gaze into her face, his blue eyes serious. "You can write to me and I'll write back."

She wiped at the stray tear running down her cheek. "Promise?" Amelia couldn't help the wobble in her voice.

"Promise." He gave her a tender smile.

When Cris straightened, Amelia tipped her head back to look at him, the sunlight glistening on his dark hair. At this angle, he seemed so grownup, so different, but inside he was still her noble, sweet friend. The smile on his face told her so.

Reassured, Amelia leaned up to press a kiss on his cheek. "Don't forget me."

His smile shifted into a grin. "Now how could I forget the little fairy who followed me around for the past six years?"

"Will you stop saying that? I haven't followed you around; you've been following *me* around," Amelia protested, her hands fisting on her hips once more.

Cris's laughter filled the woods. He reached out and tugged on her long braid again. "I'll truly miss you, Amie."

And with one last smile, he turned and walked away, his stride sure and true, his bearing grand and certain. Worthy of any fairy-tale hero. Her own personal knight. She knew she was being fanciful and that he would never do battle for her, but there was something reassuring in the thought anyway.

Yes, she knew it was silly to picture Cris as the conqueror of her fears. How could he possibly fight them? After all, her nightmares weren't of monsters and demons but of being alone and unloved. She would still have her sisters and Aunt Patricia, but none of them made her feel as secure, as loved, as Cris did. Somehow only Cris made her feel less afraid. It was as if he could look into her heart, see her darkest fears, and shed light upon them, vanquishing her terror with a few words of encouragement and a teasing smile. Now he was leaving her to fight the nightmares alone.

Amelia watched Cris until he was gone from sight, then she wrapped up all her special memories of him and tucked them into her heart.

1

London, England
July, 1827

Cris stood on the edge of the dance floor and stifled a yawn. After five years in town, the sights that had once awed him merely left him bored.

"Care to join me in cards?"

Cris Merrick turned to see Owen Chambers, Earl of Newbury, standing a step behind him. He'd met Newbury a few times at Oxford and found him to be a likable fellow. Still, the thought of staying any longer at this dull party was more than Cris could bear. "No thank you," Cris declined with a shake of his head. "I appreciate the offer, but I'm about to head off to White's."

"Understandable," Owen murmured. "These affairs get a bit tedious after a while." He tilted his head toward the dance floor. "Do you see the lovely Miss Lockley there with Lord Nowell?"

Cris saw the beauty spinning around the floor. "She's quite attractive," he acknowledged.

"And also quite ambitious. Make no mistake

about it, my dear marquess, that sweet thing is in pursuit of a title."

Cris lifted an eyebrow. "Which one of these beauties being paraded before us isn't?"

Owen laughed over the remark, nudging Cris in the side. "For truth, Merrick. So many of these young dandies see all these bits of beautiful flotsam floating around the balls, that they don't bother to look beneath the surface at a one of them."

Cris looked at Owen with a growing sense of respect. The earl was echoing the sentiments Cris himself often felt. "Do you see Lady Havershill over by the refreshments?"

Owen nodded.

Cris leaned closer. "Last season she tried to convince me she was desperately in love with me and couldn't bear to contemplate marriage to anyone else." His lips twitched. "Of course, she was Miss Pensham then. Since her wedding took place a few weeks after her declaration, I can only assume she overcame her devotion with admirable swiftness."

"Quite amazing how that works, isn't it?" Amusement danced in Owen's blue eyes. "Even more interesting is that earlier this evening, the lady in question approached me, intimating that she would not be adverse to seek a relationship with me that was of an intimate nature."

Cris felt his gut tighten, "That poor sot, Havershill. So, it would appear, sadly enough, that even her husband cannot hold her interest."

"Don't feel sorry for that old bastard," Owen said

with a shrug. "He's playing pansy with Lady Daveran."

Cris struggled to keep his expression blank. Disgust for the entire matter roiled inside of him. Instead, he said lightly, "It appears to be the newest rage."

"What does? Tasting the flowers?" Owen laughed. "It's hardly new, Merrick. Trust me, I know. My parents were experts at it. If my sister and I didn't look nearly identical, I would swear she had a different sire. By the time of her birth, my dear parents were exploring other interests." Owen brushed back a lock of his blond hair. "Of course, everyone knows that your parents are different, utterly devoted to one another."

"Hmmm." Cris pushed away the swirl of contempt caused by Owen's innocent words. Utterly devoted to one another. That described them perfectly, Cris realized. When he'd first arrived in London, he'd tried to fit into their world, to find a place for himself in their already happy home. Thank God, he'd long since grown out of that naive pursuit. Instead, he now enjoyed the social status afforded him by his rank and wealth. And if the sheen of excitement seemed a little less bright, it was merely because he needed a change of pace. The season would be over in a month, and he was planning on heading up to Scotland for some grouse hunting. Undoubtedly, all he needed was a change of scenery.

"Merrick? Are you still with me?"

Owen's question snapped Cris from his thoughts. "Sorry. I was wool-gathering for a moment."

"So glad to know you find me such a fascinating conversationalist," Owen returned, the humor in his voice softening the statement. "And here I thought I was being absolutely brilliant by pointing out that there seems to be only two choices with marriage."

Again Cris apologized. "Please continue, Owen. To what two choices are you referring?"

"You can either marry with the intention of wandering afterward, which seems perfectly acceptable to me as long as both parties are in agreement, or you can wed the lady of your heart, remaining true to her throughout time."

Cris shook his head. "The first is distasteful and the second too confining. You forgot one option, Chambers."

"That would be?"

One side of Cris's mouth tilted upward. "Why, to never marry at all."

"I didn't forget that option, Merrick, because it isn't one." Owen put his hands on his hips, pushing back his coat. "You know as well as I that with the title comes the responsibility to beget an heir. Remaining a bachelor is *not* an option for either one of us, I'm afraid."

Cris frowned at the realization that Owen was quite correct. Eventually he would have to marry. "Very well, Chambers. When it is time for me to marry, I shall look for someone who is undemanding, unassuming, and unquestioning in her loyalty to me."

"Lofty expectations. What man wouldn't want the perfect shadow of a wife? Unfortunately, my friend, it will be difficult for you to find such a paragon. Most women are unwilling to be so, shall we say, pliable?" Owen replied.

"Perhaps, but I'll find her." Cris looked around the ballroom, seeing far too easily beneath the veneer of the smiling ladies. "I will indeed."

Owen clasped a hand upon Cris's shoulder. "Then I wish you luck in your quest."

"There's no need to make it sound as if I'm about to embark upon an impossible search," Cris said, shifting away from Owen. "Besides, I'm in no rush." A grin split his face. "Simply because I have no wish to marry one of these doves doesn't mean I don't wish to play with them a bit."

Owen tossed back his head, exploding with laughter, garnering glances from the couples nearby. "Ah, Merrick," Owen wheezed finally, wiping at his eyes, "I feel as if I've found a kindred spirit."

Cris nodded in agreement, before offering, "I'm off to White's now. Would you care to join me?"

Owen accepted readily, glancing toward the main entranceway. "Our indomitable hostess, Lady Hammond, is guarding the exit. I can only assume she had no desire to let anyone escape before it is fashionable. Otherwise people might speculate on the entire affair being a bore."

Cris knew this too was another game played by

the members of the ton. Gossip spread through polite society with speed and ferocity. After all, what better way to dispel your own failing than to point out someone else's? He shook his head. "Why don't we head through the gardens. There should be a door in the rear wall through which we can make our escape."

"By Gads, Merrick. My admiration for you continues to grow." He swept out his hand. "You make your way out first, my clever marquess, and I'll follow in a few minutes."

"Fine, though I don't believe your delay is necessary. I doubt if anyone will even notice our departure."

"True, but I prefer not to take the chance of getting caught. Lord, if we were, we might have to stay even longer," Owen finished with a mock shiver.

Cris nodded in agreement, before he began to weave through the throng of people, exiting into the garden. A few couples strolled along the terrace as Cris headed down the steps onto the stone path leading toward the rear of the garden. The strains of the music followed him even as he stepped into the darkness of the night.

"Bloody damn dark out here," Cris murmured to himself, looking at the unlit torches lining the path.

The sounds of the party faded as Cris wound his way through the garden. Suddenly, a muffled scream ripped through the night air, bringing Cris to a halt. The cry cut off abruptly, only to be followed by scuffling noises. Cris peered into the darkness and was able to make out three figures holding a lady in a flowing, white gown.

"What's going on there?" he called out, hurrying toward the group.

"Stand back," one of the men called out. "This is not your concern."

"Damn if it's not!" Cris moved closer. He could almost feel the woman's fear and smell her desperate sense of faint hope. "Unhand the lady."

The man shifted in front of the girl, blocking her with his body. "This is a matter between gentlemen," he said in a gruff voice. "Leave us to our business."

"And leave that poor girl at your mercy?" Cris asked, fury bursting to life within him. Despite the fact that he was woefully outnumbered, he could not abandon the poor lady to the fate that awaited her at the hands of these so-called gentlemen. "Unhand her," Cris ground out again.

The bushes rustled, signaling someone's approach.

Cris could see the leader of the trio straighten to alertness.

"Someone's coming," whispered one of the men.

"Indeed." Frustration resonated in the leader's voice. "Let's be off."

With that bidding, the two men released their hold on their victim, and she shrank away from them, cowering against the door in the garden wall.

With muffled curses, two of the men turned and ran into the thick brush of the garden. The leader paused, pointing a finger at Cris. "You will regret your actions this evening," he rasped. "You have my word . . . as a gentleman." Then he too faded into the darkness.

The lady buried her face in her hands. "Don't touch me," she cried. "Please leave me alone."

Cris felt helpless to calm the terrified woman. Still, he had to try. "Shhh," he murmured. "I won't hurt you."

"There you are, Merrick." Owen walked into view. "It's so bloody dark out here that I lost my way for a moment. I say, what is going on here?"

Cris kept his attention focused on the weeping girl. "I came upon three men accosting this poor girl."

Owen stepped closer. "Samantha?" he asked, his tone incredulous.

"Owen?" the girl asked, her voice wavering. "Oh Owen, I was so frightened! The men grabbed me and they—" Cris was stunned when she launched herself into his companion's arms with a final wrenching sob.

Cris looked at the pair as the girl sobbed uncontrollably within Owen's tight embrace. "You know this girl?"

Even the darkness could not hide the fierce light of anger burning in Owen's gaze as he lifted his head to look at Cris. "This is Samantha, my cousin." The words scraped from him, raw and filled with pain. "I don't know what happened here, but I'm going to find out."

Samanatha lifted her head, fear etched across her

features. "No, Owen. Please, no. I couldn't bear if anything happened to you."

Owen smoothed his hands down Samantha's back. "Nothing is going to happen to me. I just want to find out who did this to you."

She shook her head. "But you might be hurt trying to find out, Owen. These men are monsters, I tell you. I came out to the garden to look for you . . . I thought you might be out here getting some air. I had no idea that there were men lurking out here . . . just waiting to—" Her voice broke on the last word, sobs overtaking her body once more.

"Oh, Samantha," Owen murmured, gathering her close.

Cris glanced around, all too aware of the darkness surrounding them. He didn't think the three men had left the garden. It seemed as though he could feel the gaze of Samantha's attackers upon him. "Let's be gone from here. My carriage is around front. I shall drop you off at your town house if you'd like."

Owen nodded. "Most appreciated."

The trio left together, hurrying out toward the security of the crowded street.

Owen tossed back his brandy and poured himself another. Cris settled into his chair, waiting until his new friend calmed himself. "Are you certain your cousin is all right?"

Owen slammed his hand down upon the sideboard. "No thanks to me," he ground out. "Those bastards almost got her."

Cris leaned forward, resting his elbows upon the arms of his chair. "What bastards? What's going on, Chambers?"

Owen's gaze narrowed on him, but Cris held steady beneath it. "Can you keep a confidence?"

"Most certainly."

Owen paused again, before finally nodding. He took the seat facing Cris. "Samantha came to live with me last year. Her father, Baron Wickham, had passed away and she had no other relatives. She's not been a bother; she is a delightful girl and a pleasure to have in my home." Owen brushed away his rambling thoughts. "A few weeks ago, my cousin told me that she felt as if someone was always watching her. She said that she had even been followed home from the modiste's. At first I scoffed it off, thinking it was merely Samantha's fanciful imaginings." A bitter sound broke from Owen. "How wrong I was. Last week, I came home early from my club one night. I wasn't quite ready to head inside, so I decided to take a stroll around the grounds. No sooner did I open the gate than I saw three men, dressed all in black with hoods, climbing over the top of my wall. At my shout, they dropped back over to the other side. By the time I got out to the street, they were gone."

Cris frowned as he tried to piece everything together. "What I don't understand is why they didn't rush you. Or why they didn't come at me tonight. It was three against one. Yet, they didn't even try to overtake us."

"I don't know. Perhaps they were startled."

Owen shrugged. "It really doesn't matter. All that concerns me is that these monsters have targeted my cousin for some reason. But even I didn't guess to what lengths they would go to capture her. It stunned me to find Samantha had been in their clutches this evening. I thought she was at a different ball with my friends, the Earl and Countess of Rawth, as escort. Ever since the incident at our home, I'd made sure Samantha didn't leave the house unescorted."

"Then how did she find herself at the Hammonds's?"

Owen thrust to his feet, pushing his hands into his pockets. "She decided to meet me at the Hammonds's affair. Her escort left her in the care of our hostess, but since Lady Hammond wouldn't leave her post by the entryway, Samantha was free to roam. She searched for me, but apparently couldn't find me in the crush. She was looking for me in the garden when she was grabbed from behind and dragged out into the bushes."

"So, the men must have been following her," Cris concluded. "Why?"

"How the devil do I know!" Owen exploded. "If I knew that, don't you think I'd have stopped them? She's been engaged to Lord Whitten all Season and is due to marry him in one week's time, so it's not as if she'd have a thwarted suitor. I can't imagine who would come after Samantha this way."

"Are you going to hire a Bow Street Runner to investigate the matter?"

Owen began to pace in front of the fireplace. "I want to, by damn, but Samantha won't hear of it. She's worried that word will leak that she was accosted, and she knows all too well how the truth can be twisted."

"If Whitten hears of it from the gossips, he'll be enraged." Cris rose, moving to pour himself a brandy. "Are you going to tell him?"

"Again, Samantha is tying me up on this one. She begged me not to tell him or to look into the matter further. No one heard or saw what happened this evening. Since we left through the garden, she believes, and rightfully so, that everyone will assume she left with us after meeting in the garden. I doubt if anyone at that party will think otherwise. Samantha doesn't wish to begin her marriage with the threat of Whitten believing the worst."

Cris lifted both of his brows. "Instead, she would prefer to start it with a lie."

Owen squirmed beneath Cris's gaze. "I know, I know, but I can't convince her otherwise."

Cris took a sip of his brandy. "Then I pray for everyone's sake that this is the end of it."

"As do I," Owen whispered fervently. "As do I."

"We nearly had her that time." The man said as he tossed his mask on a nearby table. "Right, Alonso, old man?"

"Yet, truly, Prospero, what would we have done with her if we had gotten a hold of her?" Alonso asked as he placed his mask on top of the other one. "It's not as if we've ever done this before."

"True, but hasn't it been a thrill?" the third man asked.

Prospero grinned at the suggestion. "Yes, Sebastian, it has been quite entertaining."

Alonso poured himself a drink. "I wish we'd captured our *Tempest*."

"As do we all," Prospero added. "However, she escaped our grasp once more."

"When do we try again?" asked Sebastian eagerly.

"We don't," Prospero sighed.

"Why the devil not?" asked Antonio before taking a sip of his brandy.

"She is to be wed."

Prospero's statement merely brought confusion to the other men's faces.

"What has that to do with anything?" Alonso frowned at Prospero. "Samantha is a fine choice. I want her."

"As do I," added Sebastian.

Prospero held up both of his hands. "She is to be wed next week; as Whitten's wife, she is no longer an eligible candidate for our little game."

"And why the devil not?" Alonso took a seat next to Sebastian. "What difference does her marriage make?"

"Need I remind you that we are gentlemen," Prospero chided them. "We do not poach on another man's property. I am afraid we will simply need to choose another quarry."

Sebastian sat back in his chair. "I'm still not clear

on all of this, Prospero. I know that this club of ours is the most exciting endeavor I've undertaken in years, but I'm beginning to have a few doubts about our actions." He shifted in his seat. "By following Samantha and trying to spirit her away, we've broken laws, both morally and legally."

Prospero reached out, grabbing Sebastian by the arm. "And hasn't it been marvelous. When did you last feel this alive, this invigorated? We are peers of the realm, Alonso. Do not forget that. Ever." His fingers dug in tighter. "We do not infringe on the rights of another gentleman, nor do we break any code between peers, which is precisely why we left as soon as Chambers saw us that first night. If we had fought him, it would have been against the laws of the peerage. However, we do nothing wrong in amusing ourselves with a pretty like Samantha. She is merely the daughter of a baron, therefore not of rank or consequence. Our needs override hers without question. After all, it is not only our *right*, but our *duty* to pursue our happiness."

Alonso nodded in agreement and Sebastian fell silent, shifting his arm from beneath Prospero's clasp.

"However, this evening, Merrick broke those codes. He failed to respect our rights, thus forfeiting his own." Prospero leaned back in his chair. "In fact, I do believe Merrick should be punished for his actions this evening."

"Punished?" Alonso asked, frowning. "What do you mean?"

Prospero stroked his chin. "I believe it our duty to let all the members of polite society know of his lack of respect for our rules."

"What are you proposing to do?" Sebastian's voice deepened, wariness coloring the tone.

"I propose, my dear Sebastian, that we begin to drop hints as to Merrick's despicable reputation."

"But his reputation is flawless," protested Alonso. "He's known to enjoy the ladies, but that is hardly considered a fault."

"Who mentioned anything about the rumors needing to be true?" A smile played upon Prospero's lips. "The ton is always eager to believe any savory tidbit tossed their way. If we merely make vague aspersions in the right ears, everyone will soon be whispering about Merrick's disreputable behavior."

"And soon everyone will begin to believe the rumors," concluded Alonso, slapping his knee. "By Gads, Prospero, you're brilliant!"

"At times," Prospero agreed. "Merrick should prove an interesting player in our little games, don't you think?"

Sebastian shook his head. "I don't know if we should get involved with Merrick."

"Don't be an old abigail," Prospero chided, waving a hand in dismissal. "He deserves a, shall we say, chastisement for his lack of respect."

"I'm still a bit uncomfortable about the whole idea," Sebastian said, crossing his arms.

"I assure you; there is no need to worry. In fact, I'm quite confident that you'll learn to enjoy the game." Prospero placed both hands on the arms of his chair. "So, now we need to vote on our next ladybird."

"Ladybird?" asked Sebastian, his voice loud with astonishment. "You just said we would torment Merrick for a bit."

"As we shall," agreed Prospero, grinning widely. "But why should we limit our game? Why not expand upon it, as it's already proved vastly entertaining?"

"Oh, I agree," exclaimed Alonso, the gleam in his eyes downright lascivious. "I've very much enjoyed chasing the lovely Samantha." He paused for a moment. "I admit, though, that I'm still somewhat confused. Exactly what *are* we going to do with her once we capture her?"

Slowly, a smile curled onto Prospero's mouth in deadly intent. "I'm not quite certain, my fellow Shakespearean members." His hands curled around the arms of his chair. "But we are at our leisure to decide. In the words of our dear William Shakespeare, *"Time be thine, and thy best graces spend it at thy will."*

2

Dovedale, England
June 1832

"Good heavens, Amelia. Are you still climbing trees?"

Amelia almost fell off the branch at the sound of Cris's voice, long since heard, but never forgotten. "Cris!" she shouted, hiking up her long skirt and winding her way down the tree. Her heart raced as she landed upon the ground. Cris stood next to a man Amelia didn't recognize, and promptly dismissed, having eyes only for her dear friend.

She launched herself into Cris's arms. "You're back."

"I've missed you, Amie," Cris said, embracing her.

Her heart sang at his words. Oh, how she'd waited for this day to come. For Cris to return to her, pull her into his arms, whisper how he'd missed her, how he noticed she'd grown up, that he'd waited for her, that he'd come back to make her his own. She snuggled closer, waiting for him to acknowledge all the changes in her.

"And you haven't changed a bit."

If her mouth hadn't been pressed against his shoulder, it would have surely dropped open. Shocked, she pulled back, leaning against his arms. "Of course I have, Cris. I've grown up."

His smile was tender. "You're still a little bit of a thing."

At nearly five feet seven inches, she was hardly petite. "I'm not," she protested briskly.

"You must be all of, what now, seventeen, eighteen?"

She pulled away from him. "I'm twenty-two," she announced, annoyed that he'd forgotten so much about her when she'd remembered everything about him. "A lady now."

"One who still clambers about in trees," Cris added, pushing a finger against her shoulder.

The grin on his face irritated her. How dare he not notice how much she'd changed? Besides, she was merely seeking peace and quiet in the tree, she wasn't *climbing* it.

"A lady who completely disarmed me with her refreshing vitality," the stranger interrupted, stepping forward to clasp her hand. "Allow me to introduce myself. Lord Owen Chambers, sixth earl of Newbury at your service." The affable words were accompanied by a kiss to the back of her hand.

Amelia smiled down at the blond head bent over her hand, thankful for the distraction of the stranger. "It is my pleasure."

Owen beamed at her as he straightened, retaining a hold upon her fingers. "Charming as well as beautiful," he murmured, running an admiring gaze over her features. "Lustrous brown hair, unusual gray eyes, a figure that puts to shame many—"

"I think you've gone quite far enough," Cris interrupted, slanting his friend a look as he wrapped an arm around Amelia's shoulders. "This is my dear Amelia, remember."

"You failed to mention how lovely she was," Owen returned, bowing in deference as he released Amelia's hand.

Amelia looked up expectantly at Cris.

Cris laughed, shaking his head. "I told you she was an adorable child."

"She's hardly a child now," Owen remarked, winking at Amelia.

Cris hugged her closer, smiling down at her. "Of course not, but she's . . . well . . . she's my sweet, little Amie."

And that, she supposed, was that, her dreams of a passionate reunion fading.

Suddenly, she remembered all he'd endured recently. She knew why he'd come home. "I was so sorry to hear of your parents, Cris." Amelia placed her hand softly on his arm.

"Thank you." A look of pain passed quickly across his features. "Their carriage accident was a horrible tragedy. At least they went together. They would have wanted it that way."

Amelia nodded in agreement, having heard enough stories from Aunt Patricia to know that Cris's parents were completely in love, a self-contained unit of oneness, usually to the point of excluding even their own son.

"How is your family?" Cris inquired, removing his arm from around her. "Your sisters must be all grown now, too."

"Sisters?" Owen asked, perking up again. "You mean to tell me there are more of these beautiful creatures running about?"

"Four of them," Amelia replied with a smile, enjoying Owen's exuberance. "Beatrice, Camilla, Deanna, and Emmaline."

"There is a God."

Owen's praise brought a laugh from Amelia. "Come back to the Hall for some tea and I'll introduce you." She looked at Cris. "They would love to see you again."

"I doubt the youngest ones will remember me."

With all the stories she'd told about Cris over the years, there was no doubt they'd remember him, but she didn't see any reason to tell him that. "Of course they will, Cris. We all visit with Aunt Patricia quite often."

"I'm game," Owen said, moving forward to offer his arm to Amelia. "Lead the way, my dear."

She laughed as Cris rolled his eyes at Owen's chivalrous gesture. "I am positive my sisters will enjoy your company, Lord Chambers," she replied, accepting the earl's arm.

"Owen, please. All that lord business from such a lovely woman makes me feel old and stodgy."

"Gad, Owen, not that old tired line again," Cris groaned, stepping forward to clasp Amelia's other arm, gently tugging her away from his friend. "Come with me, Amelia, and pay Owen no mind. He's annoying at times, but quite harmless, I assure you."

Amelia tilted a smile up at Cris. "I never thought otherwise."

"There's my girl," he murmured, wrapping a hand over hers. "You always were a bright child. I knew you wouldn't change."

But she had, Amelia thought. "I'm not the child you left behind," she murmured with quiet dignity.

"Of course you're not," he said. "But inside you're still the same Amie."

Amelia considered that for a moment, deciding quickly that he was right. She'd been infatuated with him before he'd left and her daydreams had only grown in proportion to her body. So, in a way, she was very much the same when it came to Cris. A little in love with the idea of him.

She laughed, chagrined. "If you only knew, Cris. If you only knew."

Owen gently placed his hand on Amelia's arm. "So, my dear Amelia, describe your sisters to me."

"You're becoming far too predictable, Owen," Cris lamented, shaking his head.

"Can I help it if I'm a creature of consistency?" Owen returned lightly.

"I find comfort in routines," Amelia soothed, smiling at Cris's friend.

"Ah, that all women possessed your intelligence," Owen said.

"She doesn't know you as well as I do, Chambers, and I say you need to watch yourself before you become a bore."

"If I didn't like you as well as I do, Cris, that would be grounds for challenging you."

"To what? Cards?"

Owen shrugged lightly, grinning all the while. "We all need to utilize our strengths, my dear friend, Crispin. Only a fool strays into dangerous territory." Owen turned his gaze back to Amelia. "Now, about your sisters—"

"There's dangerous territory," Cris interjected.

But Owen continued as if Cris hadn't uttered a word, "—I'd love to hear more about them."

Amelia lifted her brows at Owen. "Perhaps having you to tea wasn't such a wonderful idea after all."

Cris roared with laughter. "I told you she was a smart girl."

Owen pled his case for the remainder of their walk to Ralston Hall.

Cris stumbled to a halt when Amelia's family home came into sight. Once a splendid example of Georgian architecture, Ralston Hall bore little resemblance to its former glory. Chunks of rock had broken off the grand stone pillars and, in an inglorious heap, remained where they had fallen. The once splendid garden was now an overgrown patch of weeds, except for one small corner that was now filled with vegetables.

Someone had obviously taken the time to clear the walkway toward the main door, but amidst the overwhelming ill repair, it made little impact. What had happened here? Amelia hadn't mentioned anything in her letters, yet it was perfectly clear that the Ralston family was suffering from great difficulties.

"Good God, Amelia! What happened to this place?" Cris asked. He was so incredibly stunned that he was unable to keep the shock out of his voice. Aunt Patricia had mentioned that the Ralston family had fallen on hard times, but nothing she'd said had led him to believe their situation was this dire.

Amelia pulled to a halt, glancing back at Cris as a dull stain spread across her cheeks. "We've had to let go a few of the staff," she said in a firm voice.

"Quite understandable," Owen quickly interjected, glaring at Cris over Amelia's shoulder before once again steering her toward the front entrance. "Let's continue on, shall we? I simply cannot wait to meet the rest of your family."

Cris remained behind for a moment, feeling like an unpolished schoolboy for his outburst. It was hardly proper to ask Amelia about embarrassing financial matters—especially in front of a stranger. Besides, she wouldn't be aware of the family's financial situation. No, that would fall to her father. And it was obvious that Lord Ralston had not been upholding his duties as provider for his family.

As awkward as it would be to approach Lord Ralston about this matter, Cris felt he had no choice. After all, he also had a responsibility to protect those he considered family and, in his mind,

Amelia fell into that category. It was up to him to find out what had happened and make it right.

"Are you coming, Merrick?"

Cris nodded, following Owen and Amie inside. His mood darkened further as he was faced with even more signs of their obvious hardship. The delicate vases that had once lined the corridor were gone and it didn't take a keen eye to discern the marks on the walls where valuable paintings had once hung.

In the formal parlor, Cris and Owen sat on worn, faded chairs as Amelia excused herself to fetch the tea and refreshments. The moment the door closed behind Amelia, Owen turned on Cris. "What were you thinking to shout out like that when you saw the house?"

"I wasn't," Cris admitted honestly, chagrined. "I couldn't restrain myself; the change shocked me. This place is falling down around them."

"Well, you thoroughly embarrassed her. It was all I could do to charm another smile out of her." Owen shook his head in exasperation.

That last statement made Cris frown. "Cease the outrageous flirtations with Amelia. She's unprepared for your practiced attentions."

Owen waved off the observation. "I wasn't flirting at all. Merely exchanging pleasantries."

"Perhaps that is your intention," Cris conceded, "but for Amelia it will seem like more."

"She's hardly a young chit," Owen retorted.

"Her age is immaterial when weighed against her upbringing. She's never left this estate, Owen. She's an innocent, unsophisticated, trusting woman who deserves better than to pin her hopes on a lothario from London."

Owen pressed a hand to his chest. "I'm flattered, Cris."

A lopsided grin curved on Cris's mouth. "You would be," he said, shaking his head. He leaned back in his chair. "My concern at the moment is for Amelia."

"I'll leave her unscathed," Owen returned blithely.

"Of that I am quite certain." Cris lifted a hand, studying his nails nonchalantly. "For if you don't, I will tell the lovely Sophia that you are not only courting the pretty Elizabeth, but that you also have a mistress tucked away in a quaint little cottage near the park."

Owen straightened in his chair. "You're not serious!"

"Never more so, Owen. While I usually find your unique way of 'exchanging pleasantries' rather amusing, this time I find it quite troublesome. These women are like cousins to me—and you know all about having concern for one's cousin, don't you?"

Owen's features sobered. "All too well." He sighed loudly. "I suppose I shall need to restrain myself. Between the lash of guilt and your vile threat about my beauties back in London, I have no choice but to leave the Ralston sisters alone."

"You're not the full-fledged libertine you'd like everyone to believe, my friend," Cris replied warmly.

"Enough," Owen said, lifting his hand. "Talk like that will only ruin my reputation."

The door to the parlor opened and both men rose as Amelia walked through carrying a tray with her sisters following close behind. Owen clutched his chest as each one came into the room, all four girls wearing smiles on their beautiful faces. Cris was just as affected as Owen, but he managed to retain hold of his senses.

"Surely these four young ladies aren't your sisters? When I left you were all such little girls." Cris closed the distance between them. He stopped in front of the second oldest sister. With brown hair and gray eyes, Beatrice looked much like Amelia. "How are you, Bea?"

She gifted him with a smile. "It's so good to see you, Cris."

He leaned in to kiss her upon the cheek, before moving on to the middle sister. "Camilla?"

Her blond hair bobbed and her blue eyes sparkled as she nodded. "You've been gone far too long. You should have come home sooner."

Cris laughed at her impudence, chucking her under the chin. He walked to the last two sisters. Both were blond and blue-eyed like their sister Camilla. "Deanna and Emmaline?"

Deanna moved forward to kiss him on his cheek. "I remember how you used to carry me around on your shoulders."

Warmth spread through Cris. "That's right." He glanced at the youngest girl. "And how about you, Emma? Do you remember me at all?"

She nodded shyly, but remained silent.

When Cris turned around, he saw that Owen had already moved in upon Beatrice and was bent over the girl's hand. The expression of awe on Bea's face told Cris all too well that once again a young lady had fallen for Owen's charm. Cris held back a sigh as he reached for his friend, clasping him by the shoulder.

"Ladies, might I introduce my friend, Lord Owen Chambers, Earl of Newbury?" Before Owen could get out a word, Cris continued, "Owen, this is Lady Beatrice, Lady Camilla, Lady Deanna, Lady Emmaline, and you've already met Lady Amelia. The sisters Ralston."

"Ladies, I am enchanted by your—"

"Don't even begin, Owen, old man," Cris said, laughter deepening his voice as he cut off his friend's free-flowing words. "Shall we enjoy the tea, ladies?"

The Ralston sisters seemed a bit befuddled by Cris's chastising, but they all nodded, and moved forward to sit down. Cris joined Amelia on the settee and the girls sat in the chairs that formed a semicircle facing them.

Owen glanced at the remaining chair. It was set back, away from everyone else. "Very gallant of you, Merrick."

Cris simply smiled.

"Why don't you pull the chair a bit closer, Owen? It would make it easier to converse," Amie invited.

Cris shook his head at Owen's triumphant grin. Owen quickly scooted the chair next to the one in which Beatrice sat. As she gave Owen a beautiful, yet shy, smile, it was easy to see how enthralled Bea was with Owen. Cris bit back a groan, knowing his friend far too well to ever believe him able to resist the lure of a beautiful female, no matter the promises he made.

Cris leaned in to Amelia. "You really shouldn't encourage him, Amie. He's bad enough on his own."

She tilted her gaze up to capture his. "I think he's delightful, Cris. I imagine he's an entertaining friend."

"True, but he's earned his reputation with the ladies," he remarked, looking down at her. "Women seem to find him irresistible and they . . ." His voice trailed off as he became lost in her guileless gaze. When was the last time he'd seen such an expression of openness, of innocence? How long had it been since he'd felt that pure, that wholesome?

"Cris?"

Her whisper brought him from his thoughts. He recovered quickly, flashing a practiced smile down at her. "So, Amelia, how is your father?"

The flash of pain in her gaze concerned him, but before he could address it, she glanced away. "Would anyone care for some tea?" Amelia asked too brightly to seem natural.

"That sounds wonderful. Would you like me to pour?" Camilla offered.

"I believe it's my turn," Deanna said before Amelia could respond.

"Don't start bickering now, for heaven's sake!" Bea whispered furiously, fixing each of them with a glare. "We have company."

"I'll do it," Emmaline said softly, peeking at Bea from beneath her lashes.

"That would be wonderful, Emma," interjected Amelia quickly.

Pleasure spread across Emmaline's face as she leaned forward. "Would you like a cup, Amie?"

Amelia shook her head gently. "It is polite to serve our guests first."

"Oh." Emmaline handed a cup to Owen, before turning toward Cris. "Would you like a cup of tea?"

"Most certainly," he replied, reaching for the one she held out to him. As he took hold of the saucer, Emmaline shifted on her chair, sending the tea spilling over the edge of the cup. Hot tea splattered on Cris's hand, causing him to jerk back slightly, a movement that only sent more of the hot liquid flowing over him.

"Oh! I'm so sorry," cried Emmaline, her eyes tearing up.

Cris blew upon his burned hand before nodding reassuringly at Emma. "Lord, see what happens when I don't pay attention? At times I can be such a bumblehead." He smiled, praying she couldn't read pain in his expression. "I hope I didn't spill any on you."

"N-n-o-o," she stuttered. "I'm fine. You're the one who was hurt."

"This tiny mishap? It's nothing of concern," he

replied, taking a sip. His hand stung like the devil, but he'd be damned if he'd let anyone else know . . . especially Emmaline. Lord, from her expression, it looked as if she would burst out in tears at the least provocation.

Bea tried to smooth over the situation. "Why don't you tell Lord Chambers of your recital for the vicar next week, Camilla?"

As the middle sister launched into her explanation, Cris relaxed back against his seat. He felt a touch on his shoulder. When Cris glanced at Amelia, the glow in her eyes stunned him. "Thank you," she whispered. "I've always known you were gallant."

Gallant? Him? Cris struggled to keep from squirming on his seat. He'd all but forgotten about them, leaving these five ladies to descend into financial hardship while he played it high and fast in London. Yet, Amie still looked at him, jaded and weary though he was, and thought him gallant. Shame mingled with another emotion he couldn't quite identify, a warm stroke inside of him. It left him dazed, unable to form words, never mind a witty response.

Luckily, Owen wasn't similarly disposed. "Precisely what type of entertainment do you indulge in around here?" he asked, leaning toward Bea with a smooth motion.

The question caught Cris's attention; he was having none of Owen's practiced charm. "So, how is your father?" Cris asked again, this time directing the question at Bea.

Reluctantly, Bea pulled her attention away from the smiling Owen. "I'm afraid he's not doing well at all."

"He never comes out of his room anymore," Camilla added.

"Amelia has been running things around here for years now," Deanna confirmed.

Cris glanced over at Amelia, who looked distinctly uncomfortable with the conversation. A wave of guilt swept over him. Only now did he remember how upset she'd been when he'd left for school, telling him of the joy and burden of her sisters. And it seemed her situation had only gotten worse. All the while, he'd been lost within his parents' world—concerned only with which party to attend, which club to frequent—she'd had to worry about how to feed her family. His heart constricted. Cris reached over and placed a hand on her shoulder.

Amelia's lashes slowly lifted until she was gazing into his eyes. Cris saw the weariness within the gray depths, and wanted to take her into his arms, to assure her that she was no longer alone. He wanted to give her a worryless, fairy-tale world where she could feel safe and secure, happy within her dreams. He wanted her to feel loved. However, this was hardly the time to reassure her that everything was going to be all right.

Instead, Cris touched her hand softly. "I'm sorry to hear about your father," he murmured.

"As am I," Owen added.

Cris used his guilt to strengthen his resolve. Feeling shame at abandoning her would not help Amie now. No, he needed to focus on unburdening Amelia as soon as possible. "It sounds like you carry a heavy load."

Amelia opened her mouth to speak, but before she could utter a word, Bea answered for her.

"Oh, she does," Bea confirmed. "She's always very busy. We help, of course, but Amelia does the lion's share."

Cris nodded at Bea. "Undoubtedly she refuses to take time for herself."

"Now, Cris—" Amelia began, only to be cut off by Deanna this time.

"Never. At least not anymore," Deanna amended.

"Well, we'll have to do something about that," Cris announced, turning toward Amelia. "Would you care to come riding with me tomorrow?"

"Sounds like a splendid idea!" Owen said brightly.

"You're not invited," Cris returned smoothly.

Owen lifted an eyebrow, a grin playing upon his lips. "Sorry, old man. I didn't realize that was a, um, private invitation."

"Your thoughts always seem to flow in one direction, my friend," Cris said, a wrinkle of irritation marking his forehead.

Owen lifted his hands, his fingers spread wide. "Some things can't be helped."

Rolling his eyes, Cris turned his attention back to Amelia. "Would you care to accompany me?"

Her expression stiffened. "I'm sorry, but I'll be unable to join you."

"We can take the path through . . . what? You won't be able to join me?" he asked, her refusal sinking in.

"She doesn't have a horse," Camilla replied before Amelia could form an answer.

"Camilla!" hissed Bea, obviously embarrassed by the revelation.

"What's wrong, Bea?" asked Deanna. "Camilla's just telling the truth. The horses were the first thing to go."

Amelia flushed brightly. "Please. This is a family matter. Let's not discuss it further."

Emmaline frowned, confusion darkening her blue gaze. "But you told us there was no shame in our situation, Amie. You said that many genteel families have to make certain sacrifices."

A sigh broke from Amelia. An instant later, she smiled reassuringly at her youngest sister. "And I meant it, Emma. There is no shame."

An awkward silence filled the room. Cris wished he'd never brought up the subject. "Well, then there is nothing to be done except for me to provide both mounts." Cris nodded firmly, hoping that by treating their dire straits as a matter of course it would lessen everyone's embarrassment. "How does that sound, Amelia? May I lead over a horse for you so we can enjoy a ride?"

"Oh, that would be wonderful!" Deanna rushed. "Amie always loved to ride before the horses had to be sold."

"It's true," Camilla agreed. "You always told us how wonderful it felt to race across the fields."

Cris smiled at the girls before turning to gaze down at Amelia. "Your sisters seem to think it's a good idea, Amie. Shall I bring over horses for both of us? Does that sound acceptable to you?"

"It sounds utterly delightful," she rushed, her eyes beginning to sparkle.

He couldn't help but grin at her enthusiastic response. "Tomorrow, then," he promised, rising to take his leave.

Amelia stood too, clasping Cris's hand between both of hers. "I'm very excited to go riding with you again. Just like old times."

The warmth of her pleasure brushed across his soul, a balm he hadn't even known he needed. It wasn't until he was here, among friends and family, that he realized how deeply the artifice of town had affected him. He stroked his free hand down Amelia's arm. "It's so good to be home . . . among friends."

She glowed up at him.

His dearest friend. The sunlight shone upon her beautiful brown hair, turning the luxurious mane ablaze with colors. Fiery red and golden blond strands intermingled with the brown, creating a dazzling effect. For a moment he stood entranced by the utter beauty of the sight, then shook himself back to reason.

Slowly he grinned down at Amelia. "Tomorrow we'll have to race. I'm curious to see if I can still take you."

She slanted him a look. "If memory serves, *I* was the superior equestrian."

Cris drew his brows downward, frowning in jest. "Oh dear, Amie. You must be getting on in years. Your memory is extremely faulty."

"Fine gentleman you are for insulting me in my own home," Amelia exclaimed with a laugh. "You can just take yourself off, my lord Duke, for I seem to have forgotten how much I enjoy your company." She paused for a beat. "With my faulty memory, that is."

"But, my dear, we're just getting acquainted," protested Owen, shifting closer to Bea.

Amelia put a hand on Owen's arm. "You're welcome to stay." She glanced pointedly at Cris. The amusement glittering in her eyes belied her cool expression. "While I seem to have tired of the duke's presence, I'd be happy to converse with you a while longer."

Cris felt his lips twitch. "You *do* know how to make a man feel wanted, don't you, Amie?"

Delicately, she tipped her chin upward. "Most certainly. Why do you ask?"

Cris burst out laughing, unable to contain himself one moment longer. Even Amelia broke into a smile. "Come on, Owen. It's time we took our leave."

"But—"

The other girls cut off Owen's protest. "Surely you can stay a bit longer," Deanna pleaded.

"We could make a fresh pot of tea," Bea said, taking a step toward the two visitors.

"We haven't had a chance to talk about London," protested Camilla.

"We're so enjoying the company," Emma chimed in.

"See, Cris?" Owen grinned at him, waving a hand toward the Ralston sisters. "They want *me* to stay."

"I never doubted they would, but surely you haven't forgotten about our earlier agreement."

"Hmmm," Owen murmured, smiling at Bea.

"You remember, the one about Lady Sophia."

The response Cris expected wasn't long in coming. Owen straightened his shoulders. "Sorry, ladies, while this has been a pleasure, Cris is quite right. We must be off."

Owen's swift turnabout made Cris smile as he bowed slightly to the younger girls. "It has been a delight, ladies, and I am sure I'll be seeing quite a bit more of you. Please call upon my aunt and me anytime."

Not one of them hid their disappointment, but they all nodded, murmuring their farewells.

"Shall we, my fine friend?" Cris didn't wait for a reply, but began to propel Owen toward the door.

"I shall be staying with Cris for quite a while, so I promise to come back and visit with you again," Owen called over his shoulder.

Cris hurried his step, following Owen out the front door to a cheer of female voices encouraging a second visit. "If you believe for a moment that I would allow you free access to a house filled with beautiful women, you are seriously deluding yourself, my friend," Cris said the moment they were outside.

Owen pulled his arm free, straightening his jacket as he matched Cris stride for stride. "I might be offended by that if I didn't understand your reasons for being so stodgy, Cris." He tugged at his sleeves. "Besides, I know that when you're in town you play just as fast with the ladies as I do."

"And as rumor would have it, I entertain myself in a very depraved manner." Cris felt bitterness well up inside him as the nightmare of the past years came forth. "It seems as if the moment one horrid story dies away, there is another nasty one to take its place—always with me at the core of the depravity."

Owen's expression grew serious. "You can't listen to the tales, Cris. You know they're not true."

"I do, but no one else seems to believe it." Anger flickered to life. "What bothers me most is the ease with which some of my so-called friends have accepted the stories. You are one of the few who has never believed even one of the tales."

"I know you far too well," Owen returned, waving a hand in dismissal. "You might enjoy the ladies, but you are not a despoiler of young innocents. No, you have far too much of that bothersome honor running through your veins to ever even contemplate the ruination of a lady."

"Thank you," Cris said quietly, humbled by his friend's unquestioning loyalty. "Still, it is a fact that two more young ladies have been abducted since Samantha was attacked."

"Have you ever considered that perhaps those are only the ones we've heard about?" Owen slowed his steps. "What if there are even more ladies who were taken, suffering through God only knows what, before being dumped back with their families? What if the kidnapping was hushed because the family didn't want to cast a shadow of shame on their name? After all, it's not as if we ever breathed a word about what nearly happened to Samantha."

"Please, Owen. It's too horrific to think about. Whatever the true number of victims of these rogues, it still remains unexplained why *my* name has been linked to the abductions."

Owen shook his head. "I have no idea. I do suspect, however, that you left London not only because of your grief over your parents, but also to escape the rumors for a time."

"I couldn't face any more," Cris admitted.

"I know." Owen flung an arm over Cris's shoulder. "I'm sorry I brought it up, Cris. You need to forget about all that for a while."

"If only I could," Cris murmured, knowing all too well how the gossip would continue to haunt him, even here, out in the country.

"Well, I for one promise not to bring up the subject again," Owen announced broadly.

"Thank heavens for small favors," Cris said, feeling his thoughts lighten at Owen's pronouncement. He *did* need to forget about his troubles in town for a while; dealing with the problems of the Ralston family was the perfect distraction. "Agreed, then," Cris added. "No further discussion about this unpleasant business allowed."

"Fine," Owen agreed readily.

The two men resumed their walk in companionable silence. After a few minutes, Owen broke in with a remark, "I wonder if it would be too bold of me to call upon the Ralston sisters tomorrow."

"Lord help me," Cris whispered.

"What is it, Cris? Do you think two days in a row is too forward?"

A groan was Cris's only response.

3

"So our frisky marquess has taken his newly acquired title of duke and fled to the country, has he?" Prospero laid another card on the table in front of him. "It would appear that our little game is finally going to break him."

"Pity," returned Alonso, fanning his cards out in front of him. "I've truly enjoyed tormenting the man—though not as much as I've loved sampling the beauties."

Sebastian pulled a card from his hand and placed it next to Prospero's. "Don't you think Merrick has paid enough for his interference? After all, he hasn't bothered us again."

Prospero lowered his cards slowly. There was steel in the gaze he turned upon Sebastian. "No, I don't believe he has. Not nearly enough at all. The man practically drips arrogance, yet holds no respect for the pleasures of his peers. I say we continue with our little game until we break the bastard."

"Why? Why should we go to those lengths? After all, he's one of us," insisted Sebastian.

"He's not one of us," spat Alonso. "It is clear he thinks he's better than us. More often than not, he doesn't even deign to acknowledge my presence, never mind accept that I am his equal."

"So true, my dear Alonso," Prospero murmured, his lips curling into a smile. "I do believe you are the perfect candidate to take a small jaunt up north, merely to take in the country air." He widened his eyes. "However, if you happen to come across Merrick's holdings up there, you might want to see how he's faring. Merely as a concerned acquaintance, you understand."

"Perfectly." Alonso leaned forward on the table. "I would hate to see my dear friend Merrick grow bored during his respite. Wouldn't you?"

"It would pain me greatly," Prospero returned with a dark laugh. "Sebastian, are you going to join Alonso on his trip to Hunterdon?"

"Is that Merrick's estate up north?" Sebastian asked.

Prospero leaned back in his chair. "Yes, and it is also the holding where his aunt resides."

"An aunt?" Alonso straightened, excitement brightening his features. "She might make an excellent pawn in the game."

"No!" Sebastian shouted, slamming his hand down on the table. "I draw the line at tormenting an old woman who is completely harmless."

"Then perhaps it would be best if you accompanied Alonso to Merrick's estate, just to make sure he doesn't do anything rash."

Sebastian hesitated for a long moment, before slowly nodding his head. "Fine."

Prospero slapped one leg. "Excellent!" he said, well pleased at the outcome of their discussion. He slowly raised his cards again. "I do believe it is your turn," he said to Alonso.

"Ah, yes." Alonso tossed another card onto the table. "Shall we discuss which lady we'll play with next?"

Prospero burst out laughing, a wicked sound that echoed through the room. "I do so admire the way you think, Alonso. Indeed, I do."

The morning sun had just crested the horizon when Cris strode into the parlor. Aunt Patricia glanced up from her painting easel. "And where are you off to so early today? It's not yet noon."

Cris paused to press a kiss upon his aunt's cheek. "I'm going riding with Amelia."

"Not here one day and you two are already back to being fast friends," she said with a laugh. "Amelia has grown up to be a delightful young lady, hasn't she?"

Cris agreed readily, "She always was delightful."

Aunt Patricia paused in her painting, allowing the brush to rest in her lap, her head tilting upward to meet his gaze. "You mean she was a delightful young girl. I'm saying she's grown into a lovely, sweet lady."

"One and the same, Aunt Patricia," Cris remarked with a shrug.

A smile played upon his aunt's lips as she murmured lightly, "I believe you're in for a surprise, my dear."

"I've already seen her," Cris replied. "And I assure you there are no changes. She's still my dear little Amie."

Aunt Patricia reached out to tap Cris's arm with her brush. "Ah, but are you *really* looking?"

"Aunt Patricia, you are an incorrigible romantic."

"Think what you'd like," she paused, lifting an eyebrow, "but I know I'm right."

Cris shook his head. "I'm quite accustomed to your interest in the more, shall we say, sensual aspects of my life, but you're way off center on this one, you old busybody. Amie is more like a sister or cousin to me than anything else."

"Things change," she returned breezily.

"Not this."

"If you say."

"I do."

Aunt Patricia graced him with a calm smile. "We shall see."

Cris laughed again. "You'll never change, will you?"

"You'd find me deadly dull if I ever did."

"True enough." Cris leaned down to kiss his aunt's cheek once again. "True enough."

"You are a love, my darling Crispin," Aunt Patricia said as she tugged up one corner of his cravat, straightening the knot.

"Careful," Cris urged, stepping back from the paintbrush she still held in her hand. "I don't believe red is my color."

"Spoilsport," Aunt Patricia said with a laugh, before nodding at her canvas. "Before you head off, tell me what you think of my latest creation."

Cris stood back, studying the painting for a long while. He was at a loss for words.

"Well?"

He glanced down at his aunt, before returning his gaze to her painting. The blobs of paint were gelling together, creating a jumbled mess of color. There was no rhythm to the picture, no harmony in the shades, no boldness to the strokes.

It was, in a word, horrid.

Cris searched for something to say. "It's . . . it's . . . unique," he murmured at last.

His aunt's peal of laughter startled him. "You always were a miserable liar, Crispin."

Relief flooded him. How could he have forgotten his aunt's irreverent sense of humor? "I pride myself on behaving like a gentleman," he began, bending lower to whisper softly, "and as such would never tell you that your paintings are still as awful as ever."

Aunt Patricia turned her head to press a kiss upon his cheek. "And I love you too, Crispin."

Cris squeezed her shoulders, straightening up once more. "I'd best be off now. I need to see about our horses."

"Indeed," Aunt Patricia said, waving him off. "And I need to finish up my painting." She tilted her head upward. "I wager that charming friend of yours will find something complimentary to say about my artwork."

"Undoubtedly," Cris agreed, his lips curling upward. "I am continually astounded by Owen's ability to find just the right thing to say—whatever the situation."

"Where is the young man this morning?"

"Still abed. I don't believe Owen has seen this hour in years."

"No matter," Aunt Patricia returned, picking up her paintbrush. "If he's well rested, it will help him appreciate my talent all the more."

"I'm so happy you think so, Aunt Patricia, and pleased to know you still have an active imagination."

Aunt Patricia swatted Cris's arm. "Begone, you rapscallion, before I enlist you as my next subject."

The sound of Cris's amusement echoed down the corridor as he headed off to the kitchen.

A warm expression lit his aunt's face as she shook her head and turned her attention back to her painting. "The boy's right," she acknowledged, studying her composition. "It is horrible."

Shrugging, she curved a thick red line across the canvas.

4

"Hurry, Amie. Cris will be here any moment!"

Beatrice's remonstration made the knot in Amelia's stomach tighten. Her sisters had been in her room for nearly an hour, flittering about, arguing over which habit she should wear, which gloves matched best, and a multitude of other inane details. If she didn't love them all so much, she would have long since sent them from her room.

"I still believe the pearl brooch would complement your outfit splendidly," Deanna insisted.

Amelia squeezed Deanna's hand. "I agree, but I can't take the risk of wearing it. What if it came unpinned and I lost it in the woods?"

Camilla moved to stand next to Deanna. "If you're fearful of wearing it, then what's the point in keeping it?"

"Security," Amelia said firmly. "It's the only valuable piece of Mother's jewelry that we still own and it reassures me to know that if our situation ever becomes truly desperate, the brooch is here for us."

"And it was Mother's favorite piece of jewelry," Emmaline added. "Isn't that right, Amie?"

Amelia tucked a strand of Emma's hair behind her ear. "Indeed it was. Father gave it to her on their wedding night."

"How romantic," sighed Camilla.

"Yes, it was," Amelia agreed, warming to the subject. All four pairs of eyes were trained on her. Amelia loved to talk about the good years when their mother was still alive and their father had been so vibrant. Poor Emma had no recollection of their mother at all. Amelia considered it a gift of love to her mother and sisters to keep their mama's memory alive.

"What else did Papa used to do?" asked Emma, moving closer to Amelia.

Amelia stroked Emma's hair. "Papa wasn't always like he is now. Mother's death was very hard on him." Since their mother's death from a fever days after Emma's birth, their father had been so sad, so quiet, so withdrawn. Amelia knew it was painful for their father to continue on without his wife, to feel joy, to feel love, but that hadn't helped her or her sisters. They had all been very young, bewildered, and in pain. Still, as the oldest, Amelia had tried to step into the role left behind by her mother, burying her own loss.

"But why doesn't he come out of his rooms?" Deanna asked, breaking Amelia from her thoughts.

"You know he's very ill." Amelia tried to lift

their spirits. "We're luckier than a lot of people who lose their mother. At least we've always had each other."

"And Mrs. Burke." Camilla's voice lightened as she mentioned their housekeeper.

"Don't forget Aunt Patricia," Emma said with a smile.

"Yes, yes, yes, we're all very lucky," Bea interrupted briskly, "but we're wasting time with all this chatter. Have you all forgotten that our Amie has a gentleman calling on her in a few moments?"

"It's only Cris," Amelia scoffed, but there was nothing she could do to prevent the little lift in her heart at the thought.

It was all too easy for her to weave the fantasy. She imagined Cris coming to call on her, his gaze burning with ill-hidden longings, his hands placing gentle touches on her arm, her shoulder, her back. He would smile down at her, his eyes darkening, before he bent down to—

"Amie? Wherever is your mind wandering?"

Bea's question snapped Amelia from her fairy-tale daydreams. Her reunion with Cris had made one thing perfectly clear. He still saw her as a favored cousin and dear friend. Yet, yesterday, during tea, for a brief moment it was as if he'd gazed *into* her and seen her as she was, a full-grown woman with desires, longings, yearnings, passion—

"Amie!"

A guilty flush stained her cheeks. "I'm sorry, Bea. What were you saying?"

"I said that you looked wonderful. Even though

Mother's riding habit is woefully outdated, it fits you perfectly."

Amelia gazed at her reflection in the mirror. The pastel blue of the habit that had so complemented their mother did little for her coloring. Even so, the high color in her face (owing to her thoughts of Cris), combined with the pert riding hat, made her feel quite pretty.

"Thank you all so much," Amelia murmured, moving from sister to sister, hugging each one fiercely. It had taken much longer to get ready with her sisters' "help," but they were so excited about her ride with Cris that she hadn't had the heart to dissuade them. "You are so dear for helping me like this."

A knock on the door interrupted Amelia's praise. "Excuse me, Miss Amelia, His Grace is here."

"His who?" Deanna asked, pulling open the door for their housekeeper.

"She means Cris," Amelia clarified.

Mrs. Burke tipped her head to the side. "I don't believe it's fitting that you address your young man that way anymore."

"He's not *my* young man," Amelia replied quickly.

Mrs. Burke waved away the protest. "Regardless of who he belongs to, it's still not right."

"Why ever not?" Bea asked before Amelia could respond.

"Because your sister's a lovely young lady and Mr. Crispin is no longer a boy." Mrs. Burke added a firm nod to her statement. She crossed her arms across her chest, her petite body drawn up to its full height. "I love you like my own, Miss Amie, and would give you all I have. But that doesn't mean you can get away with any improprieties."

"There is nothing improper with the informal address because of our long-standing friendship." Amelia glanced at her sisters, smiling at them in assurance, before returning her attention to their housekeeper. "We're the best of friends."

"That doesn't mean that you're not a lady and he a fine gentleman, both unwed."

"I assure you, Mrs. Burke, that Cris will not be any less the gentleman if we forgo the formalities," she said, tugging on her gloves. "I shall be perfectly safe in his company."

"It's not *your* safety I'm worried about," muttered Mrs. Burke, laughter glinting in her eyes.

"Mrs. Burke!"

Amelia's shocked exclamation joined the gasps of her sisters.

The housekeeper patted her gray hair, lifting her eyebrows in innocence. "There's no need to get so riled. I'm merely stating a fact."

"Who wouldn't be safe?" asked Emma in bewilderment.

"Mrs. Burke, you can't think that Amelia would compromise Cris!" Bea's astonishment reflected Amelia's.

Mrs. Burke lifted one shoulder. "I'm not saying she would or she wouldn't. All I'm saying is that your sister has done nothing but prattle on about the lad for more years than I care to remember.

Now that he's back . . ." She allowed the sentence to trail off with heavy innuendo.

It was all Amelia could do to keep from rolling her eyes. "I promise to be the soul of propriety."

Mrs. Burke snorted, giving Amelia a sharp look.

"Amelia would never do something improper," Camilla assured Mrs. Burke.

The housekeeper's expression was loving as she turned to smile at the youngest girls. "You are such sweet angels." She looked back over her shoulders. "And while you're a sweet girl, my dear Amelia, I'm not putting anything past you. Bold as brass you are. Climbing trees, wandering about, paying no mind to proper deportment." Mrs. Burke clucked her tongue at Amelia. "There's no telling what you'll do when you get that fine fellow alone today."

The smile Amelia gave their housekeeper came from her heart. "You're quite right, Mrs. Burke. I suppose there's nothing left to do but ravish poor, unsuspecting Crispin."

Mrs. Burke's eyes widened, before a look of chagrin crossed her face. "Well, I hope Mr. Cris can fend you off himself for I'm through trying to reason with you, Amelia. Now get on with you," she said, nudging Amelia toward the open door. "I've had quite enough of your sass."

Amelia chose to ignore Mrs. Burke's tartness as she hurried toward the foyer . . . and Cris. Her sisters followed after, calling for her to wait, but Amelia was too excited to slow her steps.

* * *

"Ahhh," Amelia sighed, leaning back on her hands, her legs stretched out in front of her, crossed at the ankles. Cris lay next to her, propped up on his elbow. They'd ridden to the waterfalls a mile from their homes and were now resting in the warm sun.

Cris glanced at her. "Nice to get away, I'll wager."

She lifted her face, savoring the heat from the sun. "It's wonderful." To have a glorious day, her favorite companion, and be at her beloved falls—well, there was nothing better. "Perfect, in fact," she murmured.

"It's been difficult for you these past few years, hasn't it?" Cris asked softly.

Amelia fought to keep from frowning. Ever since they'd left Ralston Hall, Cris had been probing into her family's situation. She didn't want to think about their father, their lack of financial security, or any of their other many problems right now. "I've missed you," she said instead of answering his question.

"I've been gone too long," Cris acknowledged. "I'd forgotten how much I enjoyed Dovedale, how much I'd left behind, but never once did I forget you."

Amelia felt her heart catch at his words, before she chided herself silently. He meant he'd never forgotten his childhood friend. She couldn't allow herself to look for a deeper meaning. "These past few years have been so busy for me that I've taken little time to relax and simply enjoy myself." She looked at her friend. "Yet, you're home but two days and here I am taking a leisurely ride. You're good for me, Cris."

Cris raised himself up into a sitting position, angling toward her. "We're good for each other."

She couldn't help but gaze up into Cris's face. So dear. So close.

Cris reached for her. "You've grown up on me, Amie," he whispered.

Amelia stopped breathing at his words. Did he mean it? As he moved closer, her lips parted in anticipation of his kiss. Finally, after all these years of wanting him, she was going to feel his lips upon hers. Her first kiss from her only love. Amelia's eyes fluttered closed as she waited for his mouth to touch hers.

"But you're still a hoyden underneath, aren't you?" Cris said lightly, fondness softening his voice.

Her eyes flew open as she felt him pluck something from her hair.

He held up a leaf, twirling it between his fingers. "See?"

All she saw was the man of her dreams. She ached for him to see the woman in her, to enfold her in his arms, to mold their lips into one. Instead, she received a teasing memory from a dear friend. "Yes. I see it all perfectly," she said, hiding her disappointment.

Cris leaned closer still, the very nature of his position intimate. "So much has changed here."

She was utterly confused. Why was he staying so

close to her if he didn't mean to kiss her? Uncertain, Amelia nodded at his statement.

"I know that it's hard for you to talk about your situation." He laid his hand upon hers. "I want you to know that I'm here now. For you."

Her heart began to race with unbidden longings, but Amelia struggled to suppress them. "I know, Cris."

"When I saw you again, it made me realize how much you mean to me . . . and your family too," he added quickly.

"Of course," she replied, anticipation building again as she began to grasp his meaning. Her long-held dream of becoming Cris's wife awakened beneath his words. Still, it was hard for her to focus on the meaning hidden in his carefully worded statements when all she could do was think about him pulling her into his arms and kissing her until all she knew was his name, his touch.

Cris stroked the back of her hand. "I can't allow things to remain as they are between us."

Her heart stopped. "What are you saying?" she whispered, needing him to speak plainly. All of her life she'd dreamed of this moment. Her head was spinning too fast to even think clearly.

Cris lifted his hand to cup her face. "I need to speak boldly to you, Amelia, even though I know—" He broke off his words, his gaze shifting to where his hand lay upon her cheek. He gently trailed his fingers downward, stroking the curve of her jaw. "What I meant to say was that I know—"

Once again he broke off, his gaze lifting to capture hers.

Her heart started again with a thump, pounding against her chest, drumming out a beat of desire as Cris bent slowly toward her. Coming ever nearer, so close, soon touching her lips. Her eyes drifted closed, waiting for . . .

Nothing.

Her eyes flew open in time to capture Cris's expression of shock as he jumped to his feet. Once again, confusion filled Amelia at his behavior.

Cris reached a hand down to her, his features schooled into a calm expression. "May I call upon you tomorrow so we can continue our discussion?"

"Which discussion?"

He looked startled. "The one about our future."

The words *our* and *future* could only mean one thing—marriage. Relief followed understanding as his odd behavior made sense. Of course Cris couldn't follow through with his desire to kiss her. He was far too much of a gentleman to take advantage of her in even the slightest manner. It was quite obvious that he simply wished to ignore his own desires until their betrothal was formalized.

Amelia could barely control the happiness racing through her as she reached up to accept his proffered hand. "Oh, that discussion," she murmured softly, unable to take her eyes off him.

Cris held onto her hand even as Amelia rose to her feet. "I was wondering if perhaps your father might be feeling well enough to be there."

Elation soared through Amelia. "I'm not sure if my father will be able to meet with us, but I would be honored if you would call upon me tomorrow."

His smile melted her very soul. "Around three then?"

"Perfect." She gazed into his eyes. "Absolutely perfect."

5

"Do tell how your visit with the beautiful Amelia went today," Owen beckoned from his chair on the terrace.

Cris strolled over to his friend, then leaned back against the stone railing. "We had a delightful time."

"I'll wager you did," Owen murmured, lifting one eyebrow.

Cris scowled at the implication. "Don't be crass, Chambers. Nothing improper occurred . . ." His words trailed off as he remembered how he'd leaned in toward Amelia, thinking of nothing but tasting her luscious lips, to see if they were as soft as they looked. Flustered, Cris tried to keep his expression impassive. "Nothing at all."

Owen's eyes twinkled. "The strength of your denial is quite telling, my friend."

Cris waved a hand at Owen in dismissal. "Believe what you like, Owen, but nothing untoward occurred today." Only because he'd finally come to his senses. Cris still felt shaken at the realization that he could have, no, that he'd *wanted* to kiss her. Had he been in London so long that his moral core had completely disintegrated? How could he have looked at his dear, sweet Amie and thought such lustful thoughts? The very idea rocked him.

Cris looked at his friend, and quickly, an urge to smack the smug smile off Owen's lips filled him. Yet, to display such a violent reaction to Owen's smile would betray his inner turmoil. Instead, he forced himself to act coolly.

"You never can keep your thoughts from dipping into the dirt, can you, Owen?" He forced a light laugh. "At least you never cease to amuse."

Owen's grin remained firmly planted on his face as Cris walked away, hoping he'd kept his new and disturbing attraction toward Amelia a secret.

"The innkeep has some nerve calling this swill food," grumbled Alonso, pushing away his plate. "It's fortunate for you that this trip has proven so informative, or else I would be in a foul mood."

"As if you aren't already," muttered Sebastian, slogging his way through the horrid dinner fare, his hunger outweighing his dissatisfaction. "I still don't understand why you're so excited about seeing Merrick's neighbors today."

"You don't? Are you blind, man?" Alonso leaned closer to whisper, "Those five girls are extraordinary beauties. That Merrick is a sly one, holding out on us like that. Here he has a private treasure trove of young lovelies to dally with on a whim."

Sebastian frowned. "Simply because the ladies live next door to Merrick hardly makes them his private stable."

Alonso took a swig of his ale. "Come now, Sebastian. Surely even you could see that the chits were very fond of Merrick."

Sebastian conceded the point with a nod of his head.

"Besides, even if they aren't his little playthings, that doesn't mean they aren't fair game—for *our* game."

Sebastian's eyes widened. "No," he whispered. "They're not from London; they're living peacefully here in the country."

"And what possible difference could that make?"

"Quite a bit," insisted Sebastian. "The ladies we choose in London are flirtatious twits who purposefully twist a man up inside until he'd kill for their favor. These girls have done nothing of the sort; they are truly innocent."

Alonso shook his head, laughing. "Only you, Sebastian, would try to create distinctions between the ladies we can and the ones we can't choose." He sipped at his ale again. "Trust me, my friend, in the dark, they are all alike and you have certainly enjoyed your share of the booty."

A frown settled upon Sebastian's face, but he remained silent.

Alonso nodded firmly. "Well, then, I think the

next thing to do is to ask around to find out all we can about Merrick's luscious ladybirds."

"I'm sorry I'm late," Amelia said breathlessly, skidding to a halt in the parlor. She straightened her skirts, patting them into place, as she smiled up at Cris. "My sisters always want to help me dress for special occasions and it invariably ends up taking me twice as long to get ready."

"Special occasion?" Cris murmured, surprise tinting his voice.

His reaction flustered her. "Well, yes, I suppose. I simply wished to look—nice," she finished lamely.

"The time was well spent, Amie. You look lovely," Cris reassured her immediately.

Heat rose to her face at the compliment. Anticipation raced through her. Today was the day she would become engaged to the man of her dreams. She looked expectantly at Cris, but he seemed distracted. Suddenly she felt unsure of herself. It was so odd. Here she was with her oldest friend and she didn't know how to speak with him. "Would you care to sit down?" she offered finally.

"Thank you." Cris rubbed his hands on his thighs as he sat in the chair opposite her.

The knot of tension eased within her at Cris's actions. Why, he was just as nervous as she was. She settled back into her chair, deciding to ready the way for both of them. "You mentioned yesterday that you wished to speak with me on an urgent matter," she began.

Cris nodded, visibly calming before her. "I'm so

glad you brought that up, Amie. I do need to speak with you about something very important, but I'm not quite sure how to broach the subject."

She quelled the rush of excitement she felt as she waited for his proposal. "Ofttimes it is best to plunge straight ahead."

He nodded. "You're absolutely right."

Silence fell between them. Amelia didn't know what to do next. He'd agreed with her, but then he'd stopped talking. How should she proceed without appearing overly eager for his proposal?

Taking a deep breath, she tried again. "What was it you wished to speak with me about?"

Cris shifted on his seat, obviously uncomfortable. "Are you quite certain your father can't join us?"

"Positive." She thought of her father, wasting away upstairs and was nearly overwhelmed by grief. She couldn't talk about her papa yet . . . not even with Cris. "Most definitely," she added, trying to overcome her sadness.

Cris's breath rushed out of him. "All right then. I suppose it would be best to simply speak with you directly." He leaned forward, his elbows resting on his knees. "Amie, since my return, I've noticed quite a few changes here at Ralston Hall."

Why was he talking about Ralston Hall? she wondered. Didn't he mean changes within her? She shook her head in confusion. "Ralston Hall?"

Cris continued, not answering her query. "I can't tell you how sorry I am that I neglected all of you for so very long. My aunt wrote to me that your family had fallen on hard times, but I didn't realize to what degree. I'm just thankful I'm not too late."

Too late for what? Was Cris concerned that someone else had been courting her? Amelia responded hesitantly. "There has been no one else."

"I know, I know," he said, reaching over the table to clasp her hands. "I fully realize that no one else has been here for you and I hold myself accountable for the situation."

She gasped, surprised at his words. Had he guessed that her girlish dreams about him had been her measuring stick for the few men who'd come to court her? Shyly, she admitted, "The vicar had begun to call upon me a few years back."

"Was he able to help you?"

Confusion filled her. The vicar help her . . . how? Perhaps Cris was asking if the vicar's courtship had helped her overcome memories of him. Slowly, Amelia shook her head. "While his presence was welcome, he did nothing to make me forget the past." When Cris nodded at her, she assumed she had interpreted his question correctly.

"I'm sorry for that," Cris began, "and it makes me regret my absence even more."

His interest warmed her heart. It seemed obvious to her that he was concerned another had taken his place in her affections. Amelia smiled sweetly. "It matters not, Cris, for you are home now."

"Yes, I am," he stated firmly. "And I want to be more than your friend."

Her breath caught in her throat. Here it comes, she thought, excitement surging through her.

"But first, I want to ask you a very personal, very intimate question." Cris paused, gazing deeply into her eyes. "I want you to understand how serious I am, how important this is to me."

"I understand," she breathed, barely able to contain her excitement.

He nodded, slipping from his chair. Kneeling before her, he said, "Amelia, I know how hard the past years have been for you and I want to take away all the hardship, all your burdens."

His pause nearly slayed her. Go on, she urged silently. Go on!

"I want to be your protector. I want to support you and your family."

Her heart leapt. "Oh, yes, Cris, I've wanted this for so long. Of course I'll be your wife."

"My wife?" Cris exclaimed, rocking back onto his heels. "Good Lord, Amie. I was proposing to be your guardian, *not* your husband."

6

Mortification seared through her. She prayed the floor would open up and swallow her whole, one big gulp so she wouldn't have to face his shocked reaction.

"Amie, how . . . how could you . . ."

"Don't!" Amelia thrust out a hand to stop his stumbling words. "I've already made a fool of myself by misreading your intentions. Please don't apologize and make it worse."

He sat back down in his chair. "Marriage?"

"Yes. I thought you were going to propose." Her cheeks burned beneath his incredulous gaze. "Is it so impossible to imagine someone wanting me?"

"Of course not," he said quickly. "But me?"

She began to pray for a huge lightning bolt to strike her down. "I mistook your intentions," she replied stiffly. "Please let's leave it at that."

Cris spread his hands out. "I was offering to give you money, to support your family, to make repairs on your home."

A fresh wave of embarrassment overtook her. Why wouldn't he just let it be? "We are not paupers to beg assistance from neighbors, Crispin. We are doing fine on our own."

"Amelia, I'm not blind. I know this is a sensitive issue to discuss, but it is apparent that you need—"

"You have no concept of our needs," she interrupted, pushing to her feet. "We have no use for your charity." She said the last word as if it pained her.

"Be sensible, Amelia," Cris protested.

She couldn't bear to hear more. Lifting her chin, she strode from the room, ignoring Cris's insistence that she stay. The only thing left to her was her dignity, and she'd be Hell bound before she'd let go of that as well.

It took all of her self-control not to slam the door as she left the room, unconcerned about leaving him behind.

He could see himself out.

Cris headed for the brandy as soon as he entered the parlor where his aunt and Owen sat discussing the Ralston sisters, Owen's favorite new topic. Cris tossed back a drink, welcoming the searing rush of the liquor as it burned down his throat. Hopefully, it would dull the guilt weighing him down. He didn't even pause before pouring himself a second.

"Ho, old man, I've never seen you go at it quite like that before," Owen called.

His drink firmly in hand, Cris turned to face his

aunt and friend. He eyed Owen as he took another gulp.

"That bad?" Owen slanted a look at Aunt Patricia. "The poor boy must be worse off than we thought."

"Yes, Amelia seems to have gotten Crispin rather perturbed." Aunt Patricia's calm statement earned her a steely glare.

"Enough of that," Cris growled, taking another pull of his brandy. "I find no humor in this situation."

"Perhaps if you actually explained the situation to us, we might agree with you," Owen said smoothly, waving his hand toward a nearby chair. "Please sit down, Cris. Tell us what's gotten you so riled."

Cris accepted the offer, sinking onto the cushioned chair, his drink still in hand. "Not only have I managed to make a complete fool of myself, but I have also hurt one of my oldest and dearest friends in the process."

"Amelia?" Aunt Patricia offered.

At Cris's nod, Owen exclaimed, "Ah, the beautiful Amie. She is enough to tie any man into knots."

"It's nothing of the sort," Cris returned immediately. "Not at all."

Owen laughed. "Sorry, old chum, but I'm having trouble believing that. You are obviously distraught in a manner befitting a man entranced. Lovely ladies have that power," he added as an aside to Aunt Patricia.

She didn't comment on Owen's light-hearted remark. Instead, she continued to gaze at her nephew. "What happened?" she asked softly.

Cris closed his eyes, leaning his head back against the chair. "It shocked me to see the disrepair of Ralston Hall. You'd told me they were suffering from financial difficulties, but I had no idea as to the degree."

"Naturally, you wished to help them," she concluded.

"Of course." Cris looked at his aunt. "How could I do less?"

"How, indeed," she agreed. "I have offered many times in the past, but Amelia has always refused me. I find your offer, your sense of responsibility, quite honorable."

"But it all went wrong," Cris admitted, agitated. "She thought I was proposing to her." He pressed a hand against his chest. "It's my fault she misunderstood my intent. The things I said to her could have been easily misread. I mentioned wanting to speak with her father privately and something about deepening our relationship. I was careless with my phrasing and I see now how Amie could have misconstrued my intentions."

Owen tapped a finger against the arm of his chair. "Perhaps you're right, Merrick. You probably botched your offer of help and led her to believe you were considering marriage."

"That's *exactly* what happened," Cris returned. "I know she has no romantic feelings toward me; she only saw the logic in us marrying. Undoubtedly, she didn't even consider the possibility of my becoming her guardian, so to speak."

"Instead of her husband," Owen said.

"Exactly." Cris shifted on his chair.

Aunt Patricia took a sip of her tea. "I'm only confused about one thing, dear." She looked at Cris, her eyes wide and innocent. "Why don't you consider it?"

"Consider what? Marriage?" Cris asked, incredulous. "This is Amie we speak of. You know I consider her family. I've never even looked at her in a romantic sense before."

"Then start," Owen said bluntly.

Cris looked at his friend in surprise. "Pardon me?"

"Start," Owen repeated, this time more firmly. "She's a beautiful, witty woman, Merrick. I find it hard to believe that you've failed to notice."

Memories of their near kiss flooded him. The sensations of hunger that had swept through him as he'd gazed upon her, all warm and lazy in the sun, still fresh in his mind. For a moment, he had wanted her as he had never wanted another.

But it had been wrong, Cris told himself, fighting back the flicker of desire. All wrong. To feel lust for someone he loved as a dear friend was debasing—for both of them. "Of course I realize she's a beautiful woman, Owen. I'm not blind," Cris said tightly.

"Then why don't you marry the girl and do your duty by producing a wonderful heir." Owen shrugged when Cris stared at him.

"This is Amelia we're talking about here, not a broodmare," Cris exclaimed, scowling at Owen. "I shouldn't expect you to understand, Owen, because you only view women as lovely bits of fluff set upon this earth for your amusement."

"I'd wager a pretty farthing or two that your dear Amelia would rather have you think of her as a woman than a chum," Owen pointed out.

"You don't know her at all."

Owen leaned back in his chair, crossing his arms. "Well, then, since you have no romantic interest in her, I can safely assume that you would have no objections if I pursued my inclinations toward her."

A raw, ugly emotion roiled through Cris. "I most certainly would!"

"Why?"

A simple question, invoking only complicated answers. Why did the image of his friend pursuing Amelia disturb him so? Undoubtedly it was because he'd seen the trail of broken hearts Owen had left behind him. Relieved, Cris responded honestly. "Because you would hurt her."

"Ahhh, I believe I understand you now, Cris. You feel you're the only one allowed to hurt Amelia . . . because of your friendship and all," Owen finished softly, lifting a brow at Cris.

Guilt slashed at him again. Cris took another deep swallow of his drink. He leaned back in his chair, allowing the burning liquor to dull the ache near his heart. "The real question remains. Whatever do I do now?" He looked toward his aunt for help. "Should I return to Ralston Hall and apologize?"

Her eyes widened. "Dear heavens, *no.* I fear Amelia will need a few days to recover. It is probably best that you wait and call on her again in a week or so."

"A week?" The thought of allowing the wound he'd inflicted on Amelia's heart and pride to fester was almost unbearable. He needed to apologize for his careless wording and to assure Amie that he hadn't meant to embarrass her. "Surely that is too long."

Aunt Patricia remained silent for a moment. "No, Crispin. I believe she will need the time to recoup. Do not press the issue further."

He didn't like it, but he would accept his aunt's judgment. Lord knew, it was his own faulty judgment that had created this mess in the first place.

Cris drained his glass, pushing to his feet. "I appreciate your candor and understanding," he said, bending down to kiss his aunt's hand. "I will take your advice and give Amelia some time before I approach her again."

"Don't berate yourself too much," Aunt Patricia murmured.

"I won't," he answered, even as he wondered how he could do otherwise. The image of Amelia's mortified expression would not be easy to forget. "I'll see you this evening," he bade Owen in farewell. "I'm off for a ride to clear my head." Cris released his aunt's hand before making his way to the door, pausing to place his empty glass on the sideboard.

As soon as the door shut behind Cris, Owen began to chuckle softly.

"What's so amusing?" Aunt Patricia asked.

"He has no idea, does he?" Owen shook his head. "No bloody idea that his dear friend, Amie, is utterly and completely in love with him."

"None whatsoever," she confirmed, before wagging a finger at Owen. "And it's going to stay that way."

"Why?" He gestured toward the door. "The poor man would be much better off if we simply told him."

"You've known Crispin all these years and you don't know him any better than that?" Aunt Patricia took another sip of her tea. "If you were to tell Cris that Amie has a *tendre* for him, he would run from her as quickly as possible."

"Do you truly believe he would do that?"

"Most definitely," Aunt Patricia confirmed. "Our Crispin has an aversion to anything even remotely resembling love—of the romantic sort, that is."

Owen rubbed his temple with two fingers. "An aversion? Don't you think that's being a trifle melodramatic?"

"Not at all." Aunt Patricia set her cup down on the saucer. "Think on his history. His parents were virtually obsessed with each other, so consumed by their love for one another that they couldn't share themselves with anyone else—not even their only son. Then he enters society, only to be exposed to a few fickle beauties who professed undying love for him one moment then turned around to express the same thing to someone with more money or a bigger title." Aunt Patricia pressed her lips together for a moment. "It hardly led him to believe in true love. I'm positive that in his mind, love is an awful affliction. Either you are utterly obsessed with another person and it consumes your life, or you accept another's lies and infidelity. No, Crispin has not had any example of the joy love can bring."

"And have you?"

Bittersweet memories swept over Patricia. "Once. He was a merchant though, far too unsuitable for a duke's daughter, so my father forbid the match. I followed his dictates and sent my love away." She sighed deeply. "Still, for a brief moment, I had a taste of the power of true love. I might have it still, if only I'd had the strength to follow my heart." She focused her gaze upon Owen. "Which is precisely why I am determined to steer Crispin in the right direction."

"I fully understand your intent, but you might have a problem succeeding," Owen pointed out. "After all, Cris's knowledge of love would put anyone off."

Aunt Patricia rose gracefully. "I do believe it is best if we simply allow this romance to develop on its own."

"The seed of marriage has already been planted in his mind," Owen pointed out, rising to his feet. "Perhaps it will take root."

"I'm hopeful." Aunt Patricia clasped Owen's arm, allowing him to escort her from the room. "After all, Crispin has always had a fertile mind."

7

Brilliant sunlight streamed through Amelia's bedroom window, but it did nothing to lighten her dark mood. She lay back upon her bed, her tears gone, but her heart still aching.

For so long she'd dreamt of Cris. Her imagination had only been fed by all of Aunt Patricia's stories about Cris's life in town, tales of all the beauties he'd escorted.

How she'd envied all those faceless women. When she'd first seen Cris after their long separation, the image of him as a renowned lover had blended with that of her storybook hero. Her dreams of him had taken on the sharper edge of a woman's desires. No longer had she dreamt of him sweeping her off her feet. No, now she'd longed for him to hold her in his arms, to make her feel like a woman . . . his woman. She'd ached for him to introduce her to the delights of love.

And then, to make matters worse, she'd expanded her dreams, so bright and hopeful, to include her sisters. With Cris at her side, she could have given her sisters a glorious Season, securing marriages for each one. Marriages built on love and respect, just like her own marriage with Cris. She had fantasized such lovely things.

Such lovely, *childish* things.

Her dreams had still been those of a little girl, imagining a prince on a white horse racing up to save her from sadness, pain, and loneliness. Cris was no knight come to rescue her. He was merely a dear friend who felt concern for her, not undying love. She'd allowed herself to be caught up in her own fantasies, misunderstanding his words, the tone of his voice, twisting their meanings to fit her desires. She'd taken his innocent statements and looked at them with her heart instead of her mind. She thought to become his wife.

Instead, she'd become his fool.

It wasn't fair to blame him; he'd not led her on. No, he'd only been trying to phrase his questions in a delicate manner. She realized that now.

Unfortunately, too late.

How would she ever face him again? How could she look him in the eye and act as if she hadn't completely humiliated herself? It seemed impossible.

Her head pounded with her dark thoughts. Not only did she have Cris to confront, but she also needed to confront her own reality. Her family's financial situation was truly becoming dire. She'd sold off everything of value they possessed except for her mother's brooch—yet it still wasn't enough.

Could she afford to refuse Cris's offer of financial help simply to maintain her pride?

The thought of accepting his help made her ill. She'd rejected it out of hand this morning, her stung pride demanding no less, but could she hold true to her position? What was more important, her dignity or the loss of their family home? The answer, the only answer, was too difficult for her to contemplate.

Unable to bear her own thoughts for a moment longer, Amelia ventured out of her room in search of her sisters. The sound of laughter drew her toward the garden; or rather, what remained of their garden. Bea, Camilla, and Emma surrounded Deanna who tried to juggle three fat green peppers. Their gales of laughter were a balm to her soul.

A smile curved on her face as she walked closer. "Are you performing tricks, Deanna?"

Startled, Deanna glanced at Amelia and missed one of the peppers. It fell to the ground, cracking open, white seeds spilling forth.

Immediately, Deanna frowned as she looked down, clutching the remaining two peppers in her hands. "Blast, Amelia, you made me pop my pepper."

That was all it took to send the Ralston girls off into another fit of laughter. This time Amelia joined in as well. After a minute, a smile tugged up the corners of Deanna's mouth until she too was giggling.

"Popped your pepper," Beatrice gasped, wiping the tears from her eyes. "That's the funniest thing I ever heard, Deanna."

"Peter Piper popped his pepper. How many peppers popped on Peter Piper?" Deanna twisted the old rhyme to suit the moment.

The sisters lost themselves to laughter again.

Finally, short of breath, Amelia sank onto the grass. "Oh, thank you all. I needed that laugh so much."

"You can always count on Deanna for a giggle," Emma said, sitting at the same time as Camilla and Beatrice.

"Our personal jester," Camilla said, folding her legs beneath her.

Deanna looked at the ground, shaking her head. "If I sit down I'll land right in squashed pepper."

Amelia smiled, patting the grass next to her. "Come over here, Deanna." She glanced at her sister's skirts. "Even though it's a bit too late to be worrying about stains."

"Oh, no," Deanna exclaimed, sticking out a leg to look at the splatter marks on her skirt. Immediately, she reached for the hem, dropping the two remaining peppers in the process.

They too broke open, spattering even more green juice upon Deanna's soiled pink dress. "Oh!" She jumped back, but the damage had already been done.

"My dress is ruined," wailed Deanna, holding the skirt out wide. "Look what those popping peppers have done."

Amelia tilted her head to the side, trying not to laugh. "It doesn't look so terrible, Deanna."

"Perhaps if you drop a few more at your sides and behind you, it will even out the green splatter marks and people will assume it's the style of the dress," Camilla jested, before clutching her stomach in laughter again.

"Pay her no mind," Amelia said, once more patting the spot next to her. "Come take a seat. Don't worry about your dress. We can dye it to a darker color and the stains will blend in."

Relief softened Deanna's expression as she plopped down next to Amelia. "You always know exactly what to do to make things right."

The memories of her embarrassing mistake with Cris flooded her. "Not always," she murmured.

"You always know how to make *me* feel better." Emma reached for Amelia's hand. "Whenever I'm worried about being too shy with people, you tell me not to fret, to concentrate on being myself, and before I know it, I don't feel nervous anymore."

Amelia nodded, her gaze warm. "You've done so well overcoming your nervousness, Emma." If only all things were that easy.

"I love how you know what is truly important to us. Look how you're forever encouraging me with my piano." Camilla plucked a blade of grass. "I realize quite well that you could have sold the piano a long time ago, but you haven't."

"Music is your love, Camilla. We could never sell the piano," Amelia replied gently.

"That is precisely what I mean, Amie. My piano

would have fetched a fair price, but you felt that the value to me outweighed the money and you couldn't be more right." Camilla leaned over to kiss Amelia upon the cheek. "Thank you."

The ache in Amelia's heart began to ease, her sisters praise raising her spirits. She'd come into the garden so upset over her embarrassing scene with Cris, and yet her sisters had grounded her. With their laughter, they had broken through her misery over her utter loss of pride. They'd made her realize that she still had everything of value that she had possessed before the debacle—her family, her health, her home.

Her sisters had also helped her to realize that she would do anything to keep those treasures safe—even beggar her sense of pride.

Right now, the thought of accepting Cris's proposition stung her heart, but she now realized that if she'd lost one of her sisters or their home, her heart would be torn asunder. Her sisters had helped her put the entire incident with Cris in proper perspective.

She hoped that, regardless of the final outcome of Cris's offer, she would be able to count his friendship among her treasures. Surely, this was something they could get past.

All she needed to do was calmly explain to Cris that she had allowed her girlish fantasies to color her judgment. He had been so noble by offering to help them. It was not his fault she had wanted more, had dreamed of more.

The time had come to put aside the dreams of

her youth, to meet him on a firm footing. If she approached their next meeting calmly, logically, there was no reason why they couldn't move beyond her blunder. And if the time came that she would be forced to accept his offer, then she would feel more comfortable doing so as his friend.

Amelia felt immensely better. Sitting there in the sun with her sisters nearby, all four of them still giggling and joking, her spirits were raised.

"You know, Camilla, you said that your piano would fetch a pretty price." Deanna wore a wicked grin, "Do you suppose it would be enough to purchase a few new gowns for each of us?"

"Oh, no, you don't, Deanna," Camilla began. "Don't look at my piano and think it can be sold to pay for more fripperies for you."

"It only seems fair, don't you think, Bea?" Deanna looked to her older sister.

"Don't be pulling me into your argument," Bea returned with a laugh. "If you two want to start bickering again, I most certainly do not wish to be involved."

Emma sighed loudly. "Why are the two of you always at each other?"

"It's not me," protested Camilla. "I'm not the one who starts it."

"Yes, but you always join right in," Deanna pointed out.

Amelia just smiled as her sisters launched into yet another heated discussion. There was something so comforting in the routine, she thought, tilting her face up toward the sun. Yes, right at this moment, they were all doing just fine. And, she now knew, they'd be fine if she were ever forced to accept Cris's offer. After all, she could survive anything for her sisters.

Love made them strong.

Amelia closed her eyes, allowing herself to drift as her sisters continued arguing around her.

"Why you . . . you . . ." Camilla sputtered. "Oh, just be quiet for once, Deanna!"

Amelia grinned up at the sun.

Ah, yes, the truly important things in her life would go on untouched.

"Good evening, Papa," Amelia said as she walked toward her father's bed. "How are you feeling this evening?"

His drawn features brightened. "As well as could be expected," he replied, his voice soft and weak. "How are you, angel?"

Amelia sank onto the edge of his bed. "I'm fine, Papa." She didn't want to tell him of her misunderstanding with Cris. No, her father seemed more drained this evening than ever before, and didn't need to worry over her. "Were the other girls in to visit?"

Her father's smile was a pale version of the one she'd received as a child. "All of them."

"Wonderful," Amelia said, searching for lighter things to discuss. "Did Deanna tell you what happened in the garden earlier? It was very amusing and—"

"You are so good to your sisters," her father

rasped, reaching out to take her hand. "You care for them, love them, as if they were your own children. I just wish tha—" Her father's words were cut off as a coughing fit overtook him.

Amelia eased him into a sitting position, propping the pillows up behind him. His coughing lessened, then finally ceased and he lay quiet, his eyes closed. It terrified Amelia to see him like that, so pale, so still. It was hard for her to hide her fear, but she did it, not wanting to burden her father with that as well.

"Can I get you something, Papa? A glass of water, perhaps?"

He shook his head, opening his eyes to gaze at her. "I need to talk with you, my darling Amie. There's so much I should have done, should have told you, long before this," he said, finishing with a cough.

"Don't tax yourself, Papa. Why don't you rest now and I'll come back for a visit tomorrow morning?"

Amelia started to rise, but her father held onto her hand with surprising strength. "No, Amelia, we need to talk now."

"You're not feeling well enough now, Papa," she protested.

Sadness welled in his eyes. "I'm never going to be feeling better than this, my sweet Amie."

The finality in his tone scared her. "Why, of course you are, Papa," she said, ignoring the panic within her. "All you need is a little more rest."

"I'm dying, Amelia."

Pain, terror, and an aching sense of loss combined to claw at her heart. Amelia fought to hold back the tears. "Don't be ridiculous, Papa. We can get some medicine that will—"

"I am *dying*."

She couldn't suppress her tears any longer. They spilled down her cheeks as she collapsed onto her father's bed, pressing her face against his clasped hands. "You can't die, Papa. I don't want to lose you too."

"Shhh, Amie. It will be all right. You'll see," he comforted her.

Amie wanted to scream, to lash out at the unfairness of it all as she accepted the truth in her heart. She was going to lose her papa. "I love you," she whispered brokenly against the back of his hand.

Her father slipped a hand beneath her chin, lifting her head until she met his gaze. "Ah, Amie, you are such a loving daughter." Sadness filled his expression. "And I've wronged you so dreadfully."

"You've never wronged me," Amelia protested, sitting up.

"You're mistaken, angel. I allowed you to become responsible for your sisters when you were far too young." Her father shifted against his pillows. "After your mother died . . ." he began, pain darkening his eyes. Finally, he began again. "I was so terribly sad, so overcome with grief, that I didn't care for you girls as I should have done."

"Oh, Papa," Amelia whispered. "We always knew you were there if we needed you."

His sigh was filled with remorse. "That wasn't enough, Amie. I should have been there for everything—like you were." He trailed a finger down her cheek. "You were there every single day for your sisters, kissing their hurts, mending their disagreements, and sharing their joys. You became responsible for your sisters after your mother died—and I let you."

"I've never minded all of that, Papa. I love my sisters," Amelia insisted.

"I know you do, angel, but you were far too young to bear that burden. I am truly sorry." Papa lifted her hand to his lips, kissing the back of it before pressing her palm to his cheek. "I've made sure that you and your sisters will be secure after my death."

Amelia felt tears threatening again. "Please, Papa, don't speak of it." She pulled her hand free.

"We *must*, Amie," her father insisted. "I'm certain there isn't much time left."

Slowly, he lifted the handkerchief he'd used to cover his mouth during his coughing fit. Her breath caught in her throat at the blood dotting the material.

"For the past week, I've been coughing up blood, Amie, and it's getting worse."

Amelia wanted to clap her hands over her ears to keep from hearing any more. But she couldn't. Her papa needed her to be strong once again. Amelia swiped at the tears that rolled down her cheeks. "What do you need to tell me, Papa?"

Relief blended with love in his gaze. "That's my

girl." He wadded up the handkerchief, hiding it from her view. "I've written to a distant cousin of mine, Hubert Collings. We used to play together when we were children, but I haven't seen him in many, many years. We promised to remain close, but for no good reason we both let our friendship slip away. In any case, Hubert is coming here to Ralston Hall to care for you and your sisters. He's a merchant of some sort, a wealthy one at that, so he'll be able to ease your financial worries."

"But, Papa," Amelia began, her insides clenching at the thought of a stranger taking control of her family. "I don't know him at all . . . and . . . and you've not seen him since you were a boy. You've never talked about him or—"

"Don't worry, Amie. If he's at all as I remember, you'll like him. He always had this—" Her father's words were cut short when another cough seized him.

Amelia helped her father hold the handkerchief to his mouth, trying not to cry as spots of blood soaked through the cloth.

After a long moment, the fit passed. "Hubert Collings is—"

"Ssshhhh," Amelia hushed her father, smoothing her hand over his forehead. "I trust you, Papa. If you liked him, I'm sure he'll be a wonderful guardian." She looked down at her father, seeing him as he once was, confident, strong, vibrant. "We'll be fine."

8

"The pastor said her father was on his deathbed—literally." Alonso crossed his booted feet and stretched them toward the fireplace of the inn. "I wrote to Prospero, telling him of what we found here." He looked about the shabby parlor room of their rented lodgings. "Though I neglected to tell him that there was only one decrepit inn here in these wilds."

"Exactly what *did* you tell Prospero?" Sebastian asked, reaching toward the fire to dispel the unusual chill of the early summer evening.

Alonso shrugged. "I told him of their father. Oh, and I also told him this interesting tidbit. Apparently, the kind, loose-lipped pastor helped dear old Papa write a letter to his cousin, telling the man of his imminent death and asking the fellow to guard his five sweet babies."

"Touching," Sebastian murmured, leaning back from the fire to rest his hands on his stomach. "I think it's fairly clear now that these chits are unacceptable game."

"I beg to differ," protested Alonso. "If anything, the death of their father simply makes them more appealing. Just imagine how vulnerable they'll be now."

Sebastian scowled at his friend. "There is no sport in hunting wounded prey."

"Perhaps," Alonso agreed. "But the wealth of beauty in that family can make me overlook the lack of challenge in the game." He laid his head back against the chair in the inn's private parlor. "Come now, Sebastian, and tell me that you wouldn't care to sample one of those morsels."

Sebastian hesitated for a few seconds, finally shaking his head. "I doubt if I could hold out against such temptation."

Alonso reached over and slapped Sebastian's leg. "Now *that's* the Sebastian I know."

"No one should be buried on such a glorious day," Owen murmured, squinting against the brilliant noonday sun.

"I don't believe there's ever a good day for a funeral," Aunt Patricia returned softly. "Excuse me, gentlemen. I'm going to see to the girls."

Cris watched as his aunt walked over to the Ralston sisters, who stood on the other side of the grave, clinging to each other. Emma flew into Aunt Patricia's arms, holding tight. Cris gazed at Amelia as she offered comfort to her sobbing sisters, her eyes red and swollen from tears already spent.

He wanted nothing more than to take Amelia into his arms, to give her the freedom to let go of the pain. But he held back, all too aware of the wall that now stood between them, knowing she would never accept his comfort.

The certainty ate away at him. He'd had nothing but the best of intentions when he'd returned here to Dovedale, yet he'd ended up alienating the one person who meant so much to him.

Cris couldn't quite understand how everything had gotten so complicated between him and Amelia. He longed to talk to her, to make things right, but this was hardly the time.

He wasn't insensitive to the fact that Amelia was suffering now. She had to be feeling the pain of her loss, along with fear of the future, the unknown—not only for herself but for her family as well.

They could be perfectly fine.

Cris started at the answer floating in his thoughts,

Marry the girl.

Cris stumbled slightly, knocking into Owen who sent him a questioning look. Cris paid him no heed, too engrossed in his thoughts.

Without marriage she and her sisters will either be homeless or begging off the mercy of relatives.

Suddenly, the idea that had seemed so far-fetched mere days ago made perfect sense. When he'd first proposed to be her guardian, it had been in an informal sense; he would merely have assisted the family financially. However, now that her father was gone and Amelia was a single, vulnerable woman, such an informal guardianship would do nothing but cast aspersions on Amelia's reputation. He could hardly give moneys to aid a single woman without having quite a few people in the community lift an eyebrow at the situation.

But if he married Amelia, no one would bat a lash. If he married her, not only would he be helping Amelia, but her sisters as well. Theirs wouldn't be a love match; no, it would be even better. She only wanted what was best for her sisters just as he did. The need to protect them, all of them, pulsed through him. It would be a solid union of two like souls, aimed toward the same future, bonded in friendship and affection.

It was the perfect solution. Amelia had seen the wisdom of their union before he had. In fact, she'd already accepted his proposal . . . before he'd even made it. That thought made him smile.

It made perfect sense for them to marry. Why had he not seen that immediately? Undoubtedly the idea of marrying Amelia had seemed strange simply because of the sheer newness of the concept; a few days of thinking about her as a potential wife had cleared his thoughts.

Resolution strengthened him as he gazed over at Amelia. His decision felt so good, the perfect solution for them both. He would give her a few days to grieve, then he would call on her and propose. He wished he could wait a bit longer, realizing that the timing couldn't have been worse. However, the situation was far too precarious to put off his declaration. For all he knew, the state of their financial affairs could be extremely urgent, if the condition of Ralston Hall were any indication.

With her father's death, creditors would undoubtedly come to collect. But he could stop all of that from happening.

He would make Amelia his wife.

Five days later, Cris straightened his cravat in the mirror as his aunt smoothed the shoulders of the jacket he'd just shrugged into.

"You haven't tied it high enough," Owen pointed out.

"I think his cravat is perfect," Aunt Patricia said. "Though the shirt could use pressing."

It was all Cris could do to keep from shrugging away from their ministrations. "I am perfectly capable of dressing myself."

"It is not every day that my nephew decides to propose marriage." Aunt Patricia stood in front of Cris and smoothed his vest. "So if I feel the need to ensure that you are properly outfitted, then you should indulge me, Crispin."

Cris kissed the back of her hand. "I spoil you rotten."

Aunt Patricia laughed brightly. "I know, so you've no one to blame but yourself for my occasional interference."

"If I didn't love you so . . ." Cris trailed off, his eyes gleaming.

"What of me, Cris?" Owen asked teasingly.

Cris caught his friend's gaze in the mirror. "You really need to ask?"

Owen shook his head. "No. I just like to hear over and over again how highly you regard me."

"That's right, Owen. Continue to tell yourself that and perhaps you'll come to believe it," Cris joked as he stepped away from the mirror to retrieve his gloves.

"Enough, both of you," Aunt Patricia chided. "This is hardly the time for your nonsense."

"So true." Cris leaned down to kiss his aunt's cheek. "I have a lady to court."

"The beautiful Amie." Owen slapped Cris's back lightly. "If I didn't abhor the thought of marriage, I'd envy you your choice."

"Pay Owen no heed. I'm quite sure Amelia will make you very happy, dear." Aunt Patricia patted the front of Cris's jacket. "Now you run along and propose to your young lady while I spend time with your lovely friend."

Owen spread his fingers wide over his chest. "Do you have plans for me?"

"Most definitely," Aunt Patricia said, nodding at the earl. "I believe I'll have you pose for me. I've wanted to try my hand at portraits."

Owen's expression froze. "Pose? As in sitting for you?"

"Only for a few hours," Aunt Patricia replied. "I'll pick a comfortable pose for you, so you won't stiffen up so quickly."

"Stiffen?" Owen's eyes grew round. "Hmmm . . . I'm not sure I'll be able to spare the time, much as I'd like to. I really should be—"

"Oh, I'm sure you'll manage," Aunt Patricia

countered, stepping forward to take Owen's arm. "After all, I'm practically family."

Cris grinned as Owen began to stutter out another excuse, only to have Aunt Patricia deflect it smoothly.

"Cris . . . help?" Owen implored him.

"Sorry, old chum. You're on your own," Cris answered quickly, trying to hold back a laugh as he watched his aunt tug Owen down the hall.

"Come on with you, Owen. It won't be half so bad. I promise." Aunt Patricia turned to wave at Cris. "Enjoy yourself, darling."

"Fine friend you turned out to be," Owen tossed over his shoulder. A moment later, he'd turned around, looking down at the elderly, iron-willed woman. "If you insist on doing this, I'd prefer if you'd paint my right side. It's my better one."

Aunt Patricia smiled up at Owen. "No need to worry, dear. I highly doubt if it will matter."

"I wanted to tell you how sorry I was about your father," Cris leaned forward to squeeze Amelia's clasped hands.

"Thank you," Amelia said softly, not meeting his gaze.

Cris shifted nervously on his chair, overwhelmingly aware of the awkwardness between them. "How are you and your sisters holding up?" he asked, trying to ease into the conversation.

"Very well, thank you."

Her polite murmurings were making him feel more than anxious. Had he truly damaged their relationship to the point where they could no longer even converse as friends? "Amie, I believe we need to speak openly about our misunderstanding," he began firmly. "This wall between us bothers me greatly."

For the first time since he'd entered the parlor, Amelia's gaze lifted to meet his. "I find it distressing also," she whispered.

Cris took a deep breath, the tightness in his chest loosening. "I've thought a lot about what happened when I asked to be your guardian and I take full responsibility for the incident. The things I said to you could easily have been misconstrued."

A dull flush crept onto Amelia's face, but she kept her gaze on him. "I can't allow you to take full blame for the misunderstanding. I am guilty of reading far too much into everything you said."

The corners of his mouth quirked upward. "Let's not get into a disagreement about which one of us is *more* responsible now."

"Fine," Amelia said, her expression lightening slightly. "It's your fault then."

"Well, you certainly conceded that point quickly enough," he returned, smiling at her. Encouraged, Cris tried to ease the conversation onto marriage. "I've thought quite a bit about your situation now, Amie, and—"

"Please, oh, please do not offer financial support again," Amelia urged, this time cutting Cris off. "It truly is not necessary now."

"Amelia," Cris began softly. "I am well aware of your present situation, of your financial situation."

"But it has changed." She waved a hand about. "Everything is going to be different. You see, we've heard from a distant cousin—at least I believe he'd be considered my cousin—he is coming here to Ralston Hall."

Cris gazed into her hopeful face and felt more jaded than ever before. He'd seen enough to know that this uncle of hers would undoubtedly come along and toss her and her sisters aside once he realized there was no money involved with the estate. But how did he tell Amie without hurting her? Uncertain, Cris merely said, "I was sure that someone would show up. After all, there is a title and lands involved in this transfer."

Amelia nodded in agreement. "So, you see there is no reason for you to be concerned for us, Cris."

"I *am* concerned," he insisted. "You don't know this relative. If he's so wonderful why hasn't he come before all of this? Not even for a visit."

Her smile dimmed. "I'm not sure."

"Which should only point toward caution." He could see her hope diminish at his logic.

"Perhaps I'm being overly optimistic," she said finally.

Her expression made him feel like he'd just taken all the color from her dreams of the future. Cris moved into the chair next to hers, grasping her hand between his. "The only reason I spoke so bluntly, Amelia, is because *I* wish to be the one to care for you."

Amelia tried to tug her hand from his. "No, Cris, please. Do not offer to be our guardian again!"

"You misunderstand me, Amelia," he said in a rush, refusing to let go of her hand. "I wish to make a new offer. You made perfect sense here the other day. I just needed time to adapt to your suggestion. I care for you and your sisters already and we've proven to be fabulous companions in our youth. I would like you to consider becoming my wife."

Her eyes widened in shock. "Pardon me?"

How could he have expected anything less after his reaction a mere week ago? "I would like you to marry me, Amie," he repeated.

She sat there, looking at him as if she were having a difficult time comprehending his proposal.

Cris rose to his feet and began to pace. "It would be wonderful, Amie. There would be none of that awful pretense between us, nor any of the dreadful obsession that I observed with my parents. We're two people with like minds and similar outlooks. We could have a lovely, comfortable marriage."

Amelia watched him, her face set in serious lines. "A marriage of convenience in a way?"

He grinned at her, pleased at her astute understanding of his offer. "Exactly. It would be the perfect solution for both of us. You and your sisters would never want for anything . . ."

". . . and you would gain a wife and hopefully an heir with little trouble," she finished for him.

"See?" He gestured toward her. "We already think enough alike to finish the other's sentences."

"Cris, I am honored by your offer," she whispered, finally smiling up at him for the first time since he'd asked for her hand in marriage. "You are such a wonderful friend."

He gazed down at her upturned face. This felt right. This *was* right. Cris knelt before her to propose in a manner befitting his future wife. "Amelia, will you be my wife?"

Amelia's lips trembled as she reached out to place a gentle hand on his face. Warmth blazed out of her eyes as she whispered the one word that would seal both of their fates.

"No."

9

Startled, Cris gasped. "What did you say?"

Amelia remained calm beneath his incredulous stare. "Thank you for the generous offer, Cris, but no."

"No?"

"No. Thank you, but no." It was fairly obvious from his reaction that she'd shocked him. "I've surprised you, haven't I?"

"To say the least," Cris said, his tone stunned.

"I don't mean to cause any more tension between us. I value your friendship far too much."

He shook his head. "You've lost me, Amie. It was precisely because of our friendship that I proposed. Marriage between us would be strong and honest."

"No, it wouldn't, Cris. It would be an arrangement between friends. It wouldn't be the sort of grand passion my parents found, the perfect match your parents shared." Amelia leaned forward. "We've both seen great love, Cris. We both know what we'd be missing if we married just because it's convenient. I don't wish to marry simply because I'm comfortable with you."

Cris stood, looking down at Amelia. "Yes, Amie, we've both *seen* passionate love, but is it truly something to be desired? Your father willed himself to death. He withdrew from you and your sisters years ago, forgetting all but the loss of his beloved wife. My parents were so engrossed in each other that they ignored all else." He waved his hand in a dismissive gesture. "If that's love, I'll avoid it for all I'm worth."

Amelia rose, facing Cris. "I know that you were hurt by your parents' actions, but surely as an adult you can appreciate the love they shared."

"The only thing I appreciate is the fact that I never want to be utterly consumed by another person." His features hardened. "Never."

"But I do," she whispered softly. "I want what my parents had—the love, the laughter. My father used to look at my mother as if she were his sun, his world. I want to be someone's sunshine, Cris."

"You want to be ruled by emotions?"

"Yes. I suppose I do." A soft smile curved her lips. "I want to experience the magic of love and I'll take the bad along with the good in order to do so."

He sighed, exasperation laced in the sound. "We could have something so much better, Amie. It could be solid, sure, not a seething mass of intensity."

How could she make him understand that after

years of weaving fairy tales, she craved exactly that wealth of emotion. Amelia stepped forward, placing a hand on Cris's chest. "I want to feel love. I want a husband who looks at me as if he could not imagine being with anyone else. I dream of a man who sweeps me away with his passion." She gazed deeply into his eyes. "No, Cris. Being comfortable is not enough for me."

He reached out, his hands grasping her shoulders. "Ours would not be a marriage in name only," he whispered, drawing her nearer until her body pressed against his, her hand trapped between them. "I would give you passion."

Amelia held still, melting beneath the heat of his gaze, as Cris bent toward her. Here was the man she'd always dreamed of. This was the man she'd prayed would return to her. The man who had the power to take her.

Her thoughts skittered to a halt at the first touch of his lips. Gently, he shaped his lips to hers, learning their texture, brushing against the softness. Naturally, her lips parted beneath his mouth and she strained toward him.

Cris froze for a moment as she offered all to him, then his arms tightened around her and he deepened the kiss. When his tongue slid between her open lips, Amelia quivered beneath the onslaught of heat. She angled her head to increase the contact, feathering her own tongue against his, craving his taste, his touch. Hungers she hadn't even known existed thundered through her as she slid her hand up around his neck, curling her fingers into his hair.

Every inch of her body burst to life, awareness sizzling throughout her, as Cris began to devour her, his hunger sparking a fire within her. His hands slid down to her hips as he rocked her tightly against him. A groan broke from him and he started to pull back, but Amelia wasn't ready to end the delightful torment yet.

She leaned forward, until he moaned again, plunging into her welcoming warmth, his touch ravenous, his hold unyielding. Again and again, he took what she offered, giving back her hunger in equal measure.

Amelia arched into him as Cris kissed her until she shivered with need, her very senses bursting with desire. She ached for him. Amelia moaned a little when she felt his mouth begin to ease upward, protesting the loss.

Cris broke off their kiss, pressing his mouth against the side of her neck. "Do you not feel all we could have, Amelia? Not a cold, passionless marriage, but one of trust and desire."

She tipped her head to the side, giving Cris greater access to her burning flesh, as she listened to him, willing herself to believe.

"We would have the best of both worlds. Passion without the tentacles of obsessive love. We could enjoy the delights of desire, yet still retain a hold on our true selves. It's perfect," he murmured, nibbling on the curve of her neck. "Perfect."

Amelia closed her eyes tightly, trying to block out his whispers now. His reasoning was beginning to set off alarms within her. She ignored the twinge of discomfort, desperately wanting to believe the desire she tasted in him was true.

"See, Amie?" he said again, brushing his lips against her earlobe. "I can give you what you want. I can feel desire for you."

Her heart slowed within her breast. She felt like crying as the dream she'd indulged in for a few passionate, incredible moments faded before her. Amelia wedged her arms between them. "I now know that you can feel desire for me, Cris, but do you want to?"

A frown furrowed upon his brow. "What are you saying? Of course I want to."

"Do you truly, Cris?"

The confusion in his gaze hardened into annoyance. "Blast it all, Amie, don't start talking in riddles. I'm trying to understand your protests, truly I am, but I'm having a devil of a time just trying to follow what you're saying."

The last little light of hope flickered out. "Exactly."

Cris took a deep breath, the flush of desire gone. "I'm afraid you'll need to be a bit more specific, Amelia."

She stepped back, clasping her hands in front of her. "You can make yourself feel desire for me because I said I wished for passion in a marriage."

"I did desire you just now. Couldn't you tell?"

"Desire is a far cry from love."

"I know that, Amie; I'm just not certain what that has to do with us. Friendship mixed with desire is far more important than love in a marriage."

"How can you say that?" Amelia wondered, raw emotion choking her. "How can you believe that?"

"It's far easier than you imagine. I've experienced more of life's lessons than you, my dear Amie, so you'll have to trust me."

Undoubtedly he was speaking of his various affairs, Amelia decided, bothered by the thought more than she wanted to acknowledge. "Let me ask you a question, Cris. Did you love all those ladies that you've taken to your bed?"

She'd managed to shock him yet again. "What do you mean by that?"

"I've heard about all your tomcatting in London, about all the ladies you've dallied with," Amelia admitted, lifting her chin.

"How did you—" he broke off, a grim set to his mouth. "Aunt Patricia?"

Amelia nodded firmly. "I highly doubt your aunt would exaggerate."

"Even if she didn't, I fail to see what bearing it has on our situation. That was in the past. I never asked any of them to marry me."

"Did you even feel affection for them?" Amelia demanded.

"I'm not about to stand here and discuss—"

"Did you?"

"Yes!" Cris exploded, thrusting a hand through his hair. "Yes. I felt affection for a few of them."

"Would you say you considered them friends?"

"Dear God, Amelia, why must you continue on this—"

"Would you?"

"Yes," Cris ground out, a fierce frown darkening his expression.

Amelia remained undaunted. "Then why didn't you consider marrying any of them?" she asked in a rush. "According to you, that is all that's necessary for a successful marriage. Affection, desire. The perfect blend that leaves your physical senses fulfilled and your emotional ones uninvolved."

Cris let out an expletive. "You are deliberately twisting my words!"

"No, Cris. I'm not. I'm merely pointing out the problems that would occur if we were to marry for the wrong reasons." Amelia reached out a hand to him. "Try to understand, Cris. Let's say we were to marry. Perhaps we got along fine for a few years, even had children, but then you grew tired of being comfortable. What if you met someone who ignited all of your passions—your heart, your soul, and your body? Then what would become of us? Our family? Suddenly you would be trapped within our marriage. And I would be left to regret ever accepting your proposal."

"I will never want the type of love you describe," he asserted firmly. "Never."

"How can you be so sure?"

"I just am."

"But how, Cris? What if you met a woman who twisted you up inside until all you could think of is her?"

"I assure you, Amelia, it will never happen," he ground out. "I will never allow it to happen."

"Then I feel very sorry for you, Cris," she said

slowly. "I want to feel the delights of falling in love. I want the joy, the heartache, the whirling emotions. I want it all." Amelia walked toward the window to gaze out upon the ill-kept grounds. "For years I've dreamed of you, Cris. I built you up in my head as this wonderful hero who would return someday and sweep me off my feet."

"I'm no hero, Amie," he said in a rush, frustration coloring his voice.

She turned to smile at him. "And that is precisely the problem, Cris, for I think you are. I've thought of you in that way for so long, it's hard for me to separate my dreams from the reality of you. I don't know the man you've become and you still think of me as the little girl you left behind. We've both experienced things that have changed us, so to enter into marriage based on a ten-year-old friendship is foolish."

"We would have far more between us than most people start with," he argued.

"I am not 'most people,' Cris, and I need more from a marriage."

His hands settled on his hips. "Even if you find that type of love, you won't be happy."

"Perhaps not," she returned calmly. "But I need to find that out for myself."

Cris threw his arms wide. "How can I convince you of the logic of my proposal?"

"You already have." Amelia gazed at the man she'd woven all her dreams around and whispered farewell to him in her heart. "You have made perfect sense to my head, but not to my heart, Cris. In my heart, I believe in love and want it more than the security you offer."

"I can't believe this," he muttered, shaking his head, before inhaling deeply. "All right, Amelia. What if we spend more time together and get to know each other again? Why dismiss my proposal out of hand? Give us time to become reacquainted."

"Why? You have made it quite obvious that you wish for a future far different from the one I want. You will not search for love while I do not wish to marry for less."

"I can see there is no point in continuing this conversation. It is obvious that you will not view this situation logically," Cris finished, his voice tight with frustration.

"Ah, but that is one of the beautiful things about love. It doesn't need to be logical; it can simply be."

Cris shook his head. "I want you to think on all I've said here, Amelia, and give my proposal serious consideration. If you marry me, it will benefit not only the two of us but also your sisters as well."

"I know," Amelia said sadly. "But I've already devoted the first twenty-two years of my life to my sisters. Must I give the rest as well?"

"Lord! You make it sound as if marriage to me would be a life sentence."

"Then I apologize, Cris. I meant nothing of the sort. I truly do appreciate your kind offer."

"But not the reasons behind it," he finished.

"Precisely."

Cris's jaw grew taut. It was clear that his patience

was at an end. "I will come back after you've had some time to consider everything and we can discuss my offer again then."

Amelia shrugged. "I will not change my mind."

"I'd rather hoped you'd begin using it," he returned.

"No need to get insulting, Cris."

He flushed lightly. "True enough, Amelia. It is now my turn to offer apologies."

A charged silence fell between them. Amelia desperately wished Cris accepted her reasons for refusing him. "Do you see how awkward it could get between us?"

His eyes blazed to life an instant before he reached out and pulled her against him again. His lips crushed hers, hot, passionate, igniting the fury of desire he'd created earlier. A moment later, she was free.

Her heart raced as she lifted a trembling hand to her lips as she gazed at Cris's impassioned features. "That is what I see can grow between us. So, as you weigh the disadvantages of marriage, remember to count your desire for me into the equation."

Amelia nodded, still uncertain of her ability to speak.

Satisfaction scored his expression as he bowed lightly before leaving the room.

When the door shut behind him, Amelia sank down on the chair, her body still tingling with the storm of sensations Cris aroused within her. Confusion intermingled with desire. If Cris could desire women, yet not love them, couldn't the same hold true for her? Did she, in truth, love Cris or had she merely been dreaming of him for so long, she'd convinced herself that she did? Was her desire for him a product of her natural urges or a manifestation of her love for him?

She simply didn't know.

Amelia leaned back against the chair, wishing she had someone in whom to confide. She certainly couldn't go to Aunt Patricia. After all, the lovely woman was Cris's true aunt, not hers. Amelia considered Mrs. Burke, but dismissed the idea, feeling awkward at confiding such an intimate problem. Amelia didn't feel she could consult with her sisters as they were involved too, in a manner of speaking. Her decision would affect all of them, so they weren't in a position to be objective.

If only Cris hadn't kissed her again. It had been so clear, so easy, until he'd enflamed her senses. Was Cris right after all? Could a marriage built merely on friendship and desire thrive? In her heart, she still believed that a marriage without love would never work. She couldn't bear the thought of giving her very soul to Cris, only to receive his desire and affection in return.

Amelia rubbed her temple; trying to sort through her feelings seemed impossible. She prayed for someone to help her see things clearly.

Little did she know that Uncle Hubert was already on the way.

10

God was surely smiling upon Hubert Collings this fine day!

The merchant's thoughts were filled with naught but the happiest of dreams. Oh, he knew very well he should feel very guilty for his joy. After all, his cousin and long-ago boyhood chum had passed away. He mourned him, truly, but the excitement pounding through his veins was hard to contain. Here he was in his prime, a healthy man of six and forty, with more money than he could spend in his lifetime spilling from his coffers—and now this.

Hubert leaned back against the fine-grained leather seat as his carriage headed toward Dovedale, where his destiny lay. He had many fond memories of cousin Roland and was quite sure that the good man was comfortably resting in Heaven. Hubert laced his thick fingers over his well-rounded belly, trying to hold onto a sense of remorse. An impossible task.

Still, Hubert knew that good old Roland would be the first to understand. The fact remained that when his dear cousin had passed on, he had left him, Hubert Collings, commoner, the lovely title of baron. He stroked his embroidered waistcoat in unconcealed excitement.

Finally, he had what he'd so long been denied. Not only a delightful title, but he'd also inherited the means to become connected to some of the most important families in England. He now had an entrée to society that not even money could buy.

He now had heiresses.

Yes, dear, wonderful, generous Roland had seen fit to bequeath Hubert guardianship of five daughters!

A thrilled chuckle burst from Hubert as the carriage pulled to a halt in front of a dilapidated pile of wood and rocks known as Ralston Hall. The ill repair bothered him not, Hubert decided, as he stepped down from his conveyance. No, he had enough money to fix the estate to its former elegance, still well in evidence in the graceful lines of the manor.

His steps were eager as he hurried toward the front door, too excited to maintain a decorous pace. As the housekeeper admitted Hubert into the foyer, he sent a prayer winging upward.

Let the chits be passable.

Oh, he'd learned long ago not to be too greedy and to accept the hand he'd been dealt, but if the girls weren't too hard on the eyes, then there'd be no telling what sort of match he could arrange—

with their large dowries as the primary attraction of course. Maybe he could land a marquis or even an earl for one of them!

Negotiating was his strong point, Hubert acknowledged with a smile as he followed the housekeeper down the arched corridor. With enough financial enticement, Hubert knew he'd be able to make suitable matches. As the good Lord knew, there were lots of young aristocrats from noble families who were living on nothing but their good names and hopes of an advantageous marriage to an heiress.

And he had five of them!

It was all Hubert could do to keep from jumping up and clicking his heels together. The housekeeper knocked discreetly at the paneled door before pushing it open. Hubert nodded his thanks to the woman as he stepped into the room.

His gaze swung toward the five young women in the room, each of them rising to their feet to face him. His heart began to pound within his chest so hard he clutched at it.

"Oh, Lord," he whispered, his eyes widening as he looked from one face to the next. Hubert staggered back from the impact, his continued silence unbearably rude, he knew, but he decided to forgive himself this lapse in the manners he'd learned at those fancy etiquette lessons.

After all, it wasn't every day that God granted a mere mortal his own private miracle! All five of them were beauties.

"Uncle Hubert?"

One of the lovelies came toward him, smiling so sweetly that it made him sigh. Lord, she even sounded like an angel.

Hubert looked toward the ceiling and whispered, "Bless you, Roland, for not passing along your crooked beak."

"So it's agreed then. We'll be off to London in three days," Uncle Hubert announced at dinner.

All five of them nodded eagerly. Amelia's heart felt light for the first time in years as she saw the glowing excitement on her sisters' faces. Their uncle had breezed into their lives earlier that day, just as she had finished telling her curious sisters why Cris had called upon her.

Her sisters had all been sympathetic, but before they could begin to discuss it in depth, Uncle Hubert had entered their lives. He hadn't even been with them for a full day, yet already he had breathed new life into everyone—herself included. She felt giddy with relief. Cris's doubts about her guardian had proved unfounded. Uncle Hubert was utterly delightful.

"Will you really buy us new gowns?" asked Deanna, leaning her elbows on the table, forgetting her manners in her excitement.

"Enough to burst the biggest wardrobe in London." Uncle Hubert wagged a finger at them. "Along with all the fripperies and gewgaws and such that go along with them."

Even Emma gasped in delight.

Uncle Hubert stuffed a bit of roasted pork into

his mouth, but the forkful didn't stop him from warming to the topic. "Then there's the sparklers you'll be needing."

Camilla had no trouble understanding him, despite his full mouth. "Sparklers? Do you mean jewels?"

Nodding, he blotted his lips with the cloth napkin. "What else? I can't have my girls prancing about London without a glitter or two."

Amelia glanced at her sisters, watching as even Bea—practical, sensible Bea—grew wide-eyed at his pronouncement.

"Shall we attend many grand parties?" asked Emma, sitting on the edge of her chair.

"Every night," Hubert returned, swinging his arms wide. "And when those young bucks see you lovelies sashay into the room, they'll flock to you."

Amelia hated to dampen the mood, but she felt compelled to ask, "How can we attend parties, Uncle Hubert? We are in mourning."

Her sisters sobered at the reminder, bringing back the darkness that had covered their house for the past two weeks. "I'm sorry to spoil your plans," Amelia said, "but we must show proper respect for Papa."

Uncle Hubert sat back in his chair. "That's true, Amelia, but it seems to me that your father's own wishes should stand for something."

"Pardon?" Amelia asked, unsure of her uncle's meaning.

"Your dear late father told me in his letter that he wished for you girls to get a twirl about London." Hubert pointed a finger at Amelia. "So, don't go getting yourself in a twiddle over it, Amelia. Your papa wanted you to go and have a grand time."

"But what will people say?" Amelia couldn't help but feel there was something wrong in planning parties so soon after her father's death.

Hubert snorted. "With the dowries I'm going to settle on each of you, the old hens will be so busy talking about the money, they'll not give a whit about improprieties."

Amelia didn't know if that was true or not. She'd never been to town and didn't know how people would react.

"Besides, we won't be leaving for town right away. I'll need at least a week to make arrangements for this wreck of a house to be repaired while we're in town. And then, once we get to London, I still need to dress you out which will take a bit of time," Hubert said earnestly.

Amelia looked at her sisters who sat quietly, shadows of sorrow darkening their beautiful eyes. It was enough to push aside her concerns. How could she even think of denying her sisters the greatest excitement they'd had in their lives? Amelia relented, smiling at Hubert. "We would love to see London."

"That's my girl," Hubert boomed. "You'll all take to London, I'll wager—and I'm sure that London will take to you. Why, in the wink of an eye, you'll all be waist deep in marriage proposals."

"Marriage?" For the first time since her uncle's

arrival, Amelia felt a twinge of unease. Suddenly, she realized that her uncle had complete control of their lives. All of her dreams and hopes would be for naught if Uncle Hubert arranged marriages for them. Her thoughts whirled as she tried to calm herself. "Surely you shall give us time to mourn our father?"

"Of course, but not forever." Uncle Hubert's expansive motions stopped for a moment. "Don't you want a husband and children?"

Before she could answer, Emma did it for her. "She wants to marry for love."

Uncle Hubert burst out laughing. "You're funning with me, aren't you?"

When all five of them shook their heads, their uncle's laughter faded away. "You're not?" His eyes widened, horrified. "You want to marry for love?"

"What is so incredulous about that notion?"

Hubert eyed Amelia, who remained still beneath the intense glare. "Here I was hoping you'd be practical, not filled with all sorts of romantic nonsense."

"The idea of love is hardly nonsense," Amelia returned briskly. Her uncle's statement reminded her all too much of her argument with Cris.

Uncle Hubert snorted. "Love doesn't secure a future. Without money, a home is a fool's wish, putting food into your mouth becomes impossible, and the clothes on your back turn to rags. For all your fine ideas of love, they don't cure those needs, I can tell you."

That stopped her cold. How could she argue that point? After all, she'd lived beneath the burden of empty coffers for far too long to dismiss her uncle's logic.

Seeing her pause, Uncle Hubert pressed his advantage. "When we head off to London, you can keep your wits about you to scope out a fine gentleman for yourselves, mayhap even one you fancy yourself in love with. No one's saying you can't love a rich gent. The trick is getting them to marry you—especially when their fine titles attract ladies like foxes to a peahen."

Once again, before Amelia could reply, Emma piped in. "But she's already declined a proposal from a fine lord."

"Lord? Lord, did you say?" Hubert sat upright, glancing between Emma and Amelia. "What's this about a lord?"

"Lord Crispin Merrick, Duke of Bradford," Bea supplied. "Our nearest neighbor."

Uncle Hubert almost fell off his chair. "Neighbor? You mean to tell me that a bleeding duke lives on the next estate and asked Amelia to be his bride and she *refused him*!" He reached out to catch Amelia's hand. "Please tell me it's not so."

"I'm afraid it is," she admitted in a quiet voice. "It was the only thing I could possibly do."

"Only thing you could—" Uncle Hubert broke off his words and released her hand, thumping back against his chair. "Are you daft, girl? He's a bloomin' duke!"

"I know he doesn't love me, so accepting his proposal would have been unfair to both of us," Amelia returned quickly.

Uncle Hubert threw his hands up in the air. "And just who is asking you to be fair?"

Amelia lifted her eyebrows delicately, but she remained silent. She'd never before had someone question her like this. She'd always been of like minds with her papa, but it was obvious that she and her uncle wouldn't always see eye to eye. "I do not wish to disagree with you, Uncle—"

"I knew your papa taught you right." Hubert laced his fingers over his belly.

"Indeed he did, which is precisely why it is so difficult for me to disagree with you about this." Amie agreed calmly, before adding, "However, he also taught us to think for ourselves."

Uncle Hubert scowled, shaking his head. "Sometimes he did have peculiar notions."

Amelia had to hold back her smile at her uncle's obvious displeasure. "Perhaps my father was somewhat unconventional, but he was a wonderful man."

"No one's saying any different," Hubert sputtered. "All I'm trying to say is that you can't go around collecting proposals from grand wigs like a duke and then turn them all down."

Amelia tilted her head to the side, considering her uncle. Finally, she smiled at him. "Very well, Uncle Hubert. I promise I won't turn them *all* down," she said—understanding all too well the ambiguity of her promise.

Uncle Hubert slapped his thigh. "That's my girl. Now when we get to London, we'll have to—"

Amelia listened to Uncle Hubert's exuberant voice and felt the tightness that had gripped her heart ease a bit. If she kept her wits about her, she could guide her uncle, ensuring the happiness of her sisters. It was fairly obvious that Uncle Hubert's heart was as big as his laugh.

Yes, he was exactly what she and her sisters needed now. Amelia felt her smile inch into a grin. Oh, yes, indeed. Their lives had all just gotten a lot more colorful.

"Why did you agree to return to London today?" Sebastian asked, leaning back against the carriage cushion.

Alonso looked out the window at the passing scenery. "Because our little game up here in the wilds is over."

Sebastian stiffened. "Over? What do you mean?"

"You'd know for yourself if you hadn't refused to help find out about those lovely ladies of Merrick's." Alonso glanced at Sebastian's face, noting the paleness. "Instead you cowered in your room, drinking yourself into a stupor."

"I did no such thing," Sebastian protested. "I was enjoying the charms of that luscious serving wench as you well know."

"I know," he agreed, crossing his legs. "But you were of no use when it came to finding out details on our foe."

"Merrick is hardly our foe; he is merely the target of our amusement."

Alonso shook his head. "I fear you are hopeless and will never understand the delicacies of our little games."

Sebastian frowned, anger furrowing his brow. "Perhaps I've tired of them."

"I don't believe that for a moment," Alonso said with a laugh. "Remember, I've seen how you enjoy the ladies."

"That's true enough, but continuing to torment Merrick is different."

"Let us not argue about this yet again," Alonso protested, pressing a hand to his temple. "I would much rather talk about my meeting with the pastor yesterday."

"The pastor in Dovedale?"

"Of course." Alonso slanted a grin at Sebastian. "It would appear our little ladybirds have a new protector, some merchant from London. According to our wonderful, loose-lipped pastor, the girls are about to head off to town—undoubtedly to secure marriages."

Sebastian pressed a hand to his stomach. "Little do they know what they'll find there."

Alonso's laughter filled the carriage. "So true. The Ralston sisters will never know that the Dark Lords await them with bated breath."

11

Cris strolled into the arbor where his aunt sat painting. "Has Owen returned from Ralston Hall yet?"

"I don't believe so." Aunt Patricia brushed a streak of yellow across the canvas. "Are you in a particular hurry to speak with him?"

"You know quite well I am," Cris replied tersely. For the past week since Amelia had rejected his suit, he'd been in a foul temper.

"You wish to see how Amelia is faring?"

Cris stiffened at the casual question. "It is only natural to be concerned," he said, trying to sound nonchalant to his all too perceptive aunt.

"I'm still unclear as to why you felt Owen should visit this morning instead of going yourself." Aunt Patricia dabbed her brush in the red paint.

How could he possibly explain his reasons? Cris wondered. Even he found little sense to his jumbled emotions. Part of him ached with wounded pride, whereas the other fretted over Amie's uncertain future.

If only she had agreed to marry him, then he wouldn't need to worry about her and her family under the care of their new guardian. Her refusal of his proposal had completely astounded him. He'd been expecting her to react in a logical fashion, instead of spouting off about love. It made him realize that the person he considered one of his dearest childhood friends had become an enigma to him. Cris shifted his stance, uncomfortable with his own thoughts.

"So this is where you two are hiding." Owen stepped into the clearing. "Oh, no. She's painting again," he groaned, stopping at the edge of the arbor. "Do you think it's safe to be around her when she's wielding that paintbrush?" he asked Cris in a stage whisper.

Aunt Patricia laughed, waving Owen forward. "It's quite all right, dear. I'm working on a landscape, so I won't ask you to pose."

"In that case," Owen replied, bending down to kiss her paint-speckled hand. "Creating another masterpiece, I see."

She pulled her fingers from Owen's clasp. "I've never known anyone who could lie in such a convincing manner as you."

Owen bowed low. "I appreciate the lovely compliment."

"Don't you ever tire of the flattery, old fellow?" Cris asked dryly, studying his friend.

"It comes so naturally, I fear it to be unavoidable."

"Then tell me how you wove your magic with the Mistresses Ralston."

The shadow that passed over Owen's face gave Cris pause. It took quite a lot to make his friend feel ill at ease. "What is it?"

Owen's smile faltered. "Their guardian has arrived."

"And what did you think of the man?" Cris asked softly, knowing that Amelia's future lay in the stranger's hands.

"I found him to be a . . . colorful fellow."

Cris released a pent-up breath. "Then the Ralston girls are well."

"Yes, but I have some news that I doubt will please you," Owen said at last.

His heart lurched at Owen's prediction. "What have you heard?"

"They are leaving."

"Leaving?" echoed Aunt Patricia, turning around to face the men.

"What are you saying?" Cris asked, impatience resounding in his question.

"I'm saying that the Ralston sisters are off to London," Owen answered quietly. "Their uncle is taking all five of them to London."

Cris shook his head. "Why?"

"Well, according to Emma, their new uncle is determined to"—Owen cleared his throat before he finished—"find them husbands."

"What?"

Owen took a step backward. "Don't harm the messenger, Crispin. I am merely relaying what I was told."

Confusion and anger crashed through him. "Amie's on her way to London to secure a husband?"

"According to Uncle Hubert."

Cris thrust both of his hands through his hair as he began pacing in the small arbor. "Going to find a husband? I don't understand this. Not at all." A horrid thought took him, his steps faltering. "Is she being forced to go?"

Owen's expression held regret. "Sorry to say, Cris, but she agreed quite calmly that it would be best. She's eager to experience the pleasures of London."

Cris thought of all the rumors that had plagued him over the recent years, of the way his life in town had soured because of the false stories haunting him. London wasn't like Dovedale, safe and honest. No, all forms of monsters could be found in town—from the jaded peers wielding their smooth compliments and seducing ladies for pleasure to the reprobates looking to snatch an innocent woman from a secluded garden.

The Ralston sisters, his Amie, would be devoured whole by the hungry ton.

"Lord, it's madness to take them to London," Cris whispered, already moving toward the path. "I need to find Amie." He left without another word, leaving Aunt Patricia and Owen to stare after him.

"Do you think he realizes he's in love with her *yet*?" Owen asked, his voice alight with humor.

"Not in the least," Aunt Patricia replied. "But it's starting to look quite promising." She nodded firmly, a smile slowly easing onto her face. "Indeed it is."

"I knew I'd find you here."

Amelia spun around, startled, to face Cris. It was the first time she'd seen him since rejecting his proposal. Immediately, she blurted out the first thing that came to mind. "How did you know where I'd be?"

His expression gentled. "Your sisters told me you went out for a walk. After I checked the falls, I decided to look here." He gestured toward the valley. "You've always loved the view from the top of this hill."

Amelia continued to stroll along the crest. "You remember," she murmured, pleased at the idea. The tension inside of her eased.

Cris fell into step beside her. "Of course I do. Still, from what Owen tells me, you aren't going to enjoy this view much longer."

"It's true," Amelia acknowledged. "I shall miss it, but I'm very excited about exploring London."

Cris reached out and stopped her. "I wish you'd reconsider. I will speak to your uncle if you'd like."

"That's not necessary, Cris. As I said, I'm quite looking forward to experiencing town."

Cris clasped both of her shoulders. "London is

not a fairy-tale world, Amie. It has very real, yet very hidden, dangers."

His concern warmed her. It was as if their argument had never occurred, except for the fact that she was all too aware of his hands resting on her. His kisses had deepened her desire for him; she tried to ignore her unbidden awareness. "I appreciate your concern, Cris, but I assure you we will be fine with our uncle to guide us."

His fingers tightened. "Won't you reconsider my proposal? I know I had no right to get angry with you the other day, and I apologize for my actions. But surely now that you've had a chance to consider my offer you realize that it makes perfect—"

She pressed two fingers against his lips, halting his words. "Please, let my answer stand, Cris. Your proposal was kind and generous—and completely unnecessary. Now that my uncle has arrived all will be well; you worry for naught. No harm will befall me in London."

Cris pulled her hand from his lips and held it against his chest. "Very well, Amie. I will accept your refusal and hope that we remain friends."

"Of course."

"Wonderful," Cris said, smiling. "When do you leave for town? Soon?" He swung her clasped hand down as they continued their walk. "I shall need a bit of time to pack, of course, but I should be ready to accompany—"

Amelia stopped immediately as she realized Cris's intent. "You intend to return to London with us?"

"Most definitely," Cris replied, a frown drawing his brows together. "While I would prefer to remain in the country, I think it best if I accompany you."

Dread filled Amelia. How would she ever get over her infatuation with Cris if he continued to spend time with her? She needed distance between them to erase the fantasies she'd concocted about spending the rest of their lives together, as lovers—as husband and wife.

Amelia forced a smile. "I wish you wouldn't, Cris."

"Wouldn't what?"

"Come back to London with me, with us."

Cris's eyes widened. "Why ever not?"

Her breath rushed from her. "Because of all that is between us now, Cris."

"I thought you agreed to remain friends."

"I did," Amelia said quickly. "And as my friend, I am asking you not to follow me to town."

Cris took a step back. "I don't know what to say."

"Oh, please don't be hurt by my request," Amelia pleaded, reaching out a hand to Cris. She knew she'd wounded him, but didn't know how to make him understand her feelings. All of her life she'd lived in Dovedale, surrounded by memories of Cris everywhere she went; she couldn't start her new life in London with the same problem.

Cris rubbed at his temple, ignoring her outstretched hand until she finally dropped it to her side. Finally, he lifted his gaze to her. "Once again

I will concede to your request, Amie. I shall remain here at Hunterton."

Amelia wanted nothing more than to wipe the lingering shadows from his eyes, but she knew that their parting would not be easy. "Thank you for understanding," she whispered. "I shall miss you."

Before Cris could respond, Amelia walked away, pressing the back of her hand to her trembling lips. In her heart, she bid Cris farewell.

"Did you make her see reason?"

As he stepped onto the terrace, Cris saw the glow of Owen's cigar in the dusk of early evening. He moved to sit next to his friend. "No."

Owen remained silent.

"I have a favor to ask of you," Cris said, still reeling from his latest encounter with Amelia. She had him completely off balance. Each time he thought he understood her, she would shift before his very eyes, becoming this frustrating . . . female! It was bloody unnerving.

"Ask away," Owen invited, waving his cigar.

"I want you to follow the Ralston sisters back to London."

Owen turned toward Cris. "Are you asking me to spy on them?"

"No, of course not."

"Shame, really, for the idea is quite intriguing."

Cris shook his head over Owen's irreverent sense of humor. "Try to be serious for a moment, Owen. I want you to introduce the Ralston girls into society and make certain that no lechers entice them."

"Lechers, hmmm? In your definition, does that include anyone who shows an interest toward your beloved Amie?" Owen asked dryly.

Cris nudged his friend. "Enough. Just tell me if you'll do it or not."

Owen drew on his cigar, leaning back to blow the smoke up into the air. "Of course I will." He looked at Cris. "My only question is why aren't you going back as well?"

"I've no desire to be fodder for the rumor mill any sooner than necessary," Cris said, giving only part of his reasons for remaining in the country. His pride had already been battered enough; he still stung from Amelia's rejection.

Still, Cris hid his feelings from Owen, preferring to protect his pride from a further bashing. "I have no desire to taint their introduction to society. I shall dispatch missives to some of my friends requesting that they include my neighbors and dear friends at their parties. I shall take care to be very selective to whom I address these letters."

"I don't believe the precaution is necessary, but I understand your reasoning." Owen clapped a hand on Cris's shoulder. "Don't worry, Merrick, I'll keep a close guard on our ladies."

Cris glanced at Owen, seeing all too clearly the smile growing on his friend's face. "Why do I feel as if I've invited a fox to guard the prize hens?"

Cris bellowed for his aunt as he stormed down the long corridor, a crumpled missive clutched in his fist. It had been four weeks since Owen had returned to London and this letter was the first news he'd received from his friend.

"Aunt Patricia!"

"I'm here, Crispin. What on earth is the matter?"

"Read for yourself." Cris thrust the crumpled paper into his aunt's hand.

Quickly, she scanned the letter before raising her eyes to meet his. "So?"

"So!" he exclaimed, yanking the missive from her hand. "You read this and your only response is, 'so'?"

Her expression grew confused.

"Did you read the part where Owen says there are men converging upon the Ralston sisters?"

"Yes."

"And what of the fact that they've been dubbed 'The Fabulous Five'?"

"Of course I did, Cris."

"And . . . and what of the fact that those despicable lechers Baskins, Stevens, and Henley are hanging about them all the time?"

"I'll admit that those gentlemen have somewhat less than desirable reputations, but—"

"Somewhat less than desirable?" Cris threw his hands up in the air. "They're reprobates, the lot of them!"

"I'm sure Owen has the situation perfectly under control."

"Owen couldn't control a situation like this if his life depended on it. He's too much of a lothario himself to even notice unwarranted behavior."

"Surely not," Aunt Patricia protested.

But Cris wouldn't be calmed. He began to pace to and fro. "There's only one thing to be done."

"And that would be?"

Had his aunt lost her senses? He glanced at her. "Why, to go to London ourselves and sort out this mess." Not that he wanted to, Cris thought to himself. He was concerned about tainting the Ralstons with the ugliness that plagued him in town, but if he were very careful, extremely discreet, he could avoid harming their reputations. Cris nodded firmly to his aunt. "Yes, we must go to London."

"Ah," she murmured softly.

"Don't give me that look, Aunt Patricia. The only reason I'm going to London is to protect the Ralston sisters from making the mistake of assuming that any man possessing a title is a gentleman! Ha! Gentlemen. Nothing could be further from the truth with the three blackguards Owen mentioned."

"Of course, dear."

"It is something I would feel compelled to do for any of my neighbors, especially ones as vulnerable as the Ralston sisters."

"Perfectly understandable."

"It's not as if we know their uncle. He came completely unannounced, then whisked them away to town. I don't know if we can trust him to recognize what is best for the girls." Cris tapped the letter against his leg. "Yes, it is time I put a stop to this farce."

"Most certainly."

Cris stopped his pacing, his hands coming to rest

on his hips. "Why do I get the feeling that you are simply patronizing me?"

His aunt's smile widened as she reached up to pat him on the cheek. "I always knew you were an intelligent man."

Cris rolled his eyes before heading off toward his own rooms. It was time he helped out his friend before she dug herself in any deeper.

12

She was bored.

There was no denying the fact, Amelia thought, as she fought to keep a polite smile. With Lord Thornton prattling on about his hounds once again, it surprised her that she didn't fall asleep where she stood. It was the third time in as many days that he'd cornered her—and nearly bored her to death. Stifling a yawn, she tried to concentrate on what Lord Thornton was saying to her.

"—so you see the crossbreeding of hounds actually creates a more . . ."

Her thoughts drifted away again. It amazed her that such a nice man could be so deadly dull. Young, handsome, and titled, Lord Thornton was one of the most eligible bachelors of the Season. Still, his pedigree aside, it baffled Amelia that anyone would actually want to marry poor Lord Thornton. Perhaps some ladies just wanted more sleep.

Amelia pushed the less than charitable thought from her mind. After all, it wasn't just Lord Thornton. No, all of the gentlemen she'd met so far had seemed so . . . so bland. None of them had aroused even a spark of excitement within her. Her hopes of finding a true love faded more each day.

Oh, she'd diligently applied herself to the task of finding someone to love. She'd spoken with all of the eligible gentlemen, conversed with other ladies about the positive qualities of those men, yet nothing seemed to increase the bachelors' appeal. She found most of the gentlemen amusing and pleasant, but no one made her heart skip or her breath catch.

"Don't you agree, Miss Ralston?"

The question startled Amelia. She gazed up at Lord Thornton. "Pardon me?"

"I asked if you agreed," he repeated politely.

Amelia searched for an answer, not wanting to admit to her companion that she hadn't heard a word he'd uttered.

"Amie!"

Amelia could have hugged her sister, Camilla, for the timely interruption. Amelia's relief shifted into concern at her sister's obvious distress. "Camilla, what is it? What's happened?" she whispered, reaching out to clasp her sister's hands.

Camilla's eyes glittered with unshed tears. "Please, Amie. I need to speak with you alone."

Amelia turned to Lord Thornton. "Please excuse me, my lord. I need to attend to my sister."

Lord Thornton bowed. "Might I be of assistance?"

Amelia shook her head. "Thank you for the kind

offer, Lord Thornton, but we shall be quite fine." She drew Camilla off into one of the empty alcoves near the entranceway.

The moment they were alone, Camilla threw herself into Amelia's arms. "Oh, Amie. What am I going to do?"

Amelia stroked her sister's back. "Calm down, darling. I'm sure everything will be fine."

"No, it won't," Camilla murmured, choking on her soft sobs. "He wants to marry me off to an old goat!"

Amelia felt her heart sink. Uncle Hubert had obviously been busy this evening. "Don't worry overmuch, Camilla. Uncle Hubert has yet to carry through with any of his grand plans. He's merely trying to nudge us in that direction."

Camilla pulled back, shaking her head. "No, Amie, it's far worse than that. He's gone and accepted Lord Pendergral's offer."

"Lord Pendergral?" Amelia gasped. "Why, the man has to be ninety if he's a day."

"I know!" Camilla moaned, closing her eyes. "I can't bear the thought of marrying him. Truly I can't, Amie."

Amelia shivered at the thought of anyone marrying the old reprobate, never mind one of her sisters! Poor Camilla. Something had to be done, Amelia knew, and it was up to her to convince their uncle that the match was ill conceived. "Don't worry, Camilla. Everything will be fine. You won't have to marry Lord Pendergral."

"I won't?"

The hope in Camilla's voice hardened Amelia's resolve. "No," she answered firmly. "I'll speak with Uncle Hubert."

Camilla wiped the tears from her cheeks. "Oh, thank you, Amie. I knew you'd save me." She hugged Amelia once more before stepping back. "Thank you," she said, her eyes warm. "I love you, Amie."

"I love you too."

Camilla kissed Amelia's cheek before sliding out of the alcove, leaving Amelia alone.

Amelia struggled to quell the sickening wave of anxiety that gripped her. How would she ever dissuade Uncle Hubert?

Amelia slowly left the alcove, searching out and finding Camilla as she accepted an invitation to dance. The young buck escorting her sister onto the dance floor was Lord Harris, who was in line for a dukedom. Amelia's eyes widened at the thought. That was it!

Her steps were light as she made her way over to where Uncle Hubert stood, beaming out at the dancers. Amelia moved next to him. "Good evening, Uncle."

"Ah, Amie. Fine night it is too," he returned jovially, reaching out to pat her shoulder. "But you should be out there dancing with one of those fancy swains."

One with a title, Amelia added silently. "I'm a bit fatigued at the moment," she murmured, keeping her gaze on the dancers. "Oh, my, our Camilla appears to have entranced Lord Harris."

Hubert began to bob next to her. "Where is she?"

"Right there." Amelia tilted her head discreetly toward the couple. "They look remarkably fitting, don't you think?" She struggled to keep her voice casual. "Since he is the next Duke of Foleroy, I do believe it would be a wonderful match for Camilla."

"A duke, did you say?"

Amelia felt like grinning as Hubert accepted the lure. "Indeed," she murmured.

"Blast it all." Hubert's brows drew together. "I've already had a sit-down with Pendergral."

"A sit-down you say, but you didn't agree to anything, did you?"

"Not at all," Hubert hastened to assure her. "A good businessman considers every offer carefully. You don't just go taking the first one to step forward."

Amelia nodded at Uncle Hubert. "Quite wise of you. That way you are free to consider all of the offers Camilla might receive." She pressed a hand to her chest. "Why, just think, if you'd agreed to an engagement between Camilla and Lord Pendergral, you might have missed out on aligning yourself with a duke."

Hubert's gasp was exactly the response she wanted.

"It was a good thing I wasn't too hasty," he muttered again.

Amelia patted her uncle on the arm. "Don't worry, Uncle. No opportunity has passed." She paused, pretending that an idea had just struck her.

"On further thought, perhaps it might be better if you hold off on accepting any offers of marriage you receive for us."

His gaze narrowed. "Is this more of your marry-for-love notions?"

"Not at all," she lied smoothly. "I was merely trying to point out how advantageous it would be to wait. However, if you feel—"

"Why should I wait?" Hubert interrupted.

She prayed her expression reflected surprise. "The reason you should wait to accept an offer is so that you might give me and my sisters more time to collect proposals. There really is so much to consider."

"Like what?" Hubert asked, his attention fully on her.

Amelia spread her hands wide. "You need to look at a gentleman's entire pedigree quite carefully. After all, one might have tightfisted parents, or another with a long lifeline or—"

"What's wrong with living for a good long time?"

"Nothing, nothing at all," Amelia murmured. "All that it means is that a young lord must wait to inherit the title."

Hubert slapped his hand against his thigh. "I hadn't thought of that before today."

"I assure you it's quite a common problem."

Hubert nodded slowly. "I think you have the right of it, Amie. Perhaps I've been a bit too eager to see this through. After all, the better the title, the more influence the man will have at the House of Lords."

"And I'm certain that a more influential member would have an easier time passing bills that could help, oh, say, merchants for instance," Amelia agreed solemnly, trying to keep the glee from her voice. "No, accepting a proposal for one of us is not something that should be rushed."

"No, it's surely not." Hubert slapped his hands together. "Well, then, I'll just have to give my girls a bit more time to round up all those lovely proposals before we pick the finest one. Waiting until the end of the Season would be best."

"It certainly would," Amelia murmured, leaning in to kiss her uncle's cheek. "You're quite the cunning fellow."

"Indeed I am!"

Amelia allowed her smile to burst free as her uncle strode away, heading directly toward Lord Pendergral—undoubtedly to tell him the bad news. Amelia wanted to shout out, to kick up her heels, to let everyone know of her success.

She felt giddy from the heady sensation of challenging her guardian. True, he might not have understood her maneuverings, but she'd gotten him to agree to wait until the end of the Season before arranging any engagements.

She was still reeling when she heard the commotion. Like a huge wave, the murmurings flooded the room, frantic whispers creating a muted din. Amelia turned toward the crowd and came face to face with none other than Cris.

A brilliant smile formed on Amelia's face as she reached out to clasp Cris's glove-encased hand with her own, unmindful of the curious stares from the people milling about them in the large ballroom. "Cris," she whispered, feeling her heart pound. "You came to London."

She couldn't hide the pleasure in her voice. Amelia was overjoyed that Cris had joined them in town, despite the fact that she'd asked him to stay away. She didn't know why he'd come, but it really didn't matter. She'd missed him.

Her pleasure was such that Amelia didn't even notice the people shifting closer to hear their conversation over the swell of the music, but the darkening scowl on Cris's face made her pause. Her smile faded beneath his fierce glare as Amelia finally began to notice the anger vibrating within him. His black hair shimmered beneath the light as he bent nearer, his grip tightening upon her hand. "What in God's name do you think you're doing?"

"Excuse me?" she asked, stunned at his anger. What on earth was wrong with him?

Cris's other hand lifted to grasp her upper arm, pulling her so close that her skirts were entangled with his strong legs. "Henley? Stevens? Baskins? What the devil are you thinking of to become acquainted with those disreputable libertines?"

A gasp broke from her as understanding formed. "Why, Crispin, you've come to rescue me, haven't you?"

"Good God, Amelia!" Cris exploded, his voice rising above the music. "How can you think such a ridiculous—" He broke off abruptly, his gaze shifting to the crowd that had pushed closer to hear their exchange with unabashed curiosity.

A sound of frustration rumbled in Cris's throat as he pulled Amelia from the room, his tight hold on her hand ensuring her compliance. Her kid slippers skidded along the floor as Amelia hurried behind Cris, trying to keep up with his brisk pace, all too aware of the eyes following their retreat.

Cris tried three doors, finding each of the rooms occupied. A few of the bold gossipmongers trailed discreetly behind them, unwilling to miss one moment of the scandalous tidbit occurring before their very eyes. When at last they came upon an empty room, Cris sent her through the doorway and turned to face the brave souls who had followed them down the hall. One blast of his icy glare had them scattering like mice before a pack of hungry cats.

Amelia glanced about briefly, taking in the books and lounging chairs in the room, before she spun about to face him. "Whatever possessed you to drag me from the ballroom?"

"*I'm* the one who is asking the questions, Amelia," he stated firmly. "Now would you care to tell me why you're keeping company with men who are known for their debauchery? Where is your uncle? Why hasn't he put a stop to this madness?"

Amelia opened her mouth to respond, but before she uttered a syllable, Cris interrupted her. "Good God, Amie. What were you thinking?"

Her temper flared at Cris's question. If he'd come

to her, shown concern, she would have gladly responded to his questions. But a demand like that didn't deserve an answer. "I do not believe it is of any concern to you, Lord Merrick."

"Lord Merrick?" Cris's color deepened. "What do you mean by 'Lord Merrick'? And I *do* have a right to be concerned. Your father would have expected no less from me."

Amelia's heart sank, her anger fading away beneath her disappointment. For a moment, one glorious moment, she'd thought he was jealous of the gentlemen she'd met. But, now she understood all too well. One moment in his presence and she'd already begun to weave fantasies around him; in reality, Cris was only playing the part of 'cousin' once more, feeling it his duty to rescue her. It seemed all these weeks apart had done nothing to end her ability to build dreams around the simpliest of Cris's actions.

She turned away from him, not certain if she could hide her feelings. "You're quite correct, Cris," Amelia said softly. "We are friends."

Just friends, her aching heart added. How could she have been so foolish as to forget?

13

Her quiet response drained him of anger. Cris reached out for Amie, but she shied away from his touch. That small movement, that little shift, surprised him. She'd been angry at him, rightfully so, he acknowledged silently. But suddenly it was as if she'd drawn into herself. He was completely baffled by her abrupt mood change. "Amie? What is it?"

Her lips tremored as she gave him a brittle smile. "It's nothing, Cris. I'm fine," she murmured softly.

He knew her far too well to ever believe her denial. Cris tried again to reach her. "I must apologize for my—"

But his apology was cut off as the Ralston girls came barreling into the room, each with an offensive display of jewels.

The full implications of his actions that evening hit him under the incredulous stares of Amie's sisters. Cris staggered under the realization. Good

God! His first moments back in London and he'd not only made a fool of himself, but a spectacle of Amelia as well.

It was an ironic twist of fate. Here he'd been afraid that the painful, vile rumors following him about might sully her reputation. Never, in all his imaginings, had he thought he'd lose control so completely and damage Amie's good name directly.

He'd come to give Amie his aid and had ended up dragging her off from a crowded party into a very private room.

What had he been thinking? Actually, that was his problem exactly. He *hadn't* used his brain at all. No, he'd acted on impulse. The moment he'd seen her, smiling at him, a wave of anger had assailed him, stunning him with its force. He still couldn't believe how he'd reacted; yet, at the time, his actions had seemed perfectly reasonable. Perhaps it had been exhaustion mingled with worry that had caused such a strong response from him.

Regardless of the reason, he now had to repair his mistake. Before he could say one word to Amie, Beatrice stepped forward.

"Why on earth did you pull Amelia from the room like that?" Bea asked, her eyes wide.

"The rumors are already starting," Camilla pointed out.

"Now, Bea, Camilla, calm down," Amelia began steadily. "There was no harm done. You see, Cris was merely trying to protect—"

"Please, Amelia," Cris interrupted. Lord, to have her defend him after his thoughtless actions only made it worse. "They're quite right. I have blemished your reputation."

"Blemished it? What is wrong with Amelia's reputation?" asked Deanna, confusion in her blue eyes.

"Nothing at the moment," Bea said, "but that might not hold true after tonight. The gossip has already begun."

"Some people can be so cruel," Emmaline agreed, taking a step forward, her jewelry catching the light.

Cris's stomach rolled at the notion that he'd harmed his dear Amie. He turned toward her. "I can only apologize for my—"

But this time it was Amie who cut him off. "Please don't, Cris. I understand your actions completely."

There was a tinge of sadness to her voice that only made him feel even worse. "Still, I should never have—"

"I will be fine," Amelia interrupted again. "Surely my reputation could not be completely destroyed by an incident of such little consequence."

"That's true," Emma agreed, stepping forward into the light. "Amelia is very popular. Why, her dance card is always filled."

Cris rubbed two fingers against his temple. "No doubt with scoundrels like Stevens, Baskins, and Henley," he muttered, frustration brimming within him.

A brilliant smile creased Camilla's face. "Oh, are they friends of yours? They are such delightful gentlemen."

A groan broke from Cris as his frustration at the

entire situation grew. Lord, they were all determined to drive him insane! "Delightful? Those men, all three of them, have not one redeeming quality between them, and what's more—"

"How can you say that?" asked Deanna. "They're always so polite."

Polite? Cris stared at the Ralston sisters, realizing that they were still naive innocents, even after a month in jaded London. "What can your uncle be thinking to let innocent beauties loose amidst the most degenerate members of the ton?" Cris muttered, driving a hand through his already tousled hair.

"Cris—" Amelia began.

"Now, how are you ever going to land yourselves fine, gentlemanly husbands when you're all hiding out here in your finery?" The booming question from the newcomer cut off Amelia's answer.

Cris looked at the man who strode into the room. Uncle Hubert, he presumed. The vivid scarlet of Hubert's jacket only enhanced the girth of his rotund figure and made his florid cheeks look positively enflamed. "Haven't I told you enough times that a good merchant always displays his wares?"

Well, therein lay the answer as to why all of the Ralston sisters were displaying their jewels in such an ostentatious manner.

"I presume you are Hubert Collings?" Cris said, stepping forward. "Allow me to introduce—"

"Hold up for a moment while we send the girls from the room," Hubert interrupted. He gave Cris a broad wink. "Then we can have a cozy discussion, just the two of us."

Cris was too astonished at the older man's overly familiar manner to even respond. Where was the anger, the remonstrations at having pulled Amelia from the ballroom?

Hubert didn't appear to notice Cris's shock. "Off with you," he instructed the Ralston sisters, waving his hands at them.

"But Uncle—" Camilla protested.

"Ah, ah, none of that," he said, waggling a finger at her. "I'll handle things in here, don't you worry. His Dukeship and I will settle this as soon as you leave us men to our conversation."

His Dukeship? Cris felt as if his world was spinning wildly out of control. First his own inexplicable behavior toward Amelia threw him off balance, now her colorful uncle was reacting in a strange manner. Still, it was time he tried to regain control. Cris cleared his throat. "Sir, I must insist that we—"

"Hold up there a minute, you eager pup," Hubert said, nudging Cris with his elbow. "Let me hurry these girls along."

"But—"

His protest quieted as Hubert clapped a hand over Cris's mouth. "This is man talk," he insisted.

To say he was shocked couldn't even begin to express his reaction. As a duke, no one ever dared to touch him in such a fashion. Cris stepped back, allowing the older man's hand to fall away.

Yet before Cris could address the issue with Hubert, the man turned to the Ralston sisters again. "Go on with you."

Amie's four younger sisters filed out, mumbling protests; Amelia stayed next to Cris. "That goes for you too, Amelia," Hubert said, looking downright gleeful.

Cris frowned at Hubert's odd reaction to the entire situation. What did the man have to be so blasted happy about? His niece had just been dragged down the hallway in front of several influential members of the ton. To Cris, it was ironic that his own disgraceful behavior toward Amelia made him all that more aware of Hubert's failings as a guardian. After all, a true guardian would have already demanded marriage; Hubert's actions brought to life all of Cris's worst fears for the Ralston sisters' future.

Before Cris could address Hubert, Amelia stepped forward. "Please allow me to explain. This is all simply a misunderstanding."

Hubert's mouth slipped into a grin. "Don't fret now, lovey. His Graceness here and I can work this out like gentlemen."

For all his oddness, Amelia's uncle was quite right. Cris needed to work this out alone with Hubert. Cris placed a hand on Amelia's elbow. "Why don't you allow me to talk to your guardian?"

Cris tried to ignore the pang in his heart when Amelia shifted away from his touch. "But, Cris, I want to explain to him why you—"

"I'd prefer to explain it to him myself." Cris

clasped his hands behind his back to keep from reaching out to touch her again.

For a long moment, Amelia gazed at him, then finally nodded. "All right, but don't let Uncle Hubert bully you into anything unwarranted. After all, you only came to London to protect me. It is all just a misunderstanding."

One which damaged your reputation, Cris thought, but wisely kept that argument to himself. "I'll take care of the situation."

He could tell from her expression that she didn't like the idea of leaving him alone with Hubert. With one last warning glance at her uncle, Amelia slipped from the room, closing the door behind her.

Cris's gaze slid onto the plump man across from him, "The Honorable Mr. Collings."

The short, round man beamed at him. "So you've heard of me, I see."

For a man whose ward had just been made fodder for the gossips, Hubert Collings certainly seemed in a jovial mood. What manner of man was this? Why wasn't he railing at him for dragging Amelia from the ball?

Cris decided to face the issue directly. "You are undoubtedly upset over my treatment of your ward, Amelia."

"Indeed I am."

Hubert's smile grew wider. Cris couldn't fathom what on earth was going on, for if the man was distressed, he certainly wasn't showing it.

Hubert crossed his arms. "Now it seems to me that there's only one way out of this tight spot."

"And that would be?"

"Why, marriage, of course."

"Ah, yes, marriage." Cris felt an odd sense of relief. At least the uncle could be counted on for a bit of sense. Cris kept his expression carefully blank as he crossed his arms. "As it so happens, it was my intention all along."

"So I've been told. My girls did mention something about you wanting to marry Amie. So, it will all wrap up nice and pretty." Hubert rubbed his hands together. "We'll have to work out the arrangements."

"I don't believe we need to be so hasty," Cris replied, allowing one side of his mouth to tilt upward. "You see, the lady refused me."

Hubert threw his hands up in the air. "I still can't believe it. Despite what people might say about you, you're *still* a duke."

The muscles in his stomach clenched. He'd hoped the rumors had died in his absence from town. "What are people saying about me?" he asked quietly.

"Just bits and pieces of nothing. Something about kidnappings and the like," Hubert said in a dismissive tone. "But you don't go helping matters by dragging proper ladies from crowded balls, I'll tell you."

Bile rose in Cris's throat. What if Amelia had heard the stories? Lord, to enter into a room and imagine everyone whispering about you was bad enough, but to have someone you care for, someone you respect, hear and perhaps even wonder about those same tales was unbearable.

As Hubert went on, Cris forced his thoughts away. "Still, a duke's a duke . . . and you don't look like a bad sort of fellow. Besides, my girls seem to think right by you."

Some of Cris's tension eased. Perhaps no one had seen fit to pass along the rumors to the innocent ladies. Cris looked Hubert square in the eye. "They trust me," he said firmly. "And I would never, ever do anything that would harm them in any manner."

Hubert held his gaze for a long moment, before breaking out in a grin. "That's what I kept on telling myself. For heaven's sake, you're a Dukeness—and you fellows don't go nabbing pretties off the streets."

But beneath every title was simply a man, Cris well knew. Still, he kept that point to himself. No reason to raise questions in Hubert's mind.

"Ever since my girls told me that Amelia turned you down, I've been in a stupor." Hubert shook his head. "What can the girl be thinking? She's spouting all this romantic nonsense."

Despite his agreement with Hubert's statement, Cris felt an odd need to defend his friend. "Amelia has always been independent and, with the way she raised her sisters, I believe she's earned the right to her own opinion."

Hubert looked at him as if he'd fallen and hit his head. "Are you daft?"

"I don't believe so," Cris murmured, not taking

offense at the question. It was difficult to be upset with someone like Hubert. His audacity merely seemed to fit in with the rest of his colorful persona.

Hubert frowned at Cris. "It's true that I can't control what she thinks, but I *do* have a say about what she does."

Cris held back his smile. "My dear Mr. Collings, you don't know your niece very well if you believe she would simply agree to your demand of marriage."

"Well, who said anything about getting her to agree?" Hubert blustered.

Cris's humor frosted over. "I consider Amelia a good friend and, as such, would never force her into marriage if she did not—"

"Too late!"

"What?"

Hubert merely smiled at Cris's explosion. "No need to get angry at me, your lordness. I'm not the one who yanked her out of a crowded ballroom, dragging her across the entire place for everyone to see, before slamming doors in search of a bit of privacy."

"Hold up, sir. There is no cause—"

"No cause? What the devil are you bleating about? A girl's reputation is serious business!" Hubert interjected loudly. "You spotted her reputation is what you did. Now, how am I going to find a gentleman of title who is willing to overlook this little pickle dillo!"

"I presume you mean peccadillo," Cris said, automatically correcting Hubert.

"That's what I said," Hubert muttered. As Cris's expression remained blank, he asked, "What's the matter, your duke? Do you need me to explain what it means?"

Cris focused in on the merchant. "No, that will not be necessary," he said coldly.

Hubert's full lips pressed together. "Then don't try to distract me from my point!" The older man added a firm nod for emphasis. "None of your fancy dancing around it will change the fact that my girl is now spotted!"

Cris's head began to pound. He straightened his shoulders and met Hubert's gaze head-on. "You are quite right, sir. I offer my apologies for any insult I gave to your niece."

A loud "humf" rumbled from Hubert as he crossed his arms. "Your fancy chitter is pretty on the ears, but it doesn't change the fact that it's time to pay the piper. Yes indeedy, it's time to marry the girl."

"I respect Amelia far too much ever to marry her without her consent," Cris stated firmly.

"You weren't thinking about that when you pulled her into this room though, were you, my boy?"

"True enough," Cris conceded. He knew that the best thing he could do for Amelia now was to keep his distance. "Not only do you have my apology, but you also have my assurance that nothing untoward will occur in the future."

"But . . . but—" Hubert sputtered. "That's not good enough."

It seemed that Uncle Hubert would not be satisfied until remuneration was made. Rightfully so, Cris agreed silently. "Very well, Mr. Collings. What if I act as your guide through society?"

"Guide? But I've already had lessons in proper behavior and such," Hubert blustered.

"I don't mean to give you lessons on social etiquette, Hubert. I am proposing to assist your introduction to the ton."

"Ahhh," Hubert sighed. "You mean you'll introduce me to the best gents?"

Cris could practically see thoughts whirling in Hubert's head. "Yes," he agreed, "but it means more than that. I will ask my aunt to use her influence to ensure that the Ralston girls attend every fashionable event and secure the most advantageous places at the opera."

Hubert considered the offer for a moment before finally nodding. "Very well, your Graceness, you have a bargain."

Satisfaction filled Cris as he shook the merchant's hand. Not only would he be able to make amends for his disgraceful behavior, but Cris would also be able to better protect the girls while remaining in the background and thus keeping his own reputation from touching them.

It was the perfect solution.

14

"Oh, you poor dear," exclaimed Lady Witherstone. The matron reached out to clasp Amelia's hand and pull her into a group of elderly ladies.

"Excuse me?" Amelia's nerves were already stretched taut with worry over leaving Cris with her uncle. She'd just managed to elude her concerned sisters. The last thing she wanted at the moment was to face this pack of gossips.

"We all saw what happened with Lord Merrick, and it was shocking!" Another elderly matron, Lady Hemple, patted Amelia on the arm. "What ever happened when you were alone in the room with him?"

"Nothing! Why, nothing at all," Amelia gasped. What did they think would happen? It was Cris they were speaking of, not some uncontrollable reprobate. "Lord Merrick was the perfect gentleman."

"Gentlemen do *not* pull young ladies from crowded ballrooms." Lady Witherstone's pronouncement was met with firm nods from the other two ladies in the group.

"But His Grace's behavior comes as no shock to us," Lady Flanery confided, leaning toward Amelia. "Why, some of the things we've heard about him are, well, quite unsuitable for any lady's ears."

"Very true," Lady Hemple agreed, her eyes alight. "The stories shocked me to my very core."

Amelia took a small step back, everything within her repelled at the hungry gleam in the three pairs of eyes as the ladies leaned even closer to impart their sordid tales.

"They say he seduces young ladies before casting them aside. He merely wants to see how many innocents he can tempt to his bidding!" Lady Witherstone finished in a rush.

Amelia shook her head. "No, you must be wrong. Cris would never—"

"It's quite true," Lady Flanery insisted. "Why, it happened to the daughter of a dear friend. The poor child was literally snatched from a ball very much like this one, then forced to commit unspeakable acts." The lady's eyes grew wide and her mouth gaped open like that of a dead salmon. "In fact, the way she was taken *exactly* mirrored how Bradford pulled you from the room tonight, except she was in the garden." She nodded meaningfully at the other two matrons. "Exactly."

"Oh dear," gasped Lady Witherstone.

"I knew it!" exclaimed Lady Hemple. "I'm only thankful that Lord Merrick's parents aren't alive to witness his despicable behavior."

"Stop it!" Amelia burst out, not caring who overheard her. "All of you. Lord Merrick is a good, honest, wonderful man who would never even think of committing such vile acts." She stepped back, fighting to hold back tears of outrage. "You have no right to spread such vicious untruths. It's all lies and you are all—"

"Amie! Here you are. We've been looking for you," Bea interrupted smoothly. She grasped Amelia's elbow before smiling politely at the three elderly ladies. "Would you excuse us for a moment?"

Before anyone had a chance to speak, Bea began to guide Amelia toward the garden doors with Camilla, Deanna, and Emma following close behind. Amelia was too upset to speak, afraid that if she uttered one word, she would burst into angry tears.

The moment they were outside and alone in the darkness of the night, Amelia broke free from Beatrice's hold. "Did you hear what they were saying about Cris?"

"No, I merely saw your face from across the room and knew you were very upset," Bea replied.

"What were they saying?" asked Camilla.

"Oh, no, don't make her say!" Emma moved closer to Amelia and began to stroke her back. "It would only upset Amie more."

"I don't think I could be any more upset," Amelia told Emma. "They were utterly hideous in their attacks upon Cris's character. They said he kidnapped young ladies and forced them to do awful things."

"How horrible!" Bea whispered. "Poor Cris."

Amelia nodded, blinking back her tears. "At this moment, I'm so furious that I'm tempted to walk back into that room and tell those old nasty crows exactly what I think of them and their wagging tongues."

"Can I watch?" Deanna asked brightly.

"Deanna!" Bea remonstrated.

"What?" Deanna frowned at Bea. "It would be amusing to see Amelia topple those gossips."

"I'm not going to topple anyone," Amie replied, burying her face in her hands. "Though I am sorely tempted."

"What are you going to do then?" Camilla questioned softly.

"Do? To them?" At Camilla's nod, Amelia said, "Nothing."

"Why ever not? They deserve a dressing down," Deanna protested.

Amelia released a deep breath. "I'm well aware of that, Deanna. However, it would do no good for me to stoop to their level. No, the best way for me, for all of us, to quell the rumors is to give Cris our unswerving loyalty."

"Especially in public," Bea added.

Emma clasped her hands together in front of her. "Do you really think that it will help to stop the rumors?"

"Yes," Amelia agreed. "Anytime we hear even a whisper directed toward Cris, we should loudly denounce it as being false."

"I shall be certain to—" Deanna broke off her

statement to gaze down the garden path. "Someone's coming," she whispered.

Amelia twisted around to look behind her. Three dark figures, no more than shadows in the darkness, were moving toward her and her sisters. Unease feathered down her spine. "Perhaps it is best if we return to the house."

All four girls needed no more urging as they hurried toward the light streaming out of the large windows. Amelia followed, but she turned back around when she reached the door. Nothing moved in the garden. The shadows had blended back into the night.

"Where did they go?" Emma pressed against Amelia's back.

"Who were they?" Camilla asked.

Deanna edged her way into the circle of her sisters. "What were they doing?"

Amelia felt a bit silly for her overactive imagination. "The three gentlemen were undoubtedly taking a stroll in the garden."

"But they were headed right toward us, and they didn't even announce themselves," Bea insisted.

"We were standing in the middle of the path leading back to the house," Amelia pointed out. "They could have been returning to the party after a bit of fresh air."

"Then where did they go?"

Deanna's question made Amelia smile for the first time since the fiasco with Cris had started. "I imagine that the sight of five women running from them made them think twice about approaching us further. They're probably waiting around that bend in the path until we go inside. Then they can return to the house without fear of startling us."

"I suppose our reaction was silly," Bea admitted. "After all, I can't imagine anyone coming to harm in the garden of a private town house. The entire idea is ridiculous."

Amelia felt a twinge of uncertainty as the tales of the matrons came back to her. Hadn't one of them told of that very thing happening to a young lady at one of these gatherings? But then hadn't that very same lady then accused Cris of the act? Amelia dismissed the thought as pure gossip, made-up fodder for the bored ladies of the ton.

Still, Amelia urged her sisters back inside. "Let's return to the party, shall we? I'm feeling quite in control of myself, thanks to you four."

"I'm glad, Amie." Emma clasped Amelia's hand. "I'm very glad we were there for you."

"As am I," Amelia returned, squeezing her youngest sister's fingers. "But we really should head inside now. After all, we have rumors to stop, don't we?"

As they stepped into the brightly lit room, none of them looked back to see the three men regroup in the middle of the path.

"That was foolish of us," Prospero said as he watched the girls disappear into the safety of the house. "But to come across all five of them, just waiting for the plucking, ahhh, it was too great a temptation to resist."

"I told you they were exquisite," Alonso said as he stood to the left of his companions.

"I'd like one of the three blondes first." Sebastian shrugged his shoulders. "I've lost my appetite for any other since I caught sight of them."

"And you were the one who wasn't certain if the game should continue," chided Alonso.

"Luckily for me, my hunger for those pretties is stronger than any sense of guilt," Sebastian acknowledged with a laugh.

"Guilt?" Prospero cuffed Sebastian on the back. "What would you feel guilt for? It's not as if we don't compensate the lovelies for their trouble. We've always been generous with the purses we give them before we return them to their homes."

Alonso nodded in agreement, a grin on his face. "Some of them even ask if they can come back!"

"I wouldn't mind at all if the Ralston sisters found our entertainment pleasurable," Sebastian murmured.

Prospero threw an arm around the men on each side of him. "With those ladies, we'll not only have the honor of taunting Merrick, but we'll also feast on some of the sweetest morsels in all of London." He inhaled deeply. "Let the hunt begin."

The moment their curricle set off at a brisk pace, Amelia turned toward Cris, who was busy directing the carriage down the empty street. "I looked for you last night until Uncle Hubert told me you'd left."

"You mentioned that in the note you sent me this

morning." Cris steered their conveyance into the park. Not only had he called on Amelia early in the day when he knew the park would be deserted, but he had also driven the carriage himself to ensure their privacy. After his debacle last night, he didn't want to expose Amelia to any more gossip.

"Yes, I did, and I appreciate you calling on me so early. This is a matter of great urgency."

Her earnest tone made him smile. "I understood that as well from your message." Besides, it suited his own purposes to call on her before anyone else was about. It would be best for Amie if they weren't seen together.

"Last evening I overheard something that will greatly distress you," Amelia began, her words rushed.

Cris's hands tightened on the reins as he pulled the horses to a stop. "I see," he murmured as he turned toward Amelia. "Exactly what did you hear, Amie?"

Her fingers twisted into her gown. "Some of the ladies told me a most vile rumor about you."

Cris closed his eyes briefly. "Go on," he said finally, uncertain of Amie's reaction. Would she be able to hear the rumors and dismiss them out-of-hand or would they make her begin to doubt him? Cris simply didn't know how she'd react. True, they'd been childhood friends, but he couldn't predict how Amie, the grown woman, would handle the vile stories. Still, it was something they needed to face. "Please, Amie, tell me what they said."

"These ladies told me that you took young

women off by force," she whispered, lowering her head so Cris was unable to see her expression.

"And you want to know if it's true or not?" Everything within him froze as he awaited her response.

It was swift in coming.

Her head snapped up, fire blazing in her eyes. "Of course not!" she exclaimed vehemently. "I *know* it's not true."

Cris sagged against the seat. He hadn't fully realized how much he'd wanted, no, needed, her unwavering trust. She'd heard the worst of the rumors and hadn't believed them for an instant. Cris gazed into Amelia's face, seeing the fierceness in her expression and felt his heart tighten.

"Thank you," he whispered, lifting a finger to gently trace her jawline.

"There's no need to thank me for believing in you, Cris. I find it shocking that anyone who has even had the opportunity to meet you could believe such a thing." Amelia caught his hand and pressed it to her cheek. "You are one of the most noble men I've ever met."

The strength of her conviction moved him more than he'd thought possible. His dear, sweet Amie had grown into a wonderful, loyal friend. "I am a lucky man indeed to be able to count you among my friends."

Her smile glowed. "What a lovely compliment," she rushed, allowing their clasped hands to fall into her lap. "I consider it an honor as well, and that is precisely what I told everyone at the ball last night."

The warmth inside of him iced over. "You did what?"

"I marched up to those old biddies gossiping about you and told them that you would never do something like that."

"Oh, Amelia," Cris moaned. "Don't you realize how you jeopardize your reputation by defending me?"

"No, I don't," she protested, shaking her head.

"You do." Cris reached out his free hand and grasped her shoulder. "No one openly addresses rumors, Amie. They should simply be ignored. By challenging the ton, you place yourself at risk for the gossip to turn on you."

Amelia stiffened beneath his hold. "If society will scorn me for defending my dear friend, then let them. I have no wish to be accepted into the ton if it means I must abandon not only my integrity, but my dearest friend as well."

Admiration for her strength filled him. "I appreciate your sentiments, Amie, but you must realize—"

"What I realize is that you are being accused of something you didn't do, yet you ask me to ignore all the whispers and innuendos." She leaned toward him. "I can't do that, Cris. I will defend you to anyone who will listen."

Cris felt torn. He appreciated her loyalty more than she could ever know, but it came at a high price. Unfortunately, he now knew all too well how it felt to be ostracized by society. He knew how each stare, every veiled comment, burned at his soul. How could he allow Amelia to condemn herself to a similar fate?

Cris slid his hand from her shoulder onto her upper arm. "Please listen to me, Amie. You need to remain silent whenever someone mentions my name. If you can't stand to hear the comments, then simply walk away."

"But I can't bear—"

"No, Amie, *I* can't bear to have my good name restored at the cost of yours." As she opened her mouth to reply, he added, "Please do this for me."

"I don't want to." Her brows lowered as she frowned at him. "I don't understand any of this at all. Everything is so strange, so different here in town. No one says what they mean and everyone is quick to attack another's faults. False rumors fill the air in whispered confidences, but no one is interested in hearing the truth." Her eyes darkened with sadness. "I don't belong here and neither do you, Cris."

How was he supposed to respond to that statement? What she said was true; he couldn't deny it. But, still, for her sake, he needed to try. "Amie, you mustn't only look at the dark side of town life. There are wondrous things here as well—the theater, the clubs, the excitement of a ride on the Thames."

"None of those things are as important to me as the people I care for," Amie returned immediately. "I don't think like most of the other ladies here.

I'm more often bored than not at these parties. In fact, all the pretense is driving me a bit mad."

He smiled at her, knowing all too well how she felt. However, Amie wasn't suffering his fate. No, she was accepted, popular, and sought out. "Surely it's not that bad," he said.

"But it is," she insisted. "The inanity of it all is taking its toll on my sanity. I'm even starting to jump at shadows. Just last night, my sisters and I were in the garden talking when Deanna noticed three men approaching down the path. I completely humiliated all of us by telling them to hurry toward the house."

Cris's throat closed as he listened to Amelia's tale.

"Can you imagine how ridiculous we all looked, running toward the house, just because three men were taking a stroll around the gardens?"

Cris released Amie's hand to grasp her other arm. "You weren't hurt, were you?"

Amelia shook her head. "Absolutely not, Cris. They meant us no harm."

"Perhaps, then again, perhaps not." Cris looked down at Amie's confused expression and sighed. There could be no help for it now. The shadows of his own fate had touched her. In order to protect her, he needed to expose her to his own private nightmare. "I've never told you how I met Owen."

Amelia shook her head. "No, but I don't understand what that has to do with last night."

"You will," he predicted, before launching into his tale. He told her everything about that fateful night that had changed his life. When Cris finished, he released his hold on Amelia and sat back. "Now do you understand why the image of three men coming toward you and your sisters alarms me?"

"Yes." Amelia shivered, suddenly looking young and vulnerable.

"I have no proof, of course, but the timing is too conspicuous. I truly believe that the attack on Samantha and the rumors are somehow connected."

Amelia nodded slowly. "It certainly makes sense."

Anger swelled to life within him. For years, he'd run from the problem, ignoring the whispers, praying they would stop. But they hadn't. Instead, the rumors had gotten worse, plaguing him, until he felt like a pariah, unwelcome among his peers.

Resolution rushed through him as Cris straightened, feeling more focused than he had in years. "I can only apologize for allowing my problems to spill onto you, Amelia, but there can be no help for it now. I will contact the Bow Street Runners immediately and arrange for them to begin to look into these rumors."

"That is a good start," Amelia said. "And I can help by trying to find out who started this nasty gossip."

"No!" Cris's response was swift and harsh. It was hard enough to have her involved at all, never mind actively seeking out information.

"But, Cris, it only makes sense to try and track down the source of the rumors. If the two *are* connected, it might lead you to whoever is behind both the rumors and the kidnappings."

Cris reached up, cradling her face between his hands. "I don't want to put you at greater risk, Amie. I couldn't bear it if anything happened to you."

She curled her fingers around his wrists. "I will be perfectly fine."

Slowly, Cris stroked his thumbs over the smooth flesh of her cheeks. "I pray that is true."

Amelia turned her head and kissed the palm of his hand.

The touch of her lips burned a path into his soul, igniting a surge of age-old desire. Cris jerked his hands away.

"What is it, Cris?"

How could he answer Amelia's question? Should he tell her that for an instant, he'd imagined pulling her into his arms and tasting her once again? Or perhaps he should admit that he craved to see if her lips were as soft, as sweet, as he remembered. Either admission was completely unacceptable.

Ever since he'd come to London, he'd been having trouble ridding himself of these flashes of desire, most likely remnants of the feelings he'd entertained when he'd thought to marry her. It was perfectly natural and, given time, he was sure these yearnings would fade away.

Somehow, looking into her wide eyes and parted lips, it was hard to convince his heart of that fact.

Cris pushed the thoughts from his mind and tried to refocus his attention on the problem at hand. "Please don't fool yourself into thinking this isn't very serious, Amie. I assure you those gentlemen who were after Samantha meant business. Just ask yourself if perhaps all the rumors *are* true—but they just don't involve me. These men are not to be dismissed lightly."

"I don't dismiss them, Cris, but surely no harm can come to me if I simply ask questions," Amelia protested, placing her hand on his thigh. "And it would be much easier for me to get members of the ton to talk than it would be for any runner you hired."

The heat from her simple touch licked at his stirred desires. Subtely, he shifted from beneath her hand. "Perhaps you are right, but you are already far more involved than I'd like. It's clear that you've made your mind up, and if I can't convince you to desist in your assistance, I believe it will be best if I stay close to you and your sisters, just to be certain that you're safe."

Amelia started to speak, but Cris lifted his hand to halt her words. "I want you to understand me completely. By staying close, I shall be casting a stained reflection upon you, and your family."

"I don't care about that," she said, waving a hand in dismissal, a tremor of fear edging her voice. "If you think it would be best, if you truly think we could be in danger."

Saddened by the fact that he'd frightened her, but knowing that the danger could be all too real, Cris tucked a strand of hair behind her ear, allowing the silken lock to smooth between his fingers. He wished he could wrap her in his arms and keep her safe until all of this was over. Then she would remain untouched by the ugliness and pain of the rumors that were certain to follow her if he began to spend time with her. "I can only hope that time won't make you regret your decision today."

Amelia gazed up at him. "Never."

Her avowal created longings within him that were best left untouched.

Nodding once, Cris retrieved the reins and headed for home.

15

Amelia hurried into the parlor, following the sound of Camilla's piano playing. Emma and Deanna sat playing cards while Bea sat reading a book in the far corner of the room. "Camilla, could you stop for a bit?" Amelia asked, shutting the door behind her.

Camilla's fingers stilled on the keys as she looked up from the sheet music. "What is it, Amie?"

Amelia waved her sister over to where the others sat. "Please join us, so I can explain everything to you all at once."

Camilla's skirts swayed as she came and took a seat next to Bea.

Amelia perched on the edge of her chair. "I need all of you to help me."

Bea lay her book on her lap. "What's wrong? Are you all right, Amie?"

"Oh, I'm perfectly fine," she hastened to assure her sisters. "Actually, it is Cris who needs our help."

Deanna nodded, understanding softening her expression. "This has to do with the rumors you told us about last night, doesn't it?"

"As a matter of fact, it does," Amelia agreed, before launching into all Cris had told her on their carriage ride. She repeated for her sisters the story about Owen's cousin, Samantha, then continued on with the tales that had haunted Cris for years now. "So, Cris is now planning on hiring a Bow Street Runner to investigate the matter."

"It's more than past time that he do so," Bea pointed out. "He should have investigated those men as soon as he saved Samantha."

"He couldn't betray her trust," Camilla responded quickly. "I think it was quite noble of him to honor a lady's wish."

"I agree with you, Camilla, but his noble intentions don't help this situation. I believe it best if we remain focused on solutions for our current problem." Amelia leaned forward. "I feel that the rumors must be connected to Samantha's kidnapping attempt. The timing seems too convenient not to tie in together."

"And what if they are related? How does that help Cris?" Bea asked, her expression filled with concern.

"I'm not sure it does," Amelia said. "Still, if the investigator is able to find out who was behind Samantha's near-kidnapping, then it might end the rumors as well."

"And if they're not connected?"

Emma's question caused Amelia to lean back in her chair. "That is precisely where we come in."

"How is that?" Deanna asked, her brows drawing together.

"Whenever we hear a whisper about Cris, we can be very clever and try to find out where that person heard the story. If we backtrack all of the rumors, if we find their source, then we shall be able to find out who is starting them." Amelia glanced at each one of her sisters in turn. "Doesn't that sound like something we can do?"

"Absolutely," Bea said without hesitation.

Deanna nodded. "I can be quite clever. No one will even know I'm questioning them."

"Somehow I doubt that," Camilla said briskly, before turning toward Amelia. "But don't worry, Amie. I'll keep Deanna under control."

Amelia smiled at Deanna's loud protest.

"I'm looking forward to helping as well." Emma smiled at Amelia. "If I sit quietly next to some of the elderly ladies, they often don't notice me and speak quite freely."

"Wonderful." The tension within her relinquished some of its hold. "I knew I could count on all of you." Amelia stood, bending to kiss each one of her sisters in turn.

Bea reached up and hugged Amelia tight. "That's what family is all about."

Love warmed Amelia as she nodded. "I couldn't agree more."

Amelia looked at the gleaming diamond necklace and shuddered. Lying beside it were matching earbobs, a bracelet, a pin, and two other jeweled chokers. Her uncle specifically requested that they wear all their newly acquired jewels—at one time.

Slowly, Amelia retrieved the plainest of her necklaces and secured it around her neck. The simplicity was a perfect foil for her elegant gown. Amelia ran her fingertips down the thin chain. Yes, this was all the jewelry she needed.

It was time she began to assert herself a bit more with her uncle. Amelia nodded to her reflection in the mirror and promised she would remove any excess jewelry from her sisters as well. After all, they should look their best at the affair this evening.

It promised to be a wonderful time, and Cris had mentioned he would attend as well. Cris. Amelia allowed herself to linger over her exchange with him in the carriage, to relive each touch, each word. A sigh broke from her as her hand fell into her lap, the necklace forgotten.

True, she was naive, but for a moment today, she could have sworn that Cris looked at her with more than just desire in his eyes. When his hands had curved around her cheeks, he'd made her feel so beautiful, so loved. It had been all she could do to keep from leaning closer and pressing her lips to his.

Oh, she knew that they were merely friends, and she needed to keep reminding herself of that fact.

She had to stop thinking of Cris in any type of romantic fashion. He'd made it perfectly clear to her that he had no interest in falling in love with her or anyone else. And yet her heart still tripped at the mere sight of him, the brush of his hand, a lingering glance. She knew she had to stop the childish fantasies from filling her heart, her mind. She needed to clear her mind of such silly nonsense and see Cris for who he truly was. Cris would be spending more time with her, so she would be able to overcome her infatuation with him.

Then perhaps the other gentlemen of her acquaintance wouldn't all seem so dreadfully dull.

Cris rose as his aunt swept into the parlor. "You look quite fetching, Aunt Patricia. I'm so glad you decided to join me in town."

"Fetching?" She flicked her fan at him. "You make me sound like a young debutante."

"Well, I, for one, certainly understand how Cris could make that mistake," Owen said, stepping forward to kiss Aunt Patricia's hand.

"My heavens, you are both being so very delightful this evening." Aunt Patricia looked pointedly at Cris. "It makes me wonder what's wrong."

Chagrin filled Cris as he assisted his aunt into a chair. "Having you know me so well is not always to my advantage."

"Too late to worry about that, dear. Now tell your auntie what is bothering you."

Cris grinned at the 'auntie' remark, but he quickly sobered as he remembered exactly what he needed to tell her. "I need to speak with you before we head off to the Winston recital."

She lifted her brows. "This sounds quite serious, Crispin."

Cris saw the concern darkening his aunt's eyes

and wished he could spare her the worry of his situation. Still, he couldn't allow his aunt to walk into the recital tonight without any idea about the rumors. What if someone mentioned something to her and she was caught off guard. No, he had to forewarn her, even if he'd rather not embroil her in his nightmare. Cris's throat tightened as he gazed down at his aunt's beloved face. It would soon be over, he vowed silently.

Taking a deep breath, he began, "You haven't come to town for quite a few years and during that time, something horrible has been happening to me."

Aunt Patricia leaned closer to him. "Are you speaking of the rumors?"

He couldn't have been more surprised if she'd smashed him on the head with a vase. "You *know* about them?"

"Well, of course, dear, but I merely dismissed them as the jealous gossip of your peers." Aunt Patricia shrugged. "I can't imagine anyone actually believing such rubbish."

Her unquestioning support overwhelmed him. "How can I thank you for—"

"Thank me?" Aunt Patricia sniffed once. "You have no need to thank me for anything, Crispin. You are my family."

And for his aunt, it was that simple.

Cris felt his throat tighten with love for this woman who had been like a mother to him. Her no-nonsense acceptance of the situation eased his nerves about the upcoming evening. If Amelia and her sisters hadn't already agreed to attend, he wouldn't have set foot at the affair.

But when he weighed his discomfort against ensuring Amelia's safety, there was no other decision he could make.

Amie was worth it.

Amelia tried not to wince as Miss Winston hit another wrong key. She didn't dare peek at Camilla who sat to her right. Undoubtedly, her younger sister was in pain over the poorly executed sonata. On her other side, next to Deanna, Amelia caught a glimpse of Aunt Patricia and the telltale bobbing of the older woman's head. It was obvious that dear Aunt Patricia had succumbed to the temptations of sleep. Amelia couldn't see Bea and Emma who were seated behind her, but she could only imagine they were suffering as well. Amelia congratulated herself on her self-control. She had only to look over to where Cris stood leaning against a wall. It was impossible to hold back her smile when she saw Cris grimace and shiver at a particularly awful chord.

Finally, thankfully, the awkward Miss Winston hit her last sour note. Applause filled the room, waking Aunt Patricia with a jerk, making Amelia laugh.

Deanna leaned close to Amelia. "I think everyone is clapping because it's over."

Amelia pressed the back of her hand to her mouth to hold in her laughter. "Behave," she finally whispered to her sister.

Deanna grinned wickedly. "As if you didn't have the same thought yourself."

Amelia couldn't deny it, so she merely changed the subject. "I believe they're serving refreshments in the dining room."

It was all the invitation Deanna needed as she rose to join Bea and Emma.

"Are you coming with us, Amie?" Camilla asked, rising as well.

"In a moment." Amelia needed a minute or two to clear the ringing in her ears.

As her sisters moved off, Amelia glanced over to where Cris had been standing, only to find the spot empty. Perhaps he'd gone on into the dining room as well.

"May I join you?"

Amelia started, whirling to face a young lord. What was his name again? Henry or Langly? Or was it Laverby? They'd been introduced, but for the life of her, Amelia couldn't remember his name. Trying to bluff her way through the awkward situation, Amelia forced a bright smile onto her face. "How lovely to see you again."

The man's face lit up. "You *do* remember me then."

"Of c-c-c-ourse," she stuttered, hoping he wouldn't notice her nervousness. Was his name Haverly? Drat!

"I know we were introduced the other evening, but for some inexplicable reason, people seem to have a hard time remembering my name."

Amelia prayed that her face hid her rush of guilt. "I can't understand why," she responded lamely.

"Neither can I." He pressed his lips together for an instant. "It's not as if Lenerby is a difficult name to remember."

Lenerby! Amelia slowly released her breath. "Not difficult at all." In her relief, she placed a hand on his arm. "It is truly a pleasure to see you again, Lord Lenerby."

"Is it?" he gushed. "I was so hoping you'd think so."

Amelia's smile wavered at his unusual enthusiasm. "Yes, well, shall we join—"

"In fact, I've been wanting a private moment with you for days now." Lord Lenerby grabbed her hand and lifted it to his lips. "Your greeting lets me know that you felt the same emotion I did at our first meeting."

What the devil was the man talking about? She couldn't even remember his name! "Please, Lord Lenerby," she protested, trying to pull her hand free. "This is most unseemly."

The young lord began to kiss his way up her arm, shocking Amelia to her core. How had she ended up in this predicament? She tried again to dissuade him. "I insist you stop at once!"

But Lord Lenerby wasn't to be dissuaded. He continued upward until his mouth reached her upper arm. It was all Amelia could take. She stood abruptly, knocking Lord Lenerby off his chair, sending him sprawling onto the floor. She glared down at him. "A true gentleman would have stopped his advances with one request," she nearly shouted.

Amelia spun around only to come face to face with a grinning Crispin. Wonderful. After having her ears abused by the horrid music, then being mauled by an overeager suitor, the last thing she wanted was ribbing from Cris.

Amelia groaned as she stepped around Cris and left the room, wanting to find a very large cup of chocolate.

Cris watched her go, a grin still on his face when he turned to look down at the young buck amongst the chairs. He reached down, holding out a hand to Lord Lenerby.

"My thanks," the younger man said, accepting the aid. On his feet, Lord Lenerby began to straighten his clothes. "I don't know what came over her. She was quite encouraging and she welcomed my—"

His words were cut off as Cris grasped the young dandy by his lapels, moving in until he was inches away from Lenerby's frightened face. "If you ever so much as glance at her again, I fear I'll have to hurt you, Lenerby," Cris murmured, his voice low and deep with promise. "Badly."

He saw real fear flash in Lenerby's eyes before Cris released the young man. It took no more than a second for the dandy to scurry away.

Cris slapped his hands together as he headed for the dining room and Amelia. He'd promised to protect her, but he'd had no idea that it would be so entertaining.

16

Two days later, Cris found himself at yet another ball, watching Amelia whirl about the dance floor with Lord Westwood. He tried not to notice what a fetching picture she made as she whirled across the floor.

"Have you marked the eldest as your own?"

It took immense self-control to keep an expression of disgust from crossing his features as Cris turned to face Lords Henley, Baskins, and Stevens. Instead, Cris schooled his face into lines of cool disdain. "Excuse me?"

"The girl, the Ralston chit, have you claimed her?" prodded Lord Stephen Henley.

Cris slowly raised an eyebrow as he glared at the older gentlemen, each twenty years his senior. Their indulgent lifestyles had left them with bulging waistlines and sallow complexions, yet their soiled reputations still surrounded them like a dark and foul cloud. That they'd taken an interest in Amie and her sisters distressed him. He'd been right to worry about them when he'd first arrived in town.

"Surely you do not refer to my dear friend, Miss Amelia Ralston, in such a fashion." Cris rounded his syllables, injecting a droll, arrogant note to his voice.

Lord Henley bristled visibly. "No need to take offense, sir. I was inquiring after your involvement with the lady."

"Indeed. My *involvement* is none of your concern." Again, Cris drew out the words before glancing around, letting all three know he was bored with the conversation.

Lord Laurence Baskins cleared his throat. "With your, shall we say, attentive manner this evening, it was a natural mistake to assume you are on the verge of an engagement."

To this, Cris said nothing. He merely slanted the gentlemen a bored look.

"And we were curious to find out if she was as tasty a morsel as she appears," Lord Edward Stevens added, poking Cris with one finger.

Cris drew himself up to his full height, glaring down at them. "If I ever hear you speak of Miss Ralston in that vile fashion again, I promise you will rue the day," Cris ground out.

Stevens must have realized his mistake, for his eyes grew wide and he began to stutter, "I never meant . . . that is, I didn't intend to—"

Cris cut him off with an abrupt wave of his hand. "I've had quite enough of your prattle for one evening."

Baskins bravely raised his chin. "It was our intent to congratulate you, not insult you, Merrick. It is obvious that you suffer from a complete lack of good humor."

"There is nothing humorous in a pack of pathetic old men making insulting remarks about an innocent young lady." Cris glared at each one, until they all, in turn, looked away. "You will stay away from Miss Ralston and her family in the future. Is that understood?"

"I had no idea you were such a prig," grumbled Baskins with a deep frown.

Cris ignored the statement. "Is that understood?"

When all three nodded, Cris turned on his heel and strode from the room.

"So, how are my girls?"

The exuberant voice could only belong to one man. Cris excused himself from his conversation to turn around and face Hubert. "I believe they are all having an agreeable time."

"And?"

Hubert was looking at him expectantly, but for the life of him, Cris couldn't understand what the man wanted. "And what?"

Hubert threw his hands up. "And have any particular gentlemen of a titled nature . . . if you catch my meaning . . ."

"Subtle though it is," Cris murmured, a smile playing on his lips.

"What was that?"

Cris shook his head. "Never mind. Do go on."

Hubert eyed him up and down. "You gentry are odd fellows at times," he mumbled, shaking his head.

Cris laughed aloud. "Please continue," he urged again.

Hubert was still looking at him as if he were some unfathomable creature. "Anyhow," Hubert began slowly, "as I was saying, I wanted to know if any titled gentlem— *Good God*!!!"

Hubert's exclamation startled not only Cris, but the other gentlemen standing nearby. "What? What is it?"

"My girls!" gasped Hubert, pointing a shaking finger toward the dance floor. "They're . . . they're . . . *naked*!"

Cris spun on his heel, scanning the twirling couples for the Ralston sisters. Amelia was sitting near the open window conversing with Lady Manning. Bea was dancing with Owen. Camilla. Where was Camilla? Ah, there conversing with Lady Westwood. Deanna was dancing with Lord Perth. And Emmaline? There she was accepting a glass of punch from young Lord Conover.

All five accounted for and each one elegantly gowned.

Cris turned back to Hubert who was still gaping at the girls. "They all look beautiful, Hubert."

Hubert grasped his chest, shock widening his eyes. "I *know* that, your Dukeness. That's not the problem. Lord in Heaven, they're naked!" he said again.

Confused, Cris glanced back over his shoulder.

"I'm afraid I don't understand what you're trying to say, Hubert. They're clothed to perfection."

"Their jewels!" Hubert shook his finger toward the girls. "Where are their jewels?"

Ah, that explained it. Cris crossed his arms. "It seems to me that the Ralston ladies arrived with the perfect complement of jewels."

"How can you say that? They only have two or three baubles each!"

Cris couldn't help but laugh at Hubert's incredulous expression. "Come now, Hubert, I agreed to help guide you through society and so you must trust my judgment. Ladies accessorize with their jewels in a subtle manner."

"Is that subtle?" Hubert asked, pointing at Camilla.

"Most definitely. Lord, they were practically dripping in gems at some of the other functions."

"As they should have been." Hubert pounded his fist against his open palm to emphasize his point. "I've told you before—a good merchant always displays his wares."

Cris knew that Hubert would never be able to understand the concept of subtlety. Still, Cris found himself saying, "Agreed, Hubert, but they aren't merchants; they're ladies and as such, they do not advertise their wealth."

"Then how are they going to snare a titled gentleman? Explain that to me, if you please." Hubert shook his finger at Cris. "Most of these dandies are shopping for a wealthy wife."

Cris placed his hand on Hubert's shoulder.

"Don't worry, Hubert. At this point, everyone knows the Ralston girls have large dowries."

"Perhaps, but it still can't hurt to keep reminding them."

It was impossible not to like the merchant. Cris patted Hubert once on the back. "You are a practical man, Hubert."

The older man puffed out his chest. "I consider myself so." He smiled at Cris. "In fact, I've been thinking that it was a bit too crowded in my carriage on the way here."

Cris's lips twitched. "Was it now?"

Hubert nodded, a sly glint in his eye. "If you wouldn't mind escorting Amelia home, your graceful, I would be much obliged."

Cris ignored the ridiculous title as he bowed to Hubert. "It would be my pleasure." It would give Cris the perfect opportunity to tease Amelia about the earlier incident with Lenerby. Perhaps, if they could return to the playful friendship they'd shared when they were children, it would help him to forget about his desire for her—and the images of her, in his arms, that plagued his sleep.

"I'm hoping pleasure is the right word to use, Lord Duke," Hubert said with a chuckle.

Cris sighed at Hubert's off-color joke before moving to find Owen. Two steps away, Cris paused, turning back to Hubert. "By the way, Hubert, I would be honored if you would call me Cris." Cris wanted to stop all of the dukey, graceness, and dukeship nonsense.

Hubert tugged down his vest. "I will indeed—Cris. Now go fetch my Amie."

"Did you see Merrick escort the oldest of The Fabulous Five, the luscious Amelia, out the door?" Prospero murmured to his companions as he sipped at his punch and watched the dancers.

"He appears to favor her," Alonso agreed.

Sebastian tugged at his cravat. "He couldn't keep his eyes off her the entire time he was here."

"His infatuation with her only sweetens Amelia's appeal," Prospero said. "Not that the other four are any less attractive."

"Not at all," Alonso whispered, watching as Emma danced past them.

A corner of Prospero's mouth tilted upward. "Watch them move so gracefully across the dance floor . . . and imagine how they will dance for us when we finally get them alone."

17

As the footman closed the door, encasing them within the private comfort of the carriage, Amelia turned to face Cris. "Very well, Cris. I know you've been waiting to tease me about Lord Lenerby."

"Me?" he asked innocently. "I would never think to torment you about such a fascinating encounter."

"As if I believe you." Amelia swatted Cris on the arm. "A true gentleman would have come to my rescue."

"You seemed quite capable of handling yourself," Cris said, rubbing where she'd hit him. He wasn't about to tell her of his little chat with Lenerby.

"The point is, Lord Merrick, I shouldn't have had to defend myself." She blew out her breath. "Must I explain this knight-in-shining-armor idea to you in detail?"

The teasing lilt in her voice made him smile. "Oh, please do, just to refresh my memory." Cris began to relax next to her as they fell into the light banter of old.

"I'm the princess," Amelia began in a slow drawl, "and you're the knight."

"That part I remember." Cris shifted closer to her. "What comes next?"

Amelia patted him on the leg. "You poor dear, you don't remember anything at all, do you?"

"A sign of age, I suppose," Cris sighed dramatically. "You must remind me, or I'll never be able to rescue you, the princess." He paused for a moment. "Or were you the fair maiden?"

"Whichever you prefer," Amelia pronounced, turning toward him. "The most important thing for you to remember is that it is your duty to vanquish any evil foe."

"Do you count Lenerby as an evil foe?" Cris burst out laughing. "I'm sorry, Amie, but my imagination isn't *that* good!"

"You have a point," she acknowledged.

"Indeed I do. Lord, the man was certainly earnest about his, er, affections, but you were able to 'vanquish' him quite on your own." Cris tucked a strand of her hair behind her ear. "A challenge he is not."

"Well . . ."

"Well, nothing." Cris grabbed Amelia's hand. "Your evil foe sounded something like this." He raised her fingers to his lips. "Oh, my darling, dearest Amelia," he murmured in a high-pitched voice.

"He said nothing of the sort," Amelia protested with a laugh.

"That's true; he was far too busy kissing his way up your arm," Cris amended, before proceeding to demonstrate. He pressed loud kisses along her arm, up to the curve of her shoulder.

"That is much higher than Lenerby ever got." Amelia smiled at him. "I suppose the only thing left for me to do is to rid myself of you as well."

Cris pulled her closer, pressing her against his chest. "I fear I shall be a more difficult foe to vanquish, my lady," he murmured.

Amelia wriggled against his hold, but Cris held her tight. Gales of laughter swept from Amelia as she writhed, trying to break free.

Suddenly, Cris became aware of the fact that this was a woman he was holding in his arms, not the little girl he used to torment and tease. The points of her breasts pressed into his chest as their bodies stilled.

Slowly, Cris turned his head until he gazed down into Amelia's upturned face. Her lips parted as her breath rushed from her. Cris struggled to retain a hold on his sensibility, but it had deserted him. All he could remember was how deliciously soft, how incredibly appealing, her lips were against his.

He knew it was a bad idea to kiss her, but for the life of him, he couldn't remember why. Slowly, Cris lowered his head gently, touching his mouth to hers. Amelia released her breath into his mouth on a sigh as if this kiss was something she'd longed for as well.

One taste and he was gone.

Cris deepened the touch, molding her mouth to his, enfolding her body even closer. Like the finest nectar, she tempted him to take more. Cris angled his head as he swept his tongue into her mouth, sating himself. Amelia curled her arms up and around his shoulders, sinking her fingers into his hair. She shifted against him, aligning her body with his.

She was a perfect fit.

Cris couldn't get enough of her. All of his senses clamored for her—he yearned to touch her tender flesh, he ached to hear her soft cries of fulfillment, he craved her sweet scent of desire, he longed to look upon her as he taught her the delights of passion. He knew he should stop, should pull away from her, but he couldn't seem to get his body to acknowledge the thought. She filled his senses, overwhelming logic with a blaze of desire.

Cris broke off their kiss, moving his mouth across the gentle curve of her jaw, down the sensuous line of her neck, to lick at the base of her throat. "You're so beautiful, Amie," he whispered close against her, brushing his lips along her collarbone.

Amelia arched her head back, giving him welcome. "Oh, Cris. I've dreamed of this moment for years."

Her words jarred inside his head. She'd dreamed of him for years. The only problem was . . . she hadn't *known* him for years. The person she'd dreamed of was her knight in shining armor. That person was someone who didn't even exist.

Cris fought down the desire still clamoring through him as he slowly eased Amelia away from him.

"Cris?"

Her soft whisper reached inside of him, making him want nothing more than to ignore his awakened sense of honor. But he couldn't. Above all else, Amelia was his friend, and it wasn't fair to either one of them to continue indulging their passion. She wanted something from him that he was unable to give.

Cris cupped her cheek. "Amelia, this was a mistake," he began softly. "We both were swept away in the moment, engrossed in fantasy, but if we take this further than a kiss, it wouldn't be right." He forced himself to ignore just how right she had felt to him.

Amelia drew away, breaking his hold.

At her continued silence, Cris tried to explain himself further. "Our friendship means too much to me. I don't ever want to be less than honest with you." He gazed into her eyes. "I'm no fairy-tale hero."

Amelia's lashes fluttered shut for a moment, before she took a deep breath and looked at him. "You're right, Cris. We did get caught up in the moment." The smile she gave him wavered. "We both got carried away."

Carried away? Cris thought. That's exactly what his senses urged him to do—carry Amie away into his bedroom and keep her there until he'd filled himself with her, satisfying every pounding urge, every burning hunger, every—

Cris broke off his thoughts. He had to remember that Amelia was his friend—his dear friend who dreamed of storybook love and happily ever after.

It seemed the ultimate irony: the woman who felt so right in his arms dreamed of someone he could never be.

"Amie, I wish you had stayed and listened to me wind the conversation around those battle-axes, Lady Witherstone and Lady Hemple." Deanna flounced onto Amelia's bed.

Amelia reached out and tugged on one of Deanna's long blond curls. "I wish I could have seen it as well." If she'd stayed, she would have avoided the embarrassing scene with Cris. "Tell me what happened," Amelia urged, wanting to forget how wonderful Cris had felt against her and how very much she wanted him to show her the heights of passion.

"I sat down next to Lady Witherstone and pretended I was too fatigued to dance. I knew that she wouldn't be able to resist gossiping if I remained quiet." Deanna curled her legs beneath her. "It took no more than a minute for Lady Witherstone to turn toward me and ask about Cris."

Amelia leaned forward. "What did she ask?"

"She wanted to know if he'd visited us last evening."

"Why on earth would she want to know that?"

Deanna's expression darkened. "Because someone said that there was a strange man lurking in Lady Hemple's garden last night. Lady Witherstone wanted to know if it was Cris."

Amelia shook her head. "Just how ridiculous can these rumors become?"

"There doesn't appear to be any limit to them," Deanna agreed. "There is some good news though. Lady Witherstone told me she'd just overheard this latest rumor."

"From whom? Did you find out?" Amelia asked eagerly.

Deanna nodded, smiling brightly. "I knew you'd be very impressed with me."

"I am, Deanna," Amelia agreed, reaching out to clasp her sister's hand. "Who was it?"

"She said it came from a very reliable source." Deanna quoted, "Lord Henley."

Amelia sat back against her pillows, amazed at the twist of fate. "It appears Cris was right after all when he warned us away from Henley."

"That Merrick is an obnoxious chap," Henley grumbled, propping his feet against the table in front of him.

"Make yourself comfortable," Stevens said, laughing.

"It's my home and I can bloody well do what I want to the furniture. I've just been set down by that bloody Duke of Bradford and you're worried about my boots being on the table?" Henley waved a hand at his friend. "The devil to that."

"No need to be testy, Henley. I'm not disagreeing

with you. In fact, I'd say he's due for a little comeuppance," said Stevens, tugging his vest down over his ever-burgeoning stomach.

"If we were younger . . ." Baskins trailed off. He smoothed back his still-thick gray hair.

"Speak for yourself, Baskins," snorted Stevens. "I'm still in my prime."

"Prime?" Henley laughed. "Perhaps if you plan on living until you're a hundred."

"So, we're a bit old, what of it?" Baskins straightened in his chair. "Does it mean we're less entitled to respect?"

"Absolutely not," Henley responded immediately. He swirled his brandy about the bottom of his glass. "Do you remember the glory of our younger days? Do you remember what it was like when we were four and twenty . . . like our sons are now?"

Both Stevens and Baskins nodded immediately. Smiles of fond memories curved their mouths. "We were a wild group. The Dark Lords," Stevens said wistfully. "Who ever would have imagined us, each married and widowed within a year, all having produced an heir in the interim?"

"If I remember correctly, none of us particularly wanted to marry, but a man's got to have an heir. Luckily for each of us, our wives were generous enough to pass on, leaving us free to our pleasures again." Baskins lifted his glass.

"Ha!" shouted Henley. "You were fairly free with your pleasures even while your wife was alive."

Baskins merely smiled. "Ah, yes, but for the past twenty and some years there has been no one to list all my sins against me in a shrill, raised voice."

Stevens shivered. "Your wife did have the most piercing of wails."

"Yours didn't lack for pitch either."

"Don't remind me."

All three men laughed at the retort.

Henley leaned back in his chair, sighing deeply. "We certainly had some lovely times in our youth."

"I often think back on some of our antics and wish I were young again." Baskins stared down at his drink. "All the women, the games, and the challenges."

Their smiles slowly faded. Henley took a long drink of brandy. "I still think Merrick deserves to be taken down a peg or two."

"Exactly what do you propose we do?" Baskins asked.

Henley widened his eyes. "Did I say we were going to do anything?"

"No, but wouldn't it be sweet?" Stevens leaned forward.

Henley stretched out his feet. "You know old chap, I think you're correct." Excitement lit within him. "I do believe, gentlemen, that we should give Merrick a final lesson in what it means to be a true gentleman of rank and meaning."

18

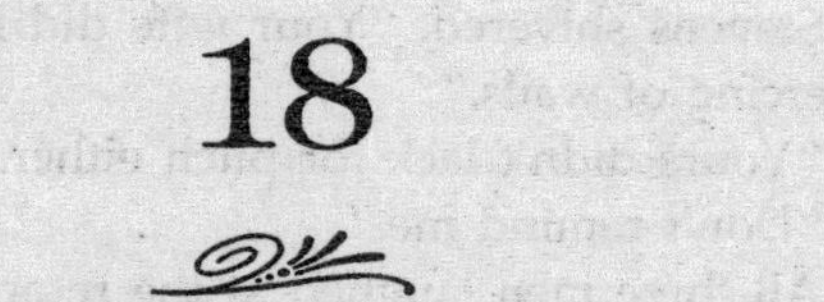

The fierce rush of satisfaction took him aback. How could he have known, even guessed, that Amelia would blend into his home so perfectly? He stood up from behind his desk. "This is an unexpected pleasure," Cris said, coming around to welcome Amelia into his study.

"I'm sorry to call on you unannounced, but it is a most urgent matter."

Cris reached out for Amelia, but he pulled back at the last moment. He remembered all too well what had happened the last time he'd touched her. Hell, it had kept him up most of the night. "What is it? What's wrong, Amie?"

"Nothing's wrong, Cris. In fact I have news that I think you'll find very interesting." Amelia sat down on the settee. "One of the ladies at the soiree last evening mentioned another rumor about you to Deanna. Then my sister asked a few more questions and she found out that the rumor had come from Lord Henley."

"Henley?" Cris sank down into one of his high-backed chairs. "Henley. My God. Have those old bastards been the ones carefully stripping me of my good name?"

Amelia's eyes darkened. "Lady Witherstone only mentioned Henley's name."

"Oh, I assure you, Amie, Henley, Baskins, and Stevens never do anything without each other. If Henley was involved, I know that the other two were as well."

"Even so, we only know that Henley was behind this particular rumor, not all of them," Amelia pointed out.

"I know, but it is all too easy to believe that they have been behind them all." And if they were, he would make sure they paid for their actions. Another thought struck him, causing Cris to slam his fist against the arm of his chair. "Damn. Now I can give up any hope that the rumors are connected with Samantha's attackers."

"Why?" Amelia asked with a shake of her head.

"Because those three are far too old to be the men I saw that night."

"It was many years ago, perhaps they looked different back then."

Cris shook his head. "Not that different, Amie. The three who tried to kidnap Owen's cousin were extremely fit."

"Perhaps they were completely unrelated incidents, but it must be a relief to know at least where one of the rumors started."

Cris agreed readily. "It certainly is. It will give

me a place to begin my investigation." Cris stood and began to pace. After years of uncertainty, of not knowing who had started any of the vicious tales, Cris found himself awash with an odd combination of anger, relief, and a hunger for vengeance. He felt as if his entire body vibrated with these intense emotions, heightening every sensation.

"Perhaps it is best if I leave now," Amelia said as she rose to her feet.

"No!" His response was swift and strong. Cris gazed at her and fought to keep from pulling her into his arms, holding onto her until he calmed. Something inside him clamored for Amelia.

By her expression, he knew that his response had surprised her. "I'd like you to stay," Cris said, more calmly this time.

Her features softened as she placed her hand on his arm. "I understand perfectly, Cris."

He drew in his breath sharply and moved away from Amelia, praying that she didn't notice his fierce reaction to her touch. The spot where her fingers had rested on him tingled as if fire had licked at his flesh. He felt Amie's touch throughout his entire body . . . and he'd liked it far too much.

"Perhaps I should be alone," he stuttered, clasping his hands behind his back to keep from reaching for her.

"Don't be silly, Cris. Everyone needs a friend at times like this."

The smile she gave him created an ache in his heart. He'd never known another like her, such a wonderful combination of innocence and unconcious allure, of integrity and loyalty.

Amelia walked around his study, trailing her fingers over the woodwork. "Your home is beautiful, Cris." She faced him. "Truly lovely."

"Thank you," he murmured in a strangled voice. It took little imagination to picture her fingers stroking down his body. The force of his desire alarmed him. He needed to leave this room immediately. Perhaps if he showed her the rest of the house, played the proper host, these odd, intense sensations sweeping through him would ease. "Come. Let me show you the most magnificent room in the house," he urged, opening the door to the study.

Immediately, Amelia moved closer, pausing in front of him. "Is it the solarium?"

Her question surprised him. "How did you know?"

"Aunt Patricia told me it was one of the best things about London." Amelia tilted her face up. "She said it brought her garden inside."

Cris looked down at her, drowning in the warmth of her gaze. "Yes, she still spends much time in that room," he murmured, not knowing or even caring if his response made sense.

"I can picture her there." Amelia moved forward, heading down the hall, breaking the intimacy of the moment.

Cris led Amelia into the solarium. Her gasp of sheer pleasure delighted him. The sunlight shone through the glass ceiling, filtering down through the lush plants filling the room, to create bold patterns against the stone floor.

"Oh, Cris, it's breathtaking." Amelia wandered into the heart of the room, brushing against leafy plants, pausing to smell a delicate bloom.

"My aunt has a way with plants." Cris trailed after her, watching how the sunlight played with her hair. "I knew you'd like this room."

"Like it?" Amelia whirled about, tilting her face upward to catch the sun. "I love it."

If he went to her, touched her, would he too feel some of her joy, share in her happiness?

Cris thrust away his thoughts, fighting to retain a hold on his self-control.

"Oh, look, there's Aunt Patricia's settee." Amelia rushed over to the velvet seat. "I've always wanted to have my portrait painted."

Cris grinned at Amelia as she lay down upon the settee, arching one arm over her head. "How do I look?" she asked in a playful tone.

The simmering desire that had plagued him all morning gave way to his laughter. "I'm sorry, madam," he began in a French accent, "but you are not in the correct position for your portrait." He held an arm across his stomach and one over his head. "You need to be like this."

Amelia giggled, a girlish sound that lent itself to their make-believe game, as she shifted into the new position. "How is this?"

Cris pursed his lips, tapping a finger against them. "Not quite perfect, *ma petite*." He stepped closer and began to drape her gown over the edge of the seat. "You need an elegant look with your skirt like thus."

Amelia remained still beneath Cris's ministrations as he perched himself on the edge of the seat.

"Now the angle of your shoulders is all wrong," he announced with a tisking noise. "You should be facing into the stream of sunlight." Cris grasped her shoulders, moving her into the position he wanted. "There." He leaned back, pressing a finger to his chin. "Perfect."

Amelia laughed brightly.

"Ah, ah," Cris reprimanded her, continuing to use the accent. "You must not move, not one inch."

Her eyes sparkled. "What if I get stiff?"

"It is a small price to pay for immortality upon my canvas," he said, airily waving his hand. "Now, the last item to discuss is your expression. You must project an aura of sultry awareness for me."

Amelia tilted her head back, exposing the long column of her neck to him. Her lashes lowered and her lips parted. "How is this?" she murmured, her voice low and alluring.

Suddenly, the game ceased to exist as Cris was caught up in the fantasy of his own making. Her gaze beckoned, calling him to her, and he was powerless to resist.

Slowly, Cris leaned down to her, craving, no, needing to kiss her once more, just one last time.

His desire reflected in her eyes as he neared her lips. He'd promised himself last night that he wouldn't kiss her again, but all of his good intentions had fled.

An inch from her mouth, he paused, gazing into her beautiful face. "Amie," he whispered before he moved to close the distance between them.

A gasp broke from Amelia an instant before she rolled away from him and off the settee, landing on the floor with a loud thump.

19

Cris found himself kissing the velvet cushion. Quickly, he sat up and peered over the edge of the settee, to see Amelia sprawled below him. "Amie?" he asked, reaching down to her.

Amelia felt the heat rise to her face. She was thoroughly embarrassed, but she'd reacted instinctively to avoid Cris's kiss. Ignoring his outstretched hand, she scrambled to her feet, smoothing down her skirts.

"Are you hurt?" Cris stood also, rubbing a hand down her arm.

"I'm fine," she responded, thankful that her voice was level. "It was rather clumsy of me."

Cris's eyes narrowed. "Clumsy? I thought you moved off the settee quite purposefully."

Amelia pasted a bright smile upon her face. "I did, but I certainly didn't mean to end up on the floor."

Concern gentled his expression. "Are you positive that you aren't hurt?"

Amelia forced herself to push away the flood of warmth at his concern. "I am perfectly fine," she assured him again.

Cris cleared his throat as he took a step away from her. "I must apologize for almost—"

"Please don't," she interrupted, unwilling to hear his apology. She was just as guilty as he for getting caught up in their playacting again. It was apparent that their friendship could never go back to the way it once was. There was too much between them now.

But where did they go from here?

The answer in her heart saddened Amelia. It was painfully apparent that Cris would always possess the ability to make her believe in fairy tales; he would always be able to sweep her off her feet. Whenever she was with him, she became the foolish girl desperately in love with him all over again.

The problem was she no longer wished to be that girl.

Since she'd come to London, she'd asserted herself with her uncle, found a place for herself within the ton, such as it was, and had begun to grow as a person. She had no desire to return to that little girl who hung all of her hopes and dreams on a knight in shining armor.

Amelia certainly couldn't be angry at Cris; he'd always been honest with her. No, the fault was hers alone. She was the one unable to forget her childhood fantasies.

Today's near kiss convinced her that she could

no longer spend her time by his side. Cris was far too much of a temptation for her heart to resist.

Amelia focused her attention back on Cris, who was wearing a confused expression. She smiled reassuringly at him. "There is no need for any apology, Cris. We must simply ensure that in the future it never happens again."

He nodded slowly. "I agree, Amie."

Amelia held back a sigh of regret. From now on, their past would remain just that—past.

Cris rapped his knuckles fiercely on Henley's door. His day had been horrendous and he was ready to take out his frustrations on the lecherous old man.

Cris couldn't rid himself of the niggling feeling that something was wrong with Amelia. She'd been polite and understanding after he'd nearly kissed her in the solarium, but she hadn't let him apologize or explain his actions.

No, she had cut him off every time.

What bothered him most was that he didn't know how he would even begin to explain his actions. What could he tell her? That he'd seen her on the settee, looking so incredibly beautiful, and the urge to kiss her had overwhelmed him? Or should he admit to the fact that the memory of their embrace in the carriage had kept him awake all evening?

And if he did, how could he explain his desire? The emotions inside him were a jumbled mess. Perhaps if they talked it out, if he admitted to being plagued with desire for her, then they would be able to overcome the awkwardness and resume their friendship. He so enjoyed their conversations, yet he risked losing her every time he gave into his desires.

His jaw tightened as he pounded on the door once more. Still no one answered. It struck Cris as being very odd that not even a servant was about, but he was too annoyed to care.

There would be time enough to deal with Henley.

Now, it was time he headed for home and prepare for his evening at the opera with Amelia and her family. Satisfaction calmed his jagged nerves. Perhaps there they would finally have a chance to talk.

"Gentlemen, it is time to capture our next prize," Prospero announced, putting his booted feet upon the table.

"Which one did you choose?" Alonso leaned forward.

"The eldest, of course." Prospero smoothed an eyebrow. "After all, she is Merrick's chosen one, so it is only fitting she be ours as well."

Sebastian glanced toward the open door of Prospero's study. "Shouldn't we take a care with what we say here?"

Prospero dismissed the open door with a wave of his hand. "I've given all the servants leave for the day." His fingers tapped out a staccato noise. "I've prepared a neat trap for our Miss Ralston at the opera tonight. My sources tell me that she and her entire family are going to be in attendance this evening."

"What have you planned?" Alonso asked, an expectant grin on his face.

"I've sent Miss Ralston a missive asking her to meet me in the powder room just before the beginning of the second half."

"You asked her to meet you?" Sebastian fell back against his chair. "How could you reveal yourself to her that way?"

"I didn't, you fool." Prospero glared at his companion. "In fact, I didn't sign it at all. I merely said that I had vital information that would aid her dear friend, Crispin."

"And if the way she's been defending him in public is any indication, she will come scurrying along quick as can be."

"That is my hope," Prospero agreed. "Just think, gentlemen. Tonight, we shall again taste the sweetness of forbidden fruit."

"I still don't see why my girls couldn't wear their glitters here," Uncle Hubert grumbled, crossing his arms with a "humpf."

Cris sat back, unfazed by Hubert's complaints. "Don't worry, Hubert. The Ralston sisters are all so lovely, they need no enhancements to attract suitors."

Emma leaned over and pressed a kiss upon Cris's cheek while he accepted grateful smiles from Camilla and Deanna. Owen and Beatrice were side by side at the other end of the box, whereas he and Amelia sat in front of Aunt Patricia and Uncle Hubert. With Emma sitting next to him and the other two younger girls in front, he was surrounded. There would be no discreet conversation between him and Amelia. He cast a longing glance at the privacy surrounding his friend and Beatrice.

Somehow the wily Owen had yet again secured the best position for himself.

All he'd wanted this evening was an opportunity to speak privately with Amelia, but there didn't seem to be any way to accomplish that goal. Even worse, Amelia had been unfailingly polite all evening. Her murmured nothings made him grind his teeth. Cris muffled a sigh and settled back in his chair.

The orchestra began to tune their instruments, the sign that the second half of the opera would soon begin. Amelia jumped in her seat. A pretty flush stained her cheeks. "Please excuse me, Cris. I wish to refresh myself," she murmured.

He rose to his feet, allowing her room to pass by him. "Would you like me to escort you?"

She seemed oddly nervous. "There is no need, thank you. I shall be back momentarily."

"I'll accompany you," Deanna offered, standing also.

Cris tried to quell his disappointment. It would have been the perfect opportunity for their discussion . . . or the perfect time to claim a kiss.

Shocked at his own thoughts, Cris sat down

abruptly, and let the sisters leave the box with no further delay.

The moment Amelia was beyond the curtains, she began to breathe a bit easier. It had been impossible for her to sit next to Cris and act as if everything were perfectly normal between them. Every time he looked at her, she wondered if he was picturing her lying on the settee. She'd ached for his kiss, but coming to that realization had been what saved her. Amelia pressed her hands against her cheeks.

It was hard to hide her emotions from him, but she forced herself to do just that. She didn't want to hurt him by ending their friendship, but she feared she had no choice.

"I believe the powder room is over here," Deanna said, pointing down the empty hallway.

Amelia nodded, gathering her control. The note she'd received earlier in the evening was tucked into her reticule. A footman had handed it to her as she'd entered the hall. A burst of anger pushed her worries aside. Amelia didn't know if she was going to berate or thank the person who wrote the note. At least it gave her something to think about other than her love for Cris. True, it still involved him, but it didn't go against her new-found resolve.

She merely considered it a favor from one friend to another.

Satisfied with her conclusion, Amelia linked arms with Deanna and started down the hallway. They passed an unlit wall sconce and a shadowy section of hall, yet Amelia didn't think much of it until they came to another darkened wall lamp. Uneasy, she paused, pulling Deanna to a halt next to her. All around her, she could hear the low murmur of people behind the curtains, but she and Deanna were alone in the corridor.

"Amie?" Deanna whispered, her voice echoing in the empty hall.

Amelia thrust aside her own apprehensions. "Two of the sconces have gone out, Deanna. There is nothing to fear."

"Where are the footmen?"

That question disturbed Amelia more than she let Deanna realize. There were usually footmen stationed at each box. The hallway was, however, completely empty. They passed a staircase leading downward and had almost reached the door to the powder room when two men appeared at the end of the hall.

Amelia gasped, the tale of Samantha's fate filling her thoughts. Fear raced through her, but she forced herself to remain calm. "Might we be of assistance?" In the darkened hallway, she couldn't make out their features.

The taller of the two men laughed, a low, dark sound. "So nice of you to inquire, Amelia."

She started at her name. They knew her. They had been waiting for her. There was no one waiting to talk to her about Cris; no, there were only these men—perhaps the same ones who had tried to snatch Samantha. Amelia stiffened her spine.

"What do you want?" she demanded in the firmest voice she could manage.

The man's dark laugh made her shiver as she heard the malicious promise in its depths. "You, Amelia. We want you, though we are quite pleased that you brought along your delightful sister, Deanna."

Her heart began to pound in fright. Amelia took a step backward, pressing Deanna back as well. "I don't understand," Amelia said, trying to distract them from noticing her stealthy movements.

The two men took a step forward. "Oh, I believe you are beginning to understand quite well," the second man rasped.

Amelia struggled to remain calm. She and Deanna took another step backward. "This is mad."

"No. This is tradition."

The third voice brought a tiny shriek from Amelia as she whirled around to face another man behind Deanna. He stood as tall as the first two.

They were trapped.

Amelia held onto Deanna's arm as the men began to close in upon them. Fear clawed at her, but she fought it back. If she lost her head, she would have no hope of escape.

Suddenly a nearby curtain thrust open and a gentleman stepped out. "I say, what is the meaning of this? Why is it so bloody dark out here?"

The three men immediately turned to face the newcomer. Amelia saw her chance. She twisted and headed down the stairs, dragging Deanna after her.

The sound of pounding footsteps on the stairs above told of their pursuit.

Amelia increased her speed as she flew down the flight of stairs. When she reached the foyer, she realized it was empty. Instinctively, she turned to her left, pushing open the door there. As soon as Deanna cleared the opening, Amelia locked it behind them.

The tumbler had just clicked when a body slammed into the door. Amelia jolted at the sound. She had to find a way out. Her blood pulsed fiercely through her body as she ran through the cluttered room backstage; Deanna following close behind. A loud cracking sound told them that the men had managed to break through the door.

Amelia glanced at her sister who was pale and frightened, but still in control. Behind her she heard crashing noises as the men fought their way through the props and costumes. Suddenly, she heard the crowd roar with laughter.

Resolve lifted her chin as Amelia tugged Deanna toward the stage. Heavy curtains pulled at them, but Amelia shoved them aside, desperate to reach the bright lights before her. Deanna tripped on a rope, tugging down on Amelia's arm.

"Hurry, Deanna," Amelia rasped, her voice quivering with fear, as she pulled her sister upward. Amelia could see three dark figures running toward them. "They're coming."

Her hand tightened upon Deanna's as Amelia practically fell onto the stage. After the dimness backstage, the bright lights blinded her. Her chest heaved in and out as she pulled to a halt in the middle of the stage.

The singers stuttered into silence, each one turning to stare at Amelia and Deanna in surprise. Amelia glanced behind her and saw three faint shadows. As she watched, they faded back into the darkness.

Relief made her shoulders sag. She and Deanna were safe. Amelia looked out at the sea of questioning faces. Reputations be damned. She had never before been so glad to have so many people staring at her.

"Now *that's* how to market yourself!" shouted Hubert, leaping to his feet. "I always knew my Amelia was a smart one."

Cris had been on his way to fetch Deanna and Amelia, but at Hubert's exclamation, he turned back toward the stage. "What did you say?"

Hubert cackled like a giddy hen. "Come see for yourself." He pointed toward the stage.

Cris moved to the edge of their box, peering down at the singers below. He couldn't quite believe his eyes.

There, standing in the middle of the stage, was a very disheveled Amelia and her equally rumpled sister.

"How in the devil did they get down there?" Cris couldn't understand how they had gone to refresh themselves and ended up on the middle of the stage.

"I don't know and I don't care." Hubert's smile

danced with glee. "All I know is that girl of mine is one smart chit. Now, all these fancy gents will get a peek at my pretty girls and the offers will start rolling in." He slapped his hands together. "Yes, sir. Rolling right in."

Cris would have laughed at Hubert's exuberance, but something in Amelia's expression made his heart stop. Even from a distance, he could see she wore an expression of sheer terror.

20

"I've already told you everything I know." Amelia leaned back in the chair, still shaken from her ordeal.

Cris kneeled down in front of her, holding her hand. "I know, Amie, but I want you to go through it all one last time, just to make sure you didn't miss anything."

It was hard to keep from bursting into tears at Cris's gentle voice. Demands she could have dealt with, but tenderness undermined her self-control. She longed to throw herself in his arms, to unburden her heart—and the desperate urge terrified her. She'd promised herself she'd distance herself from Cris, and here she was, looking for her storybook hero once again. "Is Deanna all right?" she asked, pulling her hand free of Cris's hold.

Aunt Patricia moved forward, sitting down next to Amelia. "She's fine, dear. Your sisters have brought her upstairs and are calming her with some tea." Aunt Patricia enfolded her into an embrace. "I know this is so difficult for you, my dear. I wish you didn't have to talk about it anymore."

"Quit mollycoddling the girl, Patsy. She'd be just fine if you two would give her a chance to breathe." Uncle Hubert paced the floor, but not even his gruff tone could hide his concern. "Isn't that right, girl? You're a tough one, you are. It would take more than a good scare to break your spirit, wouldn't it?"

Amelia felt tears form, but she blinked them back. She gave her uncle a smile, hearing quite clearly the affection behind his words. "That's right, Uncle Hubert. I'm made of strong stuff."

Aunt Patricia squeezed Amelia once more before releasing her hold. The older woman shot Hubert a glance. "There now, I'm not hugging her anymore. Is that more to your liking, Hubert?"

"At least the girl can breathe without you bent over her," Hubert blustered. "And don't you be getting tart with me, Patsy."

"Enough, both of you." Cris frowned at them. "We should all be thinking about Amelia and Deanna now, not bickering over bits of nonsense."

Both Uncle Hubert and Aunt Patricia sobered immediately. "You're quite right, Cris," Aunt Patricia murmured. Then all three of them turned to look at Amelia.

She shifted beneath their stares. "I have nothing more to tell you."

"Are you quite certain they knew you?" Cris asked, leaning against the back of a chair.

Her memories assaulted her again. "They called me by name," she said softly.

He shook his head, his exasperation apparent. "It was exactly like that with Samantha, except the men seem to be getting bolder."

"Who is Samantha?" Aunt Patricia's question brought a sigh from Cris. Still, he told both her and Hubert the story.

"Twisted whoresons, the lot of them," Hubert muttered.

Cris fisted his hand. "Regardless if the two incidents are connected, we need to protect Amelia."

"Agreed," Uncle Hubert replied smartly.

Cris nodded. "Excellent. Now then, I spoke with the manager of the theater myself, since the magistrate didn't seem overly concerned by Amelia's tale. The manager could spread no light on the situation either. He didn't know where the footmen had gone, nor why those sconces were unlit." Cris looked at Hubert. "Tomorrow I'll update the runners I've hired and get the addresses of the men who were supposed to be in that corridor. Then I'll visit them myself at their homes to see if they have any additional information."

"I'll go with you," Hubert offered immediately.

Cris nodded. "I thought you might want to come along."

"Come along where?" Owen asked as he strode into the room.

"To question the footmen who should have been stationed outside the opera boxes this evening." Cris looked at his friend. "How are the girls?"

Owen's features hardened. "Still quite shaken, I'm afraid. They've managed to calm Deanna and she's resting at the moment, but the others are all distraught over it."

Amelia took a deep breath, trying to ease the ball of sickness that was roiling around inside her. "I need to go to them. They were frightened very badly this evening."

Everyone murmured their agreement, before Cris escorted Amelia to the base of the stairs. Waiting until she'd disappeared from sight, Cris returned to the parlor, finding Owen, Hubert, and Aunt Patricia deep in conversation.

". . . doesn't make any sense. Who would even think of abducting two ladies from the middle of a theater?"

Coldness seeped into Cris's bones. "It is obvious that we are not dealing with rational people. Not only did those men know who Amelia was, but they knew *where* she was going to be. From the note they sent her, it's clear that they had a plan to take her." He paused, looking at everyone in the room. "I will find these men, and when I do, God help them."

"This game of ours is getting out of control," Alonso said nervously. "We're taking too many risks."

Prospero stilled in his seat. "Poor Alonso, are you afraid?"

Alsonso bristled at the question. "No, not exactly."

"He's right. We have to be more careful," Sebastian said in support of Alonso.

Prospero waved a hand at them. "Don't be such cowards. All we need to do is arrange for a few loose ends to be tied up and then our hunt can resume again."

"A few loose ends?" Alonso asked. "Such as what?"

"The footmen who were paid to leave their posts." Prospero drummed his fingers against his leg. "They saw my face before I could pull on my mask. They could identify me."

"We wouldn't want that," Sebastian agreed. He paused for a long moment, before asking, "Exactly what do you plan to do with the footmen?"

Prospero smirked at the other man. "Do you truly wish to know?"

Quickly, Sebastian shook his head. "No. I don't like any of this. I wanted to join our little group because of the fun with the ladies, not to do . . . whatever it is you plan on doing."

Prospero laughed. "No spine, eh, Sebastian? Don't fret. I shall clean up our little problem and we can get back to the matter at hand, capturing one of The Fabulous Five."

"I don't like this at all," Amelia announced, walking to the window. "Someone could be injured."

Aunt Patricia paused in the middle of a paint-stroke. "They are merely going to question a few footmen. What harm could they come to?"

"I don't know," Amelia admitted, glancing back at where her sisters sat posing for Aunt Patricia. "Perhaps I'm still on edge from last night."

"Well, don't worry, my dear," Aunt Patricia said, resuming her painting. "Even if there is trouble, Crispin is more than capable of dealing with it."

Amelia twirled about. "But he shouldn't *have* to deal with it."

"He is a dear friend of your family. He most certainly has the right to do so." Aunt Patricia set her paintbrush down. "Camilla, stop fidgeting."

"Aunt Patricia," Camilla began, "I'm tired of sitting here."

"You won't even allow us to speak," complained Deanna. "We have to sit here and listen to you and Amie chatter on, but we can't add a word. It's torture!"

"You are all bearing up marvelously," Aunt Patricia said brightly. "Now, please, all of you stay still for a moment longer. I'm almost done here."

Amelia smiled as Bea looked suspiciously at Aunt Patricia. "Almost finished? How can you paint a portrait of four people so quickly?"

"It's an interpretation of the setting." Aunt Patricia tilted her head to the side, gazing at the canvas. "This is my second attempt at this. I'm trying to expand my abilities."

All four girls fell silent once more. Aunt Patricia took a few minutes to paint, before she glanced up at Amelia. "Are you sure you won't sit for me today?"

She shook her head. "I'm sorry, Aunt Patricia.

I'm just too concerned about Cris . . . and Uncle Hubert and Owen, of course, to be able to sit for you."

"Why didn't that excuse work for me?" Beatrice asked, shifting forward.

"Because your sister used it first. Now, turn back toward Emma and be still." Aunt Patricia resumed her painting.

Amelia gazed out into the rain. She'd slept little. Nightmares of men chasing her, shouting her name, had haunted her sleep. From the circles under Deanna's eyes, it was clear that her sister had fared the same. Amelia pressed a hand against the cool pane of glass and prayed that Cris would end this nightmare.

"If you persist in banging on the door, you'll only manage to hurt your fist."

Cris turned to glare at Owen, frustration steaming away any last remnant of patience. "They're all missing," he ground out, fighting back the urge to lash out at the door again. "Three footmen and they've all disappeared. Why? It makes no sense."

"Were you thinking they'd really be here?" Hubert asked, incredulous.

Cris looked at the older man. "Of course, I did. Why else do you think I'm standing here in the rain with an aching hand?"

Hubert rolled his eyes. "If that's the case, you're not as clever as I thought."

"What would you suggest?"

The older man glanced about him. "I thought

we'd be doing a little visiting, if you catch my meaning."

"I'm afraid I don't," Cris returned dryly.

Owen looked at Cris pointedly. "I believe dear Hubert here is referring to the questionable practice of breaking into their homes."

"I don't think he meant—" Cris began, only to have Hubert interrupt him.

"Exactly!"

Hubert's pronouncement made Cris lift his brows. "Visiting, Hubert? What a charming way to phrase an activity that could land us all in prison."

Hubert puffed out his chest. "All those fancy lessons in proper deportaclament paid off, don't you think?"

Cris shook his head as Hubert butchered the word *deportment*. "Amazingly so." He rubbed a hand to his temple. "Still, I don't think, er, visiting their *empty* homes would be the wisest course."

"Then how are you going to find out what happened to the blokes?" Hubert threw his hands up in the air. "It seems to me that being a gentleman makes you useless!"

"I'm not," Owen interjected with a laugh. "I have no qualms whatsoever about levering myself inside one of the rear windows." He leaned closer to Hubert. "So, you see, being a gentleman is only restrictive if you allow yourself to follow social dictates . . . like our good friend, Crispin, here." Owen placed a companionable hand upon Hubert's shoulder. "Luckily for me, I suffer no such compulsion."

Cris walked down the front steps, shaking his head. "I should have known better than to match the two of you up."

"Ah, Dukeness, come on, now." Hubert nudged Cris with his elbow. "We won't do any harm. Owen looks spry enough. Why, I'll wager once we shove open a window, he can be tossed up over the ledge as quick as a wink. Then he can have a look about while we cover the entrances."

"No."

"But, there's nobody about today. With this rain, everyone else is cozy warm in their houses," Hubert argued.

"No."

"But how can we be nabbed if there is no one around to see?"

"No."

Cris's calm replies flustered Hubert. "If you don't want to know who's trying to snatch my girls, then—"

Cris rounded on Hubert in an instant. Anger roiled violently through him. "I want to find the bastards who chased Amelia more than you can even imagine. I want to tear them apart for daring to threaten the Ralston sisters. And when I find them, I will do precisely that."

Hubert's brows lifted. "Cor, you're a hot-blooded one under all those manners, aren't you?"

Cris fought to regain his calm, but his insides churned at the image of Amelia, terrified, standing upon the stage, her entire body quivering with fear.

Yet Amelia needed him to find her would-be attackers, not for him to vent his anger.

"All right," Cris acquiesced finally. "I shall help you boost Owen up into one of the rear windows."

Hubert slapped a hand upon Cris's back. "That's the ticket."

Cris followed Owen and Hubert around to the rear of the house. Cris glanced around the small, neatly kept yard as Owen and Hubert looked closely at the windows.

"I don't believe we'll have to break into the house after all," Cris said slowly.

"Changed your mind already?" Owen turned to face Cris, his expression filled with exasperation.

"No." Cris pointed down at a nearby bush. "He changed it for me."

A bloody boot stuck out from beneath the foliage.

"I believe we've found one of our missing footmen."

Cris, Owen, and Hubert headed out to the street. They'd sent for the magistrate, who'd come and taken notes. Cris had questioned whether the same fate could have befallen the other two footmen. The magistrate had promised to investigate the matter, but Cris didn't trust him. It was obvious from the magistrate's tone that he didn't feel there was any connection between Amelia's narrow escape at the opera and the footman's death.

Fool, Cris thought to himself. Because of the man's attitude, Cris had also sent a note around to the Bow Street Runner he'd hired, asking him to look into that matter as well. While the runner had yet to turn up any information on Samantha, Cris had more faith in him than the bumbling magistrate.

Cris felt his stomach roll as he glanced back at the dead footman's home. It was perfectly clear that the men chasing Amelia weren't harmless. Only a fool would think the two incidents weren't related. Protectiveness rose within him, but he felt useless. "We've already questioned the director of the theater, and he didn't have any insight."

"I say it's time we take to the streets," Hubert insisted strongly.

"We are on the streets," Cris pointed out.

Hubert shook his head. "No, *take* to the streets. There are all sorts of moles and ferrets scampering about the place. You gentry don't even take notice of them."

Cris's attention was caught. "You believe someone might have seen the men stalking Amelia?" The very notion intrigued him. "Surely not at the opera."

"You're probably right, but I'll wager those footmen did some chattering."

Now that seemed a real possibility. "But even if those men did mention something, how would we begin to find who they spoke to?"

"We go have a drink."

"Excuse me?" Cris had lost him.

"We go have a drink," repeated Hubert. "There are pubs where the cost of a bit of information is merely the price of a drink."

Owen's eyes gleamed. "And I'll bet you know these places well."

Hubert smiled broadly. "You don't think I became rich by keeping my head down, do you? A fellow's got to have quick feet and big ears if he wants to get ahead."

"Words to live by," Cris pronounced. "Lead the way."

There was a fierce determination in Cris's stride as he followed Hubert toward the nearest pub.

21

"It's only been two days, Cris," Owen pointed out, taking a sip of his punch. "You need to be patient. Information doesn't come easily or quickly. I'm sure someone knows what happened to those footmen."

"Patience is hard to come by when Amelia's safety is concerned," Cris pointed out. His head was beginning to pound, the cloying scent from the perfumed ladies tightened the knot of tension in his neck. "I certainly didn't want the Ralston sisters to come to this ball tonight."

"You can't keep them locked up," Owen pointed out.

"Why not?"

Owen laughed softly. "There are times when you frighten me with your archaic ideas."

Cris knew he was being ridiculous, but the thought of Amie, his Amie, in danger made him crazed. He looked out on the dance floor, searching for her amongst the flowing gowns.

When he finally saw her, he felt his gut tighten. "Isn't that Stevens's whelp dancing with Amelia?"

Owen peered around the ladies in front of him. "I believe so."

"What do you know of him?"

Owen tipped his head to the side, eyeing Amelia's dance partner. "Phillip? I haven't heard much about him. I know he's most often seen with Baskins's and Henley's sons. The three of them are as close as their fathers."

"But what of Stevens specifically? Is he as disreputable as his sire?"

"I doubt it," Owen said reassuringly. "If he were, we would have heard of it."

Still, watching Amie in the arms of anyone even closely related to Stevens made Cris furious. That pack of old men had made his life hellish. After he'd had a drink with Owen and Hubert at the pub, spreading the word that they'd pay handsomely for information, Cris had made his way over to Henley's town house and confronted the old man with his suspicions.

Not only had Henley denied spreading all of the rumors over the past few years, but he'd also disavowed any knowledge of the recent one Deanna heard. Even though Henley's denial had been vehement, Cris doubted he'd been told the truth.

The quadrille ended and Cris watched as Amie bowed to her partner. The orchestra sounded a few strains of a waltz, announcing it as the next dance. Instead of leading Amelia to the edge of the dance floor, Phillip held her in place, preparing to dance with her again.

He'd be damned before he'd allow any other man to escort Amie in a waltz.

The violins strummed once more, signaling the dancers to take their place. Cris reached Amelia just as Phillip was about to place his hand on her waist. "Pardon me, Stevens, but I believe this dance is mine."

The younger man stiffened as he turned to face Cris. "What a pity. I so looked forward to the company of this lovely lady in a waltz."

"Naturally," Cris returned smoothly, giving him a cool smile. "I'm quite certain then that you can understand my own interest in claiming the lady."

Stevens paused for a moment, before bowing slightly to Cris. "Since I have already had the pleasure of one dance, I shall give way."

Cris returned the gesture. "Your generosity is appreciated."

Amelia frowned at Cris. "I had not promised this dance to you," she pointed out firmly.

Cris placed his hand on her waist. "Lucky for me Stevens didn't have that bit of information."

With a resigned sigh, Amelia placed her hand on his shoulder. "Very well, Cris. You have claimed your dance."

"I don't suppose you could try to sound a bit more enthused by that knowledge," Cris returned, stung by her coolness toward him.

"No, I couldn't." Her tones frosted over.

Cris tried not to let her distant attitude anger

him. After all, they'd never been afforded the opportunity to discuss either the incident (or rather the *near* incident) in the solarium or their passionate embrace in the carriage. That discussion was long past due. As Cris twirled Amelia around the dance floor, he promised to correct that this very night.

The moment the music ended, Cris escorted Amelia into a small alcove off the main room.

"Amelia, we need to discuss what's happening between us."

"There is no us, Cris," she pointed out. "I'm not sure if there can even be a friendship anymore."

Her quiet statement stunned him. "What are you talking about, Amie? Of course we're still friends."

"Are we?" She gazed up at him. "We can't talk to each other anymore without feeling awkward, nor can we pretend that we haven't shared certain . . . intimacies."

Cris opened his mouth to protest, but before he could utter a word, Amelia continued her explanation.

"I will always have a place for you in my heart, but I can't go on like this. Time and time again, I find myself slipping into old patterns with you. The trouble is we are no longer children."

Finally, he understood her clearly. They had been teasing each other when he'd kissed her in the carriage and then again in the solarium when they'd almost kissed again. "Then we need to find some new way to make our friendship work."

"I don't believe that is possible, Cris. How can we forget all that has happened between us? How could we ever start clean, no memories, no past? It simply is not possible."

Panic began to set in at the finality he heard in her voice. Certainly she couldn't mean that their friendship was over. "There has to be some way our friendship can go forward." Cris tried not to sound alarmed, but the thought of never again talking to Amelia, never spending time with her, was too painful to contemplate.

Amelia shook her head, pressing a hand to her cheek as tears filled her eyes. "I need to check on my sisters," she whispered.

And with that, she was gone.

Cris stood there, wanting to call her back, but uncertain if he could even speak with the gaping hole in his chest—the very spot where his heart used to be.

The urge to kill gripped him.

Cris stood across the room, listening to Camilla play a beautiful sonatina, and all he could think about was placing his hands around the throat of Lord Henley's whelp and squeezing tighter and tighter . . . and tighter.

His fingers twitched at the thought as he watched the dandy fawn over Amelia. It was quite obvious that she was trying desperately to listen to her sister play, but it was equally clear that the fop had no intention of giving her a moment's peace.

Then again, perhaps it was only fitting, since he'd not had a respite from his jumbled thoughts since she'd walked away from him. He'd tried to discuss their situation further, but each time Amelia cut him off, telling him there was nothing else to say.

The devil there wasn't!

The fact was, he missed Amelia. He missed laughing with her, talking to her, simply *being* with her. In truth, the depth of his feelings surprised him. He'd known he loved Amelia as a dear friend, but he would never have suspected that he could miss her so very much.

People were beginning to talk about his shameless pursuit of her, but he didn't care. The thought of allowing their friendship to end was untenable.

"Hello, Cris."

Cris glanced up to see Beatrice standing before him. He smiled gently at her. "Hello, Bea. Have you been well?"

Bea looked over to her sister. "As well as can be expected with Amelia so upset."

"Upset?" Cris prompted.

Bea leaned closer to him. "Sometimes, at night, I hear her crying."

Cris's jaw tightened. "I wish I knew what to do," he said. "I hate to think of her being unhappy."

"As do I. In fact, I think you should speak with Uncle Hubert." Beatrice shot a glance at Amelia. "There is something you don't know."

Cris frowned. "What do you mean?"

"Amelia plans on taking us all back to Dovedale tomorrow."

"She WHAT!!" Cris shouted, causing Camilla to slip, her fingers jamming down on the keys in a jarring note.

Everyone in the room glanced at him sharply. Cris smiled apologetically at Camilla.

After a moment, Camilla began at the refrain. As music filled the room, Cris turned back to Bea. "She's going to take you back to Dovedale?"

"Tomorrow," Bea clarified.

"Why?" Cris felt as if someone had knocked the breath from his lungs.

Bea shrugged. "Amelia told us that it would be safer for us at home. She said that since the Season was almost over, no one would think our departure odd."

Cris gazed at Amelia, who sat rubbing two fingers against her temple. After a moment he reached out, placing a hand on Bea's arm. "Don't worry, Bea. I shall speak to your uncle first thing tomorrow."

"Then we can stay until the end of the Season?" she asked, her eyes glowing with hope.

"I shall make sure of it," Cris guaranteed. "I don't suppose your eagerness to stay has anything at all to do with Owen?" he asked with a slow smile.

Bea's cheeks flushed a brilliant red, bringing a laugh from Cris. "You shouldn't tease me so," she whispered shyly.

Cris wrapped an arm around her shoulders, giving her a quick hug. "How could I not?"

22

"I'm afraid I must insist we leave for the country at once." Amelia sat rigidly on the edge of her seat, doing her best to ignore Cris. She focused her attention upon her uncle. "It is clear to me—as it should be to anyone—that the city is unsafe for me and my sisters. We are in danger here."

"Only when you were traipsing about town," Hubert said, tossing one hand in the air.

"That's untrue, Uncle Hubert," Amelia corrected. "The latest incident took place in the opera hall." She knew her argument was weak, but she wanted desperately to return home. If she could convince her uncle that they would be safer in the country, he would most likely allow them to leave town . . . and Cris.

Hubert scowled at her. "You catch my meaning, Amie. I know you do."

"So what do you propose we do? Remain virtual prisoners in our own home?" Amelia felt bruised inside and wanted to escape the pain of seeing Cris at every function she attended. Ignoring him was proving quite difficult.

"What your uncle is proposing, Amelia, is that you not leave this house unescorted," Cris said firmly.

She didn't even look at him. She couldn't look at him. If she allowed herself to unbend, to let Cris back into her life, she would soon find herself weaving fairy tales around him again. No, the only way to save her heart was to distance herself from Cris.

So, Amelia continued to gaze at Hubert imploringly. "Please, Uncle Hubert. I miss the country."

She knew that her voice sounded defeated, but she couldn't help that. It was how she felt.

"Come now, girl, don't be making me feel like an old troll. You'll get to see the country soon enough," Hubert mumbled, shifting in his chair. "But for now, I'm just doing what's best for you."

What would be best for her would be to protect her heart against further pain.

"This is for your own good," Cris said, coming to stand next to her chair.

Amelia straightened her shoulders, drawing upon her last reserves of strength. "Very well," she said with quiet dignity. "My sisters and I shall remain in London until the end of the Season."

Her pronouncement made, Amelia stood and left the room.

The quiet click of the door closing behind Amelia made Cris wince. He almost wished she'd slammed it shut on them. Her anger would have been far preferable to her desperate pleas to return home.

Jamming his hands into his pockets, Cris turned to Hubert. "I don't believe she was pleased with our decision. Regardless, it is for the best," he said, hoping that if he repeated the sentiment enough times he wouldn't feel so horrid. Meanwhile, she would be safe . . . and close.

Hubert snorted, disgruntled. "Fine thing for you to say. You don't live with the pack of them."

"I wouldn't mind it," replied Cris honestly.

"Sometimes I wonder about your sanity." Hubert sighed, leaning back in his chair. "I don't suppose you've found any new information that could end this whole mess."

"As a matter of fact, I have." Cris leaned against the corner of Hubert's desk. "I received a message from one of your friends at the pub, a man named Flint."

"Did you?" Hubert lifted his brows. "Don't know if I'd call him a friend. Nonetheless, what did he find?"

"I'm not sure," Cris replied. "The message merely asked for a meeting at the Swan's Tail in two days. Flint promised the information he had would be well worth the asking price."

"I'll be coming with you."

"I assumed you would. I'll also ask Owen if he will join us," Cris replied, taking the seat across from Hubert.

A slight frown darkened the older man's expression. "You mentioned that Flint is asking a stiff fee for his bit of goods. Not that it matters, mind you, but I'm curious. Who is going to be paying the man?"

Cris laughed for the first time in days. Hubert truly possessed a merchant's heart. You could give him a title and fancy clothes, but underneath, Hubert would always be interested in the bottom line. "Don't worry, Hubert. I'll pay the man."

With a nod of satisfaction, Hubert leaned back in his chair.

"I'm not sure if this is the wisest thing to do, Amie."

Emma's worried tones caught Amelia's attention, but she continued to tie her bonnet laces. "If you don't wish to come, Emma, that is fine with me."

"This idea is dangerous enough without you traipsing off alone," Beatrice said, wringing her hands in nervousness.

"I'll hardly be alone," Amelia replied calmly. "I fully intend to bring a few servants with me."

Emma worried her lip between her teeth. "I'm still not certain, Amie. What would Cris and Uncle Hubert say about this?"

Amelia tried to ignore the pang in her heart. "I don't know," she murmured. "I didn't ask them."

"I don't think they'd approve," Deanna said quickly.

Amelia knew Cris wouldn't approve, but if she didn't escape the confines of the town house for a time, it would drive her mad. For two days now, Cris had come to visit—and stayed nearly all day long. It seemed as if he was everywhere. She would seek peace in the library only to have him enter a few minutes later or she would be relaxing in the parlor and he would ask to join her.

Cris had finally left with Uncle Hubert, but he had promised to be back for tea. Amelia needed a moment out of this house to collect her composure, to ready herself for yet another evening spent in Cris's company.

Amelia turned to her sisters, fixing a smile upon her face. "Since neither Uncle Hubert nor Cris is here at the moment, it is impossible to ask for their permission, isn't it?"

"Then the best course would be to wait for them to return," Bea added.

"Perhaps," Amelia acknowledged, tying her bow at a more flattering angle. "But I'm quite sure I'll burst if I don't get some fresh air."

"I really don't think this is a good idea." Camilla gripped her hands together.

Amelia reached out and squeezed Camilla's clasped hands. "Please don't worry so. I'm only going shopping."

"I'm not sure we should go," Emma said again.

Amelia looked at her sister. "I'd quite understand if you'd prefer to remain behind, Emma. I will simply go alone." She turned back to the mirror, straightening their mother's pin on the lapel of her walking jacket.

"What if we all accompany you?" Emma suggested.

Amelia shook her head. "Camilla has lessons in

half an hour, Owen is coming to call on Bea shortly, and Deanna has invited a few of her friends over for a game of whist." She picked up her reticule. "It is quite all right with me, Emma, if you choose to remain at home."

Emma placed a bonnet on her head. "I could never allow you to go alone."

"Thank you, Emma." Amelia hugged her sister. "We'll be just fine."

The Swan's Tail stank of spilled ale, rotting food, and urine. Cris faced the wiry man who fit perfectly into the surroundings. "What information do you have for us, Flint?"

The man's fingers twitched against the table. "I've yet to see a glint of your backing."

Cris pulled a thick roll of pound notes from his vest pocket. "I believe this is sufficient to loosen your tongue."

A few teeth were missing from the man's smile. "Aye, it is." He glimpsed around before leaning forward. "Have you gents ever heard of a nasty pack that called themselves The Dark Lords?"

To a man, the three of them shook their heads. "Go on," Cris urged. "What do they have to do with my business?"

"Twenty years past, tales of this pack swarmed the thoughts and minds of *genteel* society." He sneered the word *genteel* as if it soured his tongue.

"Twenty years ago? What possible relevance does it have to us?" Cris glanced at Owen and Hubert, wondering if they'd made the connection, but both men simply shrugged.

"The way I hear it told, what happened to your lady at the opera used to happen all the time," Flint said, lifting his eyebrows.

"What sort of thing?" Owen asked, confusion coloring his voice.

"You mean to say that young women were accosted in public places by this group of Dark Lords?" Cris leaned forward, the pattern growing clearer.

"Aye," Flint agreed with a firm nod. "Not only chased like your ladies, but nabbed too. The girls would disappear for a while, then suddenly reappear at their homes. The families would shuffle them off quick as can be to the country, but not before the tales started to fly."

Repulsion filled Cris, but he pushed back his anger, focusing on Amelia's near tragedy. "Still, these things occurred twenty years ago. It hardly seems likely that this group is still practicing their debauchery today."

"It's not impossible, though," Owen pointed out.

"I'm not as spry as I used to be," Hubert admitted, "but I'm still well up to chasing a pretty thing or two if I had a mind to."

Cris looked at Uncle Hubert and just shook his head. The notion of old men chasing after young innocents seemed highly unlikely.

"Other thing that struck me odd was the way you said they called one lady by name, as if they knew her." Flint shifted on his chair. "Back then, these gents would take the pick of the litter and nab her."

"Pick of the litter?" Hubert slammed his hand down on the table. "Those are my girls you're talking about."

Cris went cold. "The first of The Fabulous Five. Amelia," he whispered, everything snapping into place. "Who are the Dark Lords?"

A sly expression passed over Flint's visage. "That will cost you extra."

Cris's chair flew out from underneath him as he lunged across the table, grabbing hold of Flint's shirt and jerking him closer. "Who are they?"

Flint's eyes flared at Cris's demand. "I only know one name," he stumbled. "Henley. Lord Stephen Henley."

Cris released Flint immediately, sending the man sprawling onto the floor. He strode to the door, with Hubert and Owen following close behind. He would hunt down that bastard Henley and make him pay. Then he would search out Baskins and Stevens and see that they too received their due.

The Dark Lords were about to enter Hell.

"What do you think of this one, Amie?" Emma held up a lovely fan delicately painted and elegantly carved.

"It's beautiful," Amelia said approvingly.

"I think so too." Emma began to examine the edges of the fan. "I didn't realize how much I missed shopping." She glanced at Amelia. "It surprises me that I could miss something I only recently began to enjoy."

"It shouldn't, Emma. After all, it's still so new for you. I'm sure once you grow accustomed to it, the excitement will begin to pale."

"I suppose," Emma sighed. "Although nothing could be more dull than being cooped up at home these past few days."

Amelia couldn't agree with her sister's statement for her days had been far too busy avoiding Cris. "I know it's hard for you, Emma, but hopefully it will all be over soon."

Emma traced the fan with her fingertip. "I hope so. I know we'll all be happy when those men are caught."

"That's true," agreed Amelia. "Especially Uncle Hubert, because then we'll be able to reenter the social whirl and collect more proposals for him to consider."

Emma laughed at Amelia's teasing. "I've done my part. At last count, four gentlemen had offered for me."

"And do any of them interest you?"

"Not a one," Emma replied firmly.

"Then I'll have to think of a way to delay Uncle Hubert's decision until he can see who will make an offer *next* Season."

"You'll need to think of an excuse for yourself as well, Amie. Don't forget that Cris offered for you," Emma pointed out. "I'm certain Uncle Hubert will insist you marry Cris."

Amelia finally stuttered, "I find that doubtful."

"I don't." Emma snapped the fan together. "And if you haven't been worried of just that, then why have you been avoiding Cris lately."

"Why, why I haven't," Amelia protested lamely.

"I've been wondering what Cris must have done to have you shun him so."

"Shun him . . . certainly I haven't done that . . . we've spent nearly every day together," Amelia said, pressing a hand to still the flutter in her stomach. Perhaps her efforts hadn't been as subtle as she'd thought.

"Yet you've clearly tried to ignore him and I thought—"

Amelia touched her sister's arm. "You thought to play matchmaker, didn't you, Emma?" Warmth filled her. "It is very sweet of you, angel, but I don't need your help."

"But, Amie, you've been—"

"Perfectly fine," she said firmly.

Emma looked doubtful. "If you say so."

"I do." Amelia pointed to the fan Emma still held. "Would you care to purchase that?"

"Though it's beautiful, I already have more than I can possibly use." Emma set it down carefully. "Where would you like to go next?"

"I want to stop in at Madame Poichard's shop and see if she's received any new shipments of fabric."

"Are you looking for a new dress?"

Amelia lifted her shoulders. "Not particularly," she answered, not wanting to tell Emma that she simply wanted to extend their outing. Cris and

Uncle Hubert could have returned by now. No, Amelia wanted to stay out as long as possible.

"I'd enjoy going to Madame Poichard's also," Emma agreed.

Amelia smiled at her sister as she stepped from the shop. A light mist of rain dampened their clothes, but not their spirits. It had, however, kept most people indoors, for the streets were empty.

As she stopped to look in a neighboring shop window, something odd caught her attention. She wasn't quite sure what was bothering her, but there was something off balance, something missing . . .

Panic reverberated through Amelia as she twisted around, searching for the servants who had shadowed their every moment all day long. Neither man was in sight. Suddenly, Amelia felt vulnerable and exposed.

"Emma?"

"Hmmm?"

"Where are the servants?"

Immediately, Emma looked down the street. "I don't see either one of them." Her eyes were wide and frightened as she turned toward Amelia. "Where did the carriage go?"

Amelia forced herself to remain calm. "All we need to do is start for home."

"Walking?"

"I don't see much choice," Amelia replied logically, keeping her voice even. "Our carriage and escorts are gone, leaving us in a precarious position at best. Besides, it's not that far to our home. Just think of it as one of our nature walks back in Dovedale."

At the end of the street, Emma bumped into Amelia as they rounded a corner. "A-a-m-m-i-e!" she stuttered.

"Come along, Emma, before it begins to rain harder." Amelia glanced back at her sister, shocked by the whiteness of Emma's complexion. "Whatever is the matter?"

Emma shook her head, mutely pointing down the street.

Terror clutched at Amelia's heart when she too saw the men heading toward them. In long black cloaks, the three men appeared to be apparitions from Hades itself. Amelia bit back a scream. With scarves wrapped about their lower faces and hats pulled down low, only their eyes were visible, adding to their terrifying appearance.

And while she and Emma were standing still, the men were moving closer. Amelia forced her muscles to respond. "Run," she whispered to Emma. "Run."

Emma turned a blank gaze toward her.

Panicked, Amelia pushed Emma ahead of her. "Go straight home, Emma, as fast as you can!"

Amelia's urgent words sunk in and Emma lifted her skirts to race down the road. Amelia followed close behind, listening over the pounding of her own heart to the sound of footsteps coming ever nearer.

They couldn't outrun them, Amelia knew, so they'd have to outsmart them. "Run home, Emma.

I'll try to draw them away from you." Out of breath, Amelia swerved off to the right, praying that the men would follow her instead of Emma.

Amelia spared a moment to glance behind her to see if her plan worked. She stumbled slightly when she saw all three of the men had followed her. Dread fueled her steps as she raced, darting down dark alleyways, uncertain of where she was at this point.

Her chest burned with her exertion as she rounded a corner, heading down a long alley. Despair ripped through her as she stumbled to a halt. The passageway before her had been boarded up. There would be no escaping them now. Bravely, she swung about to face them.

One of the men threw his cloak over her, capturing her within its black folds. She heard her captor tell his companions to keep watch at the entrance of the alley. Amelia clutched at the thick material, trying to rip it free, but the man held it too tightly. Panic ate away at her, gripping at her heart, as she struggled against her fate. She clawed at the material covering her face, and as she scratched downward, her fingers scraped over her mother's brooch pinned onto the lapel of her jacket.

A glimmer of hope strengthened Amelia's efforts. Frantically, she undid the catch on the pin, fighting back waves of dizziness as her lungs began to crave air. The latch on the pin sprang free just as Amelia swayed beneath her attacker's grasp.

"That's it, love." The harsh voice echoed in her pounding head. "Stop fighting it." He bellowed to his companions. "Wait until Merrick finds out we've snared his ladybird."

Amelia held her brooch loosely in her fingers, unable to move against the pain in her chest, but at the man's taunting words, raw and hungry, rage poured through her, energizing muscles gone lax from lack of air. With a muffled cry, Amelia swept her arm up, reaching behind her with a force that took her captor by surprise and buried the sharp point of her pin into the man's face.

He screamed, releasing her. Amelia dragged the cloak from about her face, pulling in deep breaths as she struggled to focus. Her captor clutched at his face, blood seeping between his fingers, but she wasn't safe yet.

The other two men began to run down the alley toward them, intent on recapturing her and helping their companion. Dread swamped her. Her muscles quivered with fatigue. Amelia knew she didn't have the strength to fight off another assault.

Her heart raced within her breast as she turned, stumbling to the end of the alleyway. The wall was far too high for her to climb over. Renewed fear pulsed through her as she frantically looked for a way to escape. She needed something to help her get over the wall. Something she could climb . . .

Hope flared within her breast as she spotted a towering stack of boxes leaning against one of the far corners. Quickly, she tossed her mother's pin over the wall. The men neared, their steps coming closer, closer, as Amelia began to climb up the huge boxes, all her years of tree climbing held her in good stead. Her makeshift ladder swayed precariously as she neared the top. Her hands were scraped and bleeding as she grasped the wall, levering herself on top.

The boxes lurched as one of the men began to climb up after her. Holding tightly onto the wall, Amelia kicked at the highest box. It was large and heavy and it hurt her foot to kick it. She didn't care. She was too furious to stop.

"I don't know why you're doing this," she shouted, lashing out again. "But I have had"—another swift kick sent the box teetering—*"Enough!"*

One more hard kick with her foot sent the box toppling over, hitting the other boxes on its descent, and causing the entire mountain to cascade downward. A loud crash echoed along the alley. Amelia looked down. A fierce rush of satisfaction spilled through her at the sight beneath her. Both men lay still, covered by two large boxes. Lord, she prayed that she'd hurt them.

Badly.

Shaking with a mixture of fear and rage, Amelia bellowed, *"Leave us alone!"*

Pain lanced through her body as she slid her legs over to the opposite side, banging her knees against the barricade. The rough wood bit into her raw hands, but she held on, lowering herself as far as she could. Hanging, stretched along the wall, she let go, dropping down onto the ground. Her ankle twisted beneath her, sending her sprawling onto the wet cobblestones.

She wanted so badly to burst into tears, to let go

completely, but she couldn't. She was far from safe. Every inch of her body throbbed as she pushed herself off the ground. Her ankle protested with a sharp ache as she tried to put weight on it. A sob broke from her, but she pressed her hand to her mouth, holding the rest inside.

Slowly, Amelia bent down to retrieve her mother's pin. It was still her most cherished possession, even bloody and bent. Amelia pressed the smooth brooch against her cheek. She'd always known that she needed to save this last piece of her mother's jewelry in case their situation had grown dire.

It had, indeed, saved her.

Straightening her shoulders, Amelia began the walk down another long alley toward the street. Pride aided her. Not only had she kept her younger sister safe, but she'd also defended herself against three attackers.

Amelia smiled to herself as she hobbled home.

23

Cris paced the confines of the room. "Devil take it! When is Henley going to come home?"

Owen drummed his fingers along the arm of his chair. "His butler had no idea when to expect him."

"The stiff actually tried to toss us out," Hubert added, slamming his hand against the back of the settee. "I didn't think he'd even let us stay in here and wait."

"He was persuaded," Cris returned.

Hubert grinned. "Ah, he most certainly was—that is, after you grabbed the man by the throat." A chuckle burst from the portly man. "And here I was beginning to believe you gents had been bred into pale lily-livers. By God, that was a manly sight." Hubert nodded in satisfaction. "I do believe you've inspired me to practice my own bullying. It's been a few years, but I think I can remember how it's done."

Cris didn't bother to respond, despite the fact that satisfaction still sang in his veins. Perhaps he could have been more diplomatic, but wrapping his hands about that worm's throat had been so incredibly satisfying.

The front door slammed shut, bringing all three men to attention. Cris strode over to the parlor's entrance, bumping into the butler who was hastening toward the main door.

"Henley," Cris rasped, wanting nothing more than to wrap his hands about *Henley's* throat. However, he needed answers more than he needed to vent his rage.

The older man flinched, his expression of surprise chased away by one of apprehension. He recovered in an instant. "To what do I owe this . . . honor? Have you come to accuse me of spreading more rumors?" he asked, handing his black cloak to his nervous butler.

"No. You know exactly why we're here." Cris's flat tones chilled.

Henley lifted his brows. "Do I?" He moved forward, limping slightly. "Shall we take this into the parlor or would you prefer to hash it all out here?"

Cris stepped aside, allowing Henley to enter the room first. "You're limping," he pointed out, his suspicion deepening. What had Henley done to hurt himself? Chased two women around a theater perhaps? "Did you go a round at Minton's?" Cris asked, probing.

Henley snorted, moving to pour himself a brandy. "Hardly." He lifted the bottle toward Cris, Owen, and Hubert. "Would anyone care to join me?"

"No," Cris said brusquely, wanting an answer to

his question. "Exactly how did you injure yourself?"

Henley took a sip before responding, "How nice of you to be concerned about my welfare."

"Just answer the man!" Hubert exclaimed.

Henley gave Hubert a thorough look-over, his lip curling in disdain. "And who, may I ask, are you?"

Hubert took a threatening step forward. "I'm the man who's going to plant my bloody fist in your face if you don't answer the Dukeship here."

Cris suppressed a smile. Leave it to Hubert.

Brandy splashed onto the floor as Henley flinched at Hubert's threat. "No need to get crass," he said. "If you must know, I tripped over a loose stone on the street and twisted my knee."

Hubert's derisive snort told everyone in the room of his opinion.

Owen laid a steadying hand on Hubert's shoulder. "Come now, Hubert. We should give him the benefit of doubt. Regardless of how unlikely his story sounds."

Henley slammed his glass down on the sideboard. "I have had quite enough of your insults. Need I remind you 'gentlemen' that you are in *my* house. I do not need to tolerate this type of behavior."

Cris moved swiftly, closing in on Henley. "I'm tired of playing games, Henley. Either you answer all of my questions as quickly and concisely as possible or you'll feel the wrath of my anger."

Cris clamped down on his urge to throttle the older man as Henley stumbled backward.

"You are a barbarian, sir," he rasped, glancing at

Owen and Hubert as they looked on with approving smiles. "The lot of you."

"Why, thank you, Henley," Owen said with a laugh.

Cris saw how Owen's response further confused Henley. Good, he thought, satisfaction settling in the pit of his stomach. Let the old bastard get so turned about that he answers without thinking, giving them the whole truth.

Cris leaned closer. "What do you know of the Dark Lords?"

Henley jerked at the question, his hand knocking into his glass, sending the liquid cascading over the edge of the sideboard. "The who?" he stammered, lying badly. "The Dark Lords you say?" Henley shook his head, his movement stiff. "I can't say I've ever heard of them."

Hubert growled, lunging forward. "I'll loosen your tongue for you."

Cris placed a restraining hand upon Hubert's chest. "Let's not be too hasty. We can give him the opportunity to speak." Cris saw Henley relax slightly. "However, if it becomes necessary, I will, of course, allow you to, shall we say, convince him to talk."

Hubert gave Henley a feral smile. "Good. I've been practicing."

Owen leaned against the mantle, crossing his arms. "Oh, do let him go, Crispin. I'd love to see his technique."

"You're all insane," whispered Henley, backing up until he hit the wall, his eyes wide with fright. "Completely mad."

"Most likely you're not far off the mark," Cris admitted, moving closer until Henley was boxed in against the wall. "Which is why you're going to tell us everything you know about the Dark Lords. After all, we're totally unstable, so there's no telling what we're capable of." He felt a flare of anticipation as Henley swallowed, hard. Now, the bastard would talk, Cris thought.

"All right," Henley stammered. "All right. I know of the Dark Lords."

Cris leaned closer, his eyes narrowed.

"I-I-I mean I *was* a Dark Lord." All the color drained from Henley's face.

"Tell me about it."

A frantic expression twisted Henley's features. "I can't! I took a sacred oath."

Cris scowled fiercely. "Tell me."

"I can rip the blasted oath right out of him," Hubert offered.

"Aren't you getting a tad old for that sort of stuff?" Owen asked nonchalantly.

"Ah, but I learned to pound debtors early on in my business and after a bit, I came to love it. There were days when I'd pray someone would stiff me on a bill so I could knock some sense into his miserable skull." Hubert grinned wickedly. "I'd be more than happy to show you my skills on this one here."

Henley put up his hands, warding them all off. "Enough. I'll tell. I'll tell." He shook slightly. "A group of us started the Dark Lords in Oxford. At first, we would choose a debutante of the first water, the most sought after chit of the Season, then we would set about seducing her."

"But that's not all you did." Cris felt his muscles tense as he waited for the worst part of the story.

"No, that's not all we did," he agreed. "We would then lure the girl into one of our homes and take turns with her."

"Good God," Cris breathed, revolted at the idea.

"Most of them ended up enjoying themselves in the end," Henley replied quickly. "It wasn't as if we were doing anything wrong. She gave her flower over to us." He leaned forward, trying to convince Cris of his honesty. "It's the truth. Why, we began to grow bored with it all because most of the damn chits were so hungry they were begging for it."

Cris's stomach roiled. "I find that doubtful."

"I'm telling you it's the truth. We even had to alter the game a bit because of it!" At his words, Henley's eyes widened and he snapped his head up.

Cris picked up on the slip immediately. "You altered the game? How?"

Henley shook his head. "I didn't mean anything by it."

Cris placed one hand on the wall next to Henley, leaning in even closer. "Get on with it."

Henley closed his eyes, leaning his head against the wall. "We started to take them against their will."

"You bastard," Cris hissed, wanting to hurt the man before him . . . hurt him badly.

"It was the scent of the hunt, you see," Henley whispered hoarsely. "They would fight and scream." A shiver raced over his body. "It was so damned exciting."

Cris thrust away from him, unable to bear being close to the repulsive man. "You are vile."

Henley glared at Cris. "And you are so noble and honorable," he sneered, his spirit coming back. "You have no idea as to the delights of the flesh you are missing."

"Let me shut his foul mouth," shouted Hubert, surging forward.

Once again, Cris caught Hubert, holding him back. "We still need more information," he reminded the older man. Cris pushed down the wave of loathing that threatened to overtake him. He could not afford to indulge in his emotions. The thought that Amelia was almost one of this fiend's intended victims was unbearable.

"Tell me, Henley. Are the Dark Lords still practicing their depraved vices?" Cris couldn't keep the viciousness out of his voice.

Henley laughed, a low chuckle that filled the room. "Unfortunately, the desires of the mind aren't always compatible with the capabilities of the flesh."

Cris shook with the urge to hit the man. "I'm sick of you and your damn word games. Are you still harming innocent women?"

Henley sneered up into his face. "No. The hunt has been over for quite a while for the three of us."

"Three of you? Baskins and Stevens are your cohorts, aren't they?" Owen asked, standing alert.

Henley slanted a mocking look at him. "How astute of you," he murmured, sarcasm dripping from each word.

"How do we know you're telling the truth?" Cris demanded.

Henley tugged down on his jacket. "That is a dilemma, isn't it?"

"Let me have a whack at him," Hubert urged, nudging Cris in the back.

Henley reached for his brandy. His hand shook, but his face remained blank. "Go ahead, plebeian. I've been insulted, threatened, and assaulted so often this afternoon that I hardly care anymore." He spread his arms wide, keeping the brandy in his right hand. "Do your worst."

"Why, you—" Hubert began in a shout.

Cris turned his back on Henley, facing Hubert, placing a hand upon his chest. "He's not worth it." Cris looked into Hubert's eyes. "He's below your notice, Hubert. Far below."

Hubert straightened his vest, standing tall. He glared at Henley. "Lucky for you I'm a gentleman now."

Henley glared at him before taking a long pull on his brandy.

Cris glanced back at Henley. "If I find out you're the one who threatened Amelia, I will kill you."

Henley tried to remain calm, but Cris could see the tremor that ran through him. Cris had little doubt that Henley was indeed telling the truth; the man was far too shaken to lie so convincingly. Satisfied, Cris walked from the room, followed by Owen and Hubert, the three men leaving the worthless baggage behind.

Amelia stumbled through the door, straight into Aunt Patricia's arms. Her sisters crowded around her, their questions all coming at once.

"We were attacked as we left the shop by three men who chased us. Emma and I separated as we ran and they all followed me. I managed to overcome them and escape." Exhausted, Amelia sat down on the settee in the library. "How is Emma?" she asked, anxious for news of her sister. "I need to see her. She must be terrified."

The fear that grew in Aunt Patricia's gaze alarmed Amelia.

"What is it?" She asked the question, but in her heart she knew the answer. *"Where is Emma?"*

Aunt Patricia shook her head. "I haven't seen her since yesterday."

"The last time we saw her she was with you," Beatrice answered, her expression frozen with horror. "Are you sure she got away?"

Panic clawed at her, tearing at her heart, as fear mingled with overwhelming guilt. She'd been so desperate to escape Cris's presence that she'd forsaken their safety.

And now, because of her, Emma was missing.

Dear God, please keep her safe, Amelia prayed, hoping for a miracle, for something, anything, that would save her sister.

24

Terror forced her onward.

Emma's legs quivered with the effort of running, her breath pumped from her chest, yet she continued on. She needed to get away from the monsters chasing her; she needed to find help and go back for Amelia.

The streets narrowed, becoming an unfamiliar maze of twists and turns. She didn't have any idea where she was and nothing looked familiar, but still she ran.

Finally, her strength gave out and she leaned against a building, panting, holding in the terror that had driven her this far. Now, a new fear surfaced. She was utterly and completely lost.

How would she ever find her way home safely and in time to help Amelia?

Emma pressed her hand to her mouth to hold back a sob. Crying wouldn't help anyone. For the first time in her life, she was alone with no one to help her, no one to protect her. Now it was up to her to protect the ones she loved.

Emma straightened away from the wall, resolution giving her renewed energy. She tried to piece together her location. The air smelled like rotting food, raw sewage, and something else . . . something like . . .

Water!

Emma felt a spark of hope at the realization that she must be somewhere near the docks. It was a dangerous part of town, true, but surely she could find *someone* who would help her. Taking a deep breath, Emma headed toward the loud noises that had suddenly rent the air, praying they were coming from the wharf.

As she rounded a corner, she slammed into something. Emma looked up in alarm as a man's hands reached up to clasp her shoulders. His face was shadowed from the brim of his hat and he was dressed in unrelieved black. The terror she'd held back rushed upward, crushing her spirit, destroying her last hold of self-control.

Emma screamed for help even as the man pulled her closer to him.

Amelia and Aunt Patricia had rounded up as many servants as possible and contacted the Bow Street Runners Cris had hired. They were sending men to help with the search. Amelia had squelched her fear, focused in on the best way to save Emma, and organized a search party. They would begin at the place where she and Emma separated and fan out from there.

Amelia was giving detailed instructions on how to proceed when the front door opened.

Cris, Owen, and Hubert came into the house, stopping short when they saw the crowd of people in the foyer.

"What's going on here?" Cris asked, looking toward Amelia. One glance at her face and he rushed to her side, grabbing hold of her hands. "What is it, Amie? What's wrong?"

Her wall of strength crumbled beneath Cris's kind touch. Tears burst from her as she flung herself into his arms. Amelia held on tight as the story poured from her, releasing all of her fear, knowing deep in her heart that Cris would help her.

". . . and we were about to go find her," Amelia finished, her voice tight with unshed tears.

Cris smoothed his hands down her back. "I'll take over the search, along with Owen and Hubert." He shifted her away until she could look up into his face. "I want you to wait here."

In that moment, she knew without question that she could not live without him, that her fears had been unwarranted. Her new-found independence would only suffer if she allowed herself to deny her heart. And perhaps he might not love her the way she'd always dreamed, but he cared deeply for her, enough to put himself in danger for her sister.

Cris stood before her now, vowing to find Emma, and, for the first time since she'd come to London, she allowed her love for him to flow freely, unfettered by the constraints she'd placed upon it.

"Trust me, Amie," Cris urged, whispering fervently. "I know things have grown complicated between us, but you *must* know that you can trust me to find your sister."

His plea roused her from her thoughts as she realized he must have misunderstood her hesitation. "Of course I do," she said quickly. "I know if anyone can find her, it will be you, Cris."

His eyes blazed with intensity. "Thank you for that."

Amelia looked up at the man she loved and gave him her unconditional faith. In front of her uncle, his aunt, and anyone else who cared to see, she wrapped her arms around Cris's neck and gave him a quick kiss, filled with love, trust, and hope.

She leaned back in his arms. "Be safe," she murmured as she released him.

A look of wonderment transformed his expression, making Amelia's breath catch in her throat. She didn't dare believe that it was love that flashed in his eyes.

Her heart leapt within her breast as Cris lifted her hand, pressing a kiss into the palm, before stepping back. Only worry for her sister kept Amelia from pledging her love to Cris. Instead, she asked, "Please find my sister."

Cris gave her a short nod before turning to bark out orders. Within moments, everyone had left, each group with a direction, all of them with one mission—to bring Emma home safely.

Amelia sank down on her knees in the foyer, her hands clasped on her lap, and began to pray.

They'd been searching for hours and there had been no trace of Emma. One shopkeep had told them he'd seen a young girl running down the street, but he could only tell Cris in which direction she'd been headed. It had been over an hour since he'd gotten that information. The closer Cris got to the docks, the less hope he had of finding her unharmed. Still, he wasn't going to stop looking.

Owen and Hubert had each led a group of men in different directions, but with the information Cris had from the shopkeep, he felt sure that he and the servants he'd brought along would be the ones to find Emma. Thoughts of the young girl filled him, adding determination to every step, images of holding her when she was a tiny infant, so sweet and trusting, then escorting her onto the dance floor a few evenings ago with her looking all grown up and beautiful.

He loved Emma as if she were his own true sister.

Cris rounded a corner when a young boy ran up to him.

"Are you the ones wot's lookin' for a girl, one wi' sunny 'air?"

Cris and the servants all stopped in their tracks. "Yes," Cris answered, squatting down onto his haunches to look the boy in the eye. "Do you know of her?"

The boy nodded. "'Ole Jamie told me ta fetch ya."

A flare of excitement burst within him as Cris straightened. "Show us the way."

The lad swiftly led the way through the back alleys, and Cris followed close behind. Cris realized that it could be a trap in which the boy would lead them into a dark alley filled with the boy's friends and then steal their money, but he couldn't disallow the possibility that the lad did indeed know where Emma was.

"This way," the boy said, ducking into the doorway of a dingy, broken-down house. "She's in 'ere."

Cris asked the servants to await him outside and braced himself for what he would find as he stepped through the door. Surprise echoed in him when he saw the neatly kept room. It was obvious that someone took great pains to keep it clean, despite the worn furniture and ancient, cracked walls.

"Come on," the boy urged, heading into a room at the back of the small house.

Relief flooded Cris in a great wave when he saw Emma lying on a bed, seemingly unharmed.

"Cris!" she cried, launching herself into his arms just as Amelia had done earlier that day.

He enfolded her close, holding her against his heart. "Lord, you scared us," he murmured, squeezing her tight.

"I got lost," she said, tears filling her eyes. "Those monsters were chasing Amie and I when . . .

AMIE!" Emma clutched at him. "Cris, you must go save Amie! She's—"

"Perfectly fine and waiting anxiously for you to come home," Cris assured her, stroking her hair.

Relief eased the taut lines on her face as Emma collapsed back against him. "Thank God!"

"It would take more than three men to capture Amelia," he said lightly, trying not to let Emma sense how he'd truly felt after he'd heard the story. Rage had filled him; he'd wanted to track down those bastards and destroy them. However, Amie had needed him more, so he'd choked back his anger at her attackers and concentrated on finding Emma.

Now that Emma was safe, nothing could save those men from his wrath.

Cris shoved away the thought, hoping none of his anger had shown on his face. He glanced over Emma's shoulder at the man standing silently, watchfully, beside the boy who'd led them here.

"Do I have you to thank for Emma's safety?"

The man stepped forward into the light. "I found her on the streets, half crazed with fear."

Emma lifted her head, frowning at the man. "I was not, Jamie," she protested.

The man smiled at her, the curve of his lips gentling his strong features. "Sorry to disagree, luv, but you near screamed me deaf."

The chagrined look on her face told Cris all he needed to know. Emma felt safe with this man, this Jamie. Cris took the man's measure. His youth surprised Cris as well as the fact that despite his ragged clothes, he was surprisingly well groomed: his dark hair clean, his skin washed, his brown eyes clear. Cris knew an honorable man when he saw one.

"I am indebted to you, sir." Keeping his left arm wrapped about Emma, he offered Jamie his hand. "Crispin Merrick," he said, purposely leaving off any mention of his title in order to keep the man at ease.

After a moment's pause, the younger man accepted Cris's hand. "Jamie Pruwit," he responded in kind, before releasing his grasp on Cris's hand. "This is a bad part of town for a young lady to be caught unawares."

"I am well aware of that fact, Mr. Pruwit, which only deepens my gratitude."

Jamie nodded once. "Samuel here," he began, pointing to the boy who'd led them to Emma, "heard there were groups of men looking for Emma, but once we realized from a shopkeep that you were family and not the men who chased her, we decided to bring you here."

Cris's admiration for Jamie rose. "I am very much appreciative and would like to show my gratitude," he said, reaching for his card. Cris held it out to Jamie. "Please call on me and we can discuss my appreciation in more depth."

Jamie's brows drew together as he shook his head. "I didn't help her for money." He placed a hand on the shoulder of the boy who stood next to him. "We might not have much, but we still have our honor."

Shame nudged at Cris. "It was not my intention to offend you, Jamie. It just seemed a bit unfair that you saved one of my greatest treasures and receive nothing in return."

Jamie looked at Emma, his gaze softening. "It was a privilege to come to Miss Emma's assistance. It's not often that an angel comes to these parts," he finished in a wistful tone.

Cris looked down at Emma, catching her flush, her reaction surprising him. He held out his card once more to Jamie. "In that case, please take my card just so you know how to reach me. If there is ever anything I can do for you, anything at all, from a favor to a job, please call on me."

Slowly, Jamie lifted his hand and accepted the card. "I just might do that." He glanced once more at Emma. "I just might."

Cris nodded, tightening his hold on Emma. "Let's go home, Emma."

"Henley *was* limping yesterday," Owen pointed out from his wingback chair.

Cris steepled his fingers, his elbows resting on the large desk. When he'd left young Jamie Pruwit's house, Cris had sent the servants who had been with him to notify the other search parties and had brought Emma home himself. As soon as he'd helped Emma from the hired carriage, Amelia had run down the front steps and hugged her sister fiercely. Not wanting to impose on the moment, he'd made his way inside the house to wait for

Hubert and Owen's arrival. The two men had just returned and the time for revenge was upon them.

Cris tried to piece everything together. "It's true Henley was injured, but I find it hard to imagine him moving with any adroitness." He pressed his lips together for a moment. "Those men must have been running swiftly in order to catch Amelia. Somehow I just can't see Henley, Stevens, and Baskins possessing that speed."

Hubert puffed out his chest. "I'm a fair number of years, but I consider myself a prime physical specimen."

Tension gripped Cris, making him completely overlook Hubert's posturing. "I'd certainly agree with you, Hubert, but you must remember those three men have led lives of debauchery. Their physical constitution might not be as, er, sturdy as yours."

"That's true enough," Hubert conceded with a firm nod. "I'm proud to say I've been a hard-working man since my youth."

"Years well spent," Owen commented.

Hubert smiled broadly. "Indeed they were. And if I might say, you do justice to the role of gentlemen."

As Owen opened his mouth to reply, Cris interrupted, "Now that we've all agreed on our mutual admiration, do you think that perhaps we can get back to the problem at hand? If you remember, Amelia and Emma were attacked yesterday."

Both men sobered instantly.

"You might be right about Henley," Owen conceded. "He doesn't strike me as being physically capable."

"Which leaves us back at square one," Cris concluded in a grim voice.

"Why didn't you let us know you were having a family meeting?" Amelia asked as she limped into the study.

Immediately, Cris rounded the desk and assisted her to a chair. "Amie! What are you doing downstairs?"

"That should be perfectly obvious," she insisted, before leaning forward to glance around Cris.

He followed her gaze, watching as all the Ralston girls entered, with Aunt Patricia bringing up the rear. "Ladies," he began, "it is always lovely to visit with you, but at the moment we—"

"Are discussing the steps to catch our assailants," Amelia finished.

He looked down at her. "You're quite correct," he answered, "which is why I'm sure you'll understand—"

"That you'd like our input," she said, once more ending his sentence. Amelia watched as Cris's features tightened. She bit back her smile, knowing it would annoy him.

Cris leaned against his desk. "Amelia, I promise you I will catch your attackers."

"I know you will find them, Cris. But it only makes sense for us to help you. After all, we're the only ones who have actually seen the three men."

He shook his head. "It will disturb you too much to discuss your attack."

"No, Cris, it would upset me far more to hide while you risk your life for me." Amelia leaned forward, capturing one of his hands between both of hers. "Let's find these men together."

Cris remained silent for a moment, before finally nodding, squeezing her hand once, and then releasing it. "I will need to bring you ladies up to date with the information we have already uncovered."

Amelia sat back, stunned, as Cris related the tale of the Dark Lords. She found it hard to believe that such corruptness, such immense evil, existed in the world. A shiver ran through her as she imagined her own and Emma's fate had they failed to escape their attackers yesterday.

"Amie?" Cris bent toward her. "Are you sure you're up to this?"

She nodded, forcing herself to remain strong.

"Have you notified the magistrate?" Aunt Patricia asked.

"No." Cris shook his head. "At this point all we have is information about a group of men who practiced despicable acts years ago."

"It could still be of value to them," Beatrice pointed out. "Surely they would be able to see the similarities between the two cases."

"There is no connection between the Dark Lords and your attackers, though. Henley, Stevens, and Baskins are old men. No court would believe they were capable of chasing Amie down." Cris lifted a shoulder. "I'm not even sure if *I* believe they're capable of it."

"Where does that leave us?" Deanna asked.

"Amelia and Emma were chased down in a public street. What will happen next?"

"Nothing," Cris said firmly, "because none of you are to leave this house until we find those men." He looked sternly at Amelia. "You were foolish to go shopping after your ordeal at the opera."

"Yes, I was," she admitted, feeling guilty. "I can only apologize to all of you, especially Emma, once again. I thought that we'd be safe on a public street in daylight. Especially since we brought two footmen with us. However, they'd disappeared before we emerged from the shop. What happened to them and to our carriage driver?"

Cris slid a glance at Hubert.

Amelia felt a knot in her throat. "What happened to them?"

"I'm sorry," Cris said, shaking his head.

Owen's features were grim. "All three were found dead in a nearby alley."

"Though they were only hired a few weeks ago, I have arranged for the care of their families," Cris assured her.

"Dear Lord," Amelia whispered, a wave of dizziness threatening to overtake her.

"The men who were after Amie and Emma are murderers." Camilla finished her statement with a sob.

"I'm glad you hurt them."

The fierceness in Emma's voice made Amelia smile. "So am I, Emma. So am I."

Cris straightened, moving back around the desk,

taking his seat. "I've sent servants to watch the residences of Henley, Baskins, and Stevens. Two at each house. The servants have instructions to notify me if they leave their homes. Also, the servants are to watch for any bandages that may be masking the wound Amelia inflicted on her attacker."

"So, now we wait?" Amelia asked.

Cris shook his head. "Those are just precautions. In the meantime, Hubert, Owen, and I have arranged for Stevens, Baskins, and Henley to meet each other at Henley's. When they are all together, I can see if any of them has an injury to his face."

"What have I been telling you all along, girl? You're a smart one," Hubert boomed, pride in his words. "You marked one of them where they can't hide it. You've made it easy to pick out the bastard."

"Hubert!" exclaimed Aunt Patricia. "Please, the girls are present."

Hubert spread out his hands. "What? What did I say wrong, Patsy? Was it the word *bastard?*"

Aunt Patricia rolled her eyes.

"Would you prefer if I asked your uncle to stay here with you?" Cris looked directly at Amelia, his gaze gentle and caring.

Amelia felt the warmth radiate within her. "We'll be fine here," she assured Cris.

He agreed immediately. "The house is secure and I'll put the servants on guard when we set our trap."

"It's hard for me to believe that Henley, Baskins, and Stevens would sink to this level," Owen admitted. "I knew they were reprobates, but I had no idea as to the depths of their depravity."

Aunt Patricia stood, shaking her head. "It is a shame all three of those men don't bear the marks of their true nature. It is quite a legacy to pass on to their children."

Amelia noticed how still Cris became, his widening gaze shifting onto Hubert, then Owen. It was as if all three men were communicating silently. Each one nodded in turn.

Cris rose slowly. "Aunt Patricia, you are brilliant."

She lifted a hand to her chest. "What makes you say that?"

"You have solved the crime with one word."

Aunt Patricia shook her head, confused. "What word?"

Amelia rose to her feet, her eyes gleaming as she faced Cris to whisper the answer: "Legacy."

25

"There goes Stevens's whelp into the trap." Satisfaction filled Cris's voice. "All three are now in Henley's house. Right now, they're trying to figure out who sent them the notes asking for a meeting."

"Downright sneaky plan, Dukey." Hubert slapped Cris on the back. "I'm sorry I didn't think of it."

Cris kept his attention focused on the house in front of him. "The servants said the elder Henley left over an hour ago. That would leave the three offspring of Baskins, Stevens, and Henley inside alone." Anticipation curled inside him. He'd left Amelia home with her sisters and his aunt safe and protected, and now he would face her assailants. They would pay for daring to harm Amie. "Let's go."

Owen and Hubert followed closely behind Cris as he approached the town house. The same butler answered the knock on the door, but Cris didn't wait for him to invite them in. Instead, he pushed his hand flat against the plane of the wood, shoving the butler back into the hallway.

"What is the meaning of—?" The butler fell silent as Cris angled toward him. The memory of Cris's hands about the man's throat must have stopped him short.

"Where are they?"

The butler's mouth worked open and closed but no sound came out. Cris turned away from him, striding down the hallway, glancing into every room. He came upon a closed door and shoved it open.

Three pairs of eyes shifted onto him. Cris stepped into the room, a surge of primeval rage filling him. Carefully, he looked at each of the three men. When his gaze fell upon Stevens's heir, Cris lost control. The large bandage on his cheek gave proof to the truth. Fury, fueled by the fear of losing Amelia, pulsed through Cris as he launched himself at Stevens, wrapping his hands about the younger man's neck. He'd make the bastard pay, he thought in a haze of fury. He'd strangle all the evil thoughts out of the dissolute heir.

Baskins and Henley stood, intent on fleeing, when Hubert stepped into the study. "Now where are you gentlemen off to, hmmm?"

Owen moved over to Cris, who held a now reddened Stevens in a chokehold. "Do you mean to kill him?"

Cris heard Owen in the dim recesses of his consciousness, rage having taken over his thoughts. He held in his hands the man who attacked Amie, who threatened her life, the man who could have taken everything of worth from him. Cris squeezed tighter.

Owen laid a hand on Cris's arm. "While I wouldn't mind, you need to remember that if you kill him, it will bring the law down on you."

Cris didn't care. He hungered for vengeance.

"The problem with that is you might end up in jail," Owen continued casually. "Think of poor Amelia, left alone, wasting away with love for you."

Images of Amie shimmered in his mind. He'd known her all his life, but it felt as if only recently he'd actually begun to see her—as a friend, as a woman, as a wife. Was destroying this refuse worth ruining his life with Amie?

There was only one answer.

Reason cooled his mind and loosened his hands. Slowly, Cris released his hold on Stevens. The younger man drew in great gulps of air, clutching at his chest. Part of Cris was sorry Owen calmed him down before he'd finished Stevens off.

Cris stepped back, removing himself from temptation. He turned toward the other two men, a fresh wave of anger capturing him. It was a struggle for him to contain it.

"It . . . it was only a game," Henley began, thrusting his trembling fingers through his hair. "We . . . we would have returned her to you and we didn't mean any real harm with those rumors. It was all just for sport."

"Shut your mouth," yelled Baskins, his blond hair flying out as he spun toward his companion. "The less you say, the less he'll know."

"Oh, I believe you'll be quite surprised by how much I already know about you and this sordid club of yours," Cris spat out. He didn't bother to mention that he'd assumed it was the *elder* Henley who had started all the rumors. "I also know that your fathers started these perversities. And, being true sons, you followed in their footsteps, I see."

"All for the thrill of the hunt," rasped Stevens, a cocky grin on his face.

Cris lunged toward him, but Owen held him back. "Easy, now, Crispin. I'm not sure I could stop you if you went at him again." Owen glanced at Stevens. "Nor am I sure I'd even want to."

Cris's restraint was hard won. He looked back at Henley, the most talkative one of the group. "Why?"

Henley shrugged, his expression tight. "You know how it is, Merrick. Same old balls, same old people, same old events. Nothing exciting. Nothing different." He nodded at Stevens and Baskins. "We'd grown up hearing stories of our fathers' escapades, of their adventures, and we knew we'd found the answer to relieve our boredom."

"So you decided to resurrect the Dark Lords," Cris surmised. "That was your first mistake." He leaned forward onto the settee separating him from Henley. "Your second was spreading the rumors about me." His fingers dug into the cushion. "But when you dared to go after Amelia, you made your *last* mistake."

Henley shook beneath the dark promise in Cris's voice. "You don't know that we went after her because she belonged to you," he said quickly.

"That doesn't mean spit! If it wasn't one of my girls, it would have been someone else's," Hubert shouted, reaching out to clout Baskins on the arm.

"I wasn't the one who admitted to it," protested Baskins as he rubbed his arm.

"You're so guilty you stink with it." Hubert moved to smack Baskins again, but the younger man darted out of the way.

"You can't touch us . . . even with your knowledge." Stevens straightened, dropping his hands from his chest. "We didn't do anything to her."

The *yet* at the end of his sentence was clear. Cris shifted closer. "She's home at this moment, covered in bruises and scrapes."

"Well, she stabbed poor Stevens there with a pin," Baskins replied, picking up on Stevens's lead. "And the hellion knocked boxes onto Henley and me. We fared worse from the encounter than she did."

Cris remembered all too vividly how Amelia had sobbed as she told her story, reliving each horrible moment of her ordeal. Baskins's dismissal of his actions enraged Cris further. He shook with the effort it took to suppress his fury. "I should just kill you all where you stand and be done with it."

Stevens sneered at Cris. "You can't touch us, Merrick. You've got no proof that it was us."

Cris thought about the abrasions on Amelia's neck that this man had caused and wanted to smash the words from Stevens's mouth.

"He's right," Owen murmured to Cris. It was clear from Owen's expression that he hated agreeing with Stevens. "If we bring in the magistrate and charge them, their fathers will be able to buy their freedom. These three would be set free in a matter of hours. It would also be difficult to prove that they were the ones who had killed your servants. I don't believe they'd be sent to jail."

Cris saw all too clearly the glimmer of arrogance in all three sets of eyes. "I wasn't planning on doing anything so above board, Owen." He kept his tone low and smooth. "I've devised a far more effective way of dealing with our Dark Lords."

Hubert eyed Cris. "I'm liking you more and more, Duke. Are you *sure* you don't have good, solid merchant blood in you?"

Cris flicked a glance at Hubert. "Perhaps somewhere down the line there's a drop or two," he lied smoothly.

"I *knew* it!" Hubert crowed, before shaking a finger at Henley, Baskins, and Stevens. "You'd better start praying to your Dark Lord now because all merchants know how to deal with riffraff." He leaned forward. "We make them disappear."

Cris nodded as if he were considering Hubert's idea to simply make them vanish. He wanted to make these men sweat, to imagine their worst nightmare had come true, to pay them back even in a small measure for the hell they'd put Amelia and her sisters through. Cris began to toy with them. "I believe we could arrange for that to happen. After all, no one but the butler knows we're here."

"We could take care of him too," Owen offered.

"True," Cris agreed. "But where would we dump the bodies?"

"I've got a good friend who captains a boat," Hubert suggested. "He'd drop them over the side when they were out to sea. No questions asked."

"Y-y-you can't do that," Henley stammered. "We're lords of the realm."

Cris narrowed his eyes. "Perhaps you should have thought of that little fact before you decided to terrorize innocent ladies."

Baskins shook with genuine fear, his brave façade gone. "Please, please don't kill us," he choked.

"Don't be a fool," Stevens snarled. "They wouldn't dare kill us."

Cris slammed both hands on the back of the settee, leaning forward. "You don't know me very well then, Stevens. I could kill you as easily as you killed those footmen. No, on second thought, I'd kill you slowly, drawing out the pain, making you feel each torture I inflict on your body." He lowered his voice until it was barely a whisper. "Do you have any idea how many parts of the human body can be broken before you beg for mercy and a swift death?" His fury swirled inside of him, bloodlust rising. "Neither do I, but I'm willing to find out. Are you?"

Stevens kept his disdainful expression in place,

but it was clear from the way his eyes darted away that Cris had touched fear in him.

"Please, don't kill us," Baskins begged, tears streaming down his face. "We didn't mean to kill those footmen. They just fought harder than we'd expected. It was an accident."

A sound of disgust escaped Owen. "You kill three men and it just happened." He looked at Cris. "They deserve to die."

"Can I kill one of them?" Hubert asked eagerly. "It's been many, many years since I've dirtied my hands like that, but I'm sure I'd remember how after a few tries."

Cris tilted his head to the side, fully enjoying the way they'd destroyed the trio. Baskins was sobbing uncontrollably now and Henley had buried his face in his hands, shaking his head back and forth. Only Stevens still looked at them, but even his cocky air was gone, washed away with a fine serving of abject terror.

Vengeance was indeed sweet.

Cris remained silent for a long moment, allowing each man to savor the tainted flavor of fear. Finally, he said, "The best course might be to see if these men are able to disappear by themselves."

Henley looked up from his hands, the hope in his eyes only making him more pathetic. "I could do that," he said earnestly. "If you let me go, I could disappear from London and you'd never see me again."

Cris shook his head. "Not good enough. All of England. I want you on the Continent or even the

Americas. I don't care where the hell you go, but I never want you to set foot in England again."

Henley readily agreed. "I can be gone tonight."

"Me too," Baskins interjected, wiping the tears from his eyes. "Let me go and I'll collect my money and a few of my things and be off. You'll never see me in England again."

Cris looked at Hubert. "I don't know. What do you think?"

"Kill them," Hubert replied flatly. "Then you'll be sure that they'll never set foot on English soil again."

"Owen?" Cris asked, turning to him. "What's your vote?"

Owen rubbed his chin, looking at the three men. "As much as I'd love to dump their bodies in the ocean, I think we'd avoid an inquiry into their disappearance if they were seen elsewhere on the Continent."

Cris punched the back of the settee. "Blast. I was looking forward to seeing them bleed."

Henley sat up. "You mean you'll let us go?"

"Yes," Cris said, hiding his satisfaction over the outcome of this confrontation. He hadn't been willing to kill them, regardless of how much he craved just that. No, this was the perfect solution. Deny the bastards their heritage, their homeland.

It would be a Hell on earth for them.

"Do you agree to the terms, Stevens?" Cris asked.

Stevens nodded, even as hatred glowed from his eyes. "Yes."

Elation crashed through Cris. He had defeated

the men who threatened Amelia. He drew his features into the harshest expression he could manage. "Remember, if I see you in England any time in my lifetime, I will hunt you down and kill you. Slowly and brutally."

"And I'll get to help," Owen added.

Hubert wasn't to be left out. "As will I."

Cris straightened. "I'm almost praying one of you is foolish enough to come back. I would *love* to track one of the Dark Lords down, to see how well the hunter becomes the prey."

26

The Bradford crest shone brightly on the carriage door as it rounded the corner near Hubert's town house. Amelia jumped down from her perch at the windowsill and raced out the door and down the steps, throwing herself into Cris's welcoming arms as soon as he descended from the conveyance.

"You're home," she murmured against his neck, gripping him tighter as relief overwhelmed her. "You're safe."

Cris hugged her closer. "Yes, and now you and your sisters are safe as well."

Amelia trembled with the strength of her emotions—relief, love, satisfaction, and need.

"Why don't we go on inside and see if we can't find someone to welcome *us* home like that?" Hubert blustered.

Amelia lifted her head to smile at her uncle. "I'm sure you'll be able to find any number of young ladies inside willing to thank you properly for all you've done."

Hubert waved his hand in dismissal. "I know that. I was fancying a hug from my girl Patsy."

Owen laughed, slapping Hubert on the shoulder. "Let's go, old man. I don't know if your Patsy will provide you with a hug, but I'm fairly confident that I'll be able to collect one from Beatrice."

Hubert nodded slowly. "I'm sure she'll be more than willing to toss herself into your arms." He paused for a moment. "What did you say your title was again?"

The front door closed on Owen's booming laughter.

Amelia lowered her head upon Cris's shoulder once more. "Is it really over?"

Cris shifted her back in his arms so he could gaze into her eyes. "They admitted everything, even the murders. We made sure that each one of them boarded a ship, never to return to England again. Stevens is bound for America, whereas Henley and Baskins are going on a lifelong tour of the Continent. We even had them write letters to their respective families so questions wouldn't be asked."

"It doesn't seem fair that they got away with so much," Amelia said.

"I know, but it is the best way to deal with them." The muscles in Cris's arms tightened. "When I saw the bandage on Stevens's face, I almost killed him," he admitted.

Amelia shivered in his arms. "Part of me wishes you had ended all three of their miserable lives."

Cris smiled gently at her. "You always were a bloodthirsty little thing, weren't you?"

"No more so than you, it seems."

"True," Cris admitted, his smile turning into a grin. "We are well matched, Amie."

Amelia's heart did a little flip at his words. "I can't thank you enough, Cris, for all you've done for my family."

He frowned at her. "There is no need to thank me."

"I believe there is." Amelia gazed up into his face. "I want to let you know how grateful I am."

"I've had enough misunderstandings between us, Amelia." Cris grabbed her hand and led her toward his carriage. "We are going to my home where we can finally discuss our relationship."

"We can't leave," she protested even as Cris helped her into the carriage. "My family needs—"

"Your family is fine. *I* need you now." Cris sat across from her as the carriage pulled away. "For days now, you've been avoiding me and it's time it all stopped."

"I promise I won't do that any longer, Cris." Amelia looked at him.

"Why is that? What could possibly have—" Cris broke off his questions, raising both his hands. "This is not the place for this discussion. Let us wait until we reach my home." And with that, he fell silent.

As soon as they reached his town house, Cris leapt from the carriage, reaching in to help Amelia out, before striding into his home, tugging her behind him. Cris strode down the hall and into his library.

After shutting the door behind them, Cris turned to face Amelia, grasping both of her hands. "We need to discuss what's happened between us—all of it. The distance that's grown between us is driving me mad."

Amelia pulled away from him. "I'm sorry that you've been hurt, Cris, but I thought I needed time to overcome my infatuation with you." She rubbed her hands on her arms. "Did you know that I used to fantasize about you when I was a child?"

"Amelia, I don't see what that has to do with us now."

"The only reason I mention it, Cris, is because when you first returned to Dovedale, you reawakened all of my girlish dreams about you."

Cris stiffened. "I'm no knight in shining armor, Amie."

She laughed softly at his protest. "Ah, but you are, Cris. Your sense of honor, your need to protect, is the stuff of legends."

"Amie," he began in a gruff voice. "I don't deserve . . ."

"What don't you deserve, Cris? My admiration, because you have it, or my loyalty, for you have that as well." She paused, taking a deep breath. "And you have my love."

Cris rubbed his face in his hands. "I can't be your knight, Amie. I'd only be doomed to fail."

His head jerked up at her laughter. "Don't worry, Cris, I've outgrown my childhood dreams." She moved closer to him. "I've come to know you as the man you've become . . . and I've fallen in love with you. You, Cris, not the boy of my fantasies."

Cris opened his mouth, but she cut him off.

"Please, don't feel that you have to say anything. I know you have no desire to love anyone; you've always been perfectly honest with me." She hid the sadness caused by her own words. "I just needed to tell you how I felt, especially since you raced to Emma's rescue."

"You don't know anything," he rasped, reaching out to clasp her shoulders, drawing her up until she was pressed against him. "I rescued Emma for *you*."

Amelia's heart bumped against her ribs until she calmed her hope. "What do you mean?"

Cris's fingers tightened. "If you had asked me to battle a dragon for you, I would have done it, Amie. Don't you understand that?" He gazed down at her. "I did it all because I love you."

Amelia dared not believe what she heard. "I know that you love me as a friend, Cris, but—"

A sound of disgust rippled from him as Cris released her, resuming his pacing. "Are you going to tell me *how* I love you? I didn't know what love was, so how could I know that I felt it? Lord, Amie, things have been changing so fast, so drastically, between us. I just needed a little time to grow accustomed to the idea of loving you as a woman as well as a friend."

"You shouldn't need time to know whether or

not you love me," Amie whispered, afraid to believe him.

"But I did, Amie." Cris stopped right in front of her again. "I needed time to realize that the reason I couldn't stop thinking of you, wanting you, was because I loved you." He gazed down at her. "I love the way you see everything in such a wonderful light, making even the dullest of parties fun. I love the way you are so loyal to those you love. Most of all, I love the way you embrace life, enjoying it to the fullest."

Amelia couldn't believe her ears. Could it be true? Dare she entrust her heart to him?

But Cris was far from finished. "Ever since you turned my world around with your kiss, I haven't been able to stop thinking about you. I was thoroughly confused by all of the emotions you roused within me."

Cris clasped her shoulders. "But I'm not confused any longer. I want to grow old with you, Amie. I want to have children with you. As insane as your sisters have driven me, they've also become an important part of my life and I love them as if they were my own flesh and blood."

Amelia didn't know what to say. She'd never imagined that this dream, this wonderful, incredible, stupendous dream could come true.

"When I'm with you, I see magic in the world again." Cris reached out, bringing her hand up to his chest, pressing it against his heart. "Marry me, my wonderful friend, Amie."

She wasn't sure if she would be able to stand all

of the happiness flooding her. "Yes, oh, yes," she whispered brokenly. His proposal came from love, need, and, yes, even friendship. This proposal came from his soul.

Her long-held, fairy-tale dreams came to life as Cris pledged himself to her. Her lips trembled as she pressed against his hardness, his strength, and gave him her heart.

"Amie," Cris murmured, reaching for her. "My love."

Eagerly, Amelia went into his arms.

"Let me love you, Amie." His entreaty was followed by sweet kisses along the curve of her neck.

Amelia released her pent-up desire, arching toward him in need. "Please, oh, please," she whispered.

He needed no further encouragement. Sweeping her up into his arms, Cris took the stairs swiftly, and brought her into his bedroom. He kicked the door shut behind him, before allowing her to slide down his body.

Amelia stood still as Cris leaned forward, his mouth playing with her features, feathering over her eyes, brushing down the line of her nose, flirting with the curve of her lips. His hands played over her back, moving to the fastenings on her dress.

Amelia leaned into Cris, inhaling his unique male scent, still unable to believe that he was hers. Now and forever. He eased the dress from her shoulders, pushing it over her hips, before allowing it to puddle at her feet. Amelia quivered beneath his touch as he removed the rest of her clothes, finally lifting her chemise over her head.

Then she stood before her love, bare and vulnerable—and she felt beautiful. Amelia burned beneath his molten gaze, every inch of her skin heating from his gaze. She yearned for him. "Please," Amelia whispered, reaching up to tug on his cravat.

A sensual smile curved upon Cris's face as he began to remove his clothes. As his body was revealed, Amelia felt herself grow more aroused. The curve of his muscles, the fine line of his form, combined to create the man of her dreams. Cris's broad shoulders and well-developed chest made Amelia catch her breath.

His manhood jutted boldly out of a thatch of dark hair, making Amelia flush with shyness. Yet, she didn't look away. Slowly, she allowed her gaze to travel over the length of his body, until finally she lifted her eyes to meet his.

Her love, her Cris, was magnificent.

Amelia ached for his touch. The hunger that sculpted sensual lines on Cris's face created a liquid tingle between her legs.

Cris's hand shook as he reached out for her. "You're so damn beautiful, Amie," he groaned.

A heartfelt moan slipped from Amelia at the incredible sensation of his hot flesh against her skin, his hands sliding around her waist, one moving downward to press her hips to his hardness, the other upward to hold her head steady for his kiss. All shyness was lost beneath Cris's mouth, his tongue plunging deeply to claim what was given freely, joyously.

His hand tugged at her hair, tilting her head backward, before his mouth moved from hers, across her cheeks, down her throat, and onto her aching breasts. Amelia allowed her head to fall back, arching into Cris's hardness, as he rained kisses all over her flesh.

"Cris," Amelia murmured, love swelling inside her, intensifying the sensations he was creating with his caresses.

Cris trailed his fingertips all over her body, stroking a burning need within her. His thumbs glided up the column of her neck, gently tormenting her with his touch. His fingers swirled around her shoulders, skimmed over the tops of her breasts, lightly, teasingly, until she was sure she'd go mad with hunger.

A sharp moan broke from her when his hands finally slid downward, cupping her breasts, his palms pressing against the pointed crests. She swayed into his grasp, moving side to side, the friction increasing her excitement. His hands slid around her, pulling her into his body once more.

Cris's head dipped down to capture her willing mouth as he moved their entwined bodies closer to the bed. He laved her bottom lip before breaking off their kiss. Gently, he lifted Amelia into his arms, treating her as if she were a fragile treasure, laying her down on the bed, before joining her. He entwined his fingers with hers, lifting her arms over her head, as he feasted upon her moist lips.

Cris traced the outline of her body as he moved downward, sculpting her breasts into hard points of desire, nibbling at the curve of her waist until she shifted upward, in silent beckoning. She was aglow with the sensations pulsating through her. But when Cris began to kiss her thighs, a flicker of apprehension struck Amelia.

"No," Amelia whispered, suddenly uncertain.

"Shhh. It's all right, love." Cris curved his arms underneath her knees, his body shifting between her legs. His gaze burned up the length of her body, penetrating her insecurity with his passion. "You're so beautiful, Amelia. I want to taste you, all of you. I want there to be nothing between us, no room for shyness, no thoughts of hesitation. Trust me," he said, his hot breath rushing over the pouting lips of her womanhood. Slowly Cris bent to press a gentle kiss high on her inner thigh. "Trust me."

His breath whispered over her, sending pulsating anticipation throughout her entire body. Amelia stopped fighting her own desire. She didn't know where Cris would take her, but she would trust him. Her head fell back on the bed and her eyes closed, as she waited breathlessly for his caress.

Cris gifted Amelia with his mouth. Sensual pleasure rushed through her at his touch, bringing a cry of unknown delights to her lips. Her back arched up off of the bed as she slid her fingers into his hair, unconsciously pressing Cris closer. The most unimagined colors of ecstasy swirled inside her as Cris drank deeply of her essence, creating a maelstrom of desire within her.

Finally, Cris pulled away, kissing his way back up her body. Amelia slipped her hands from his hair onto his back as he levered up onto his hands, his hardness poised at her womanhood.

"My Amie," Cris whispered and with one slow push, he joined them in the most elemental way, melding two bodies into one.

The sweeping sensation of overwhelming fulfillment made Amelia gasp as she clutched at Cris, the only solid point in her spinning world. Cris's features tightened into a mask of masculine desire as he began to move within her, sliding into her again and again, driving them both higher, pushing them faster, harder, closer to that pinnacle of blinding light dancing just beyond them.

Amelia watched the emotions play over Cris's face, certain they were reflected on her own, as she moved with him, racing toward the ultimate satisfaction, wanting, needing, craving all he was giving her, hungry for more.

Stars burst to life within her soul, a cry ripped from her as she crashed over the precipice of desire. Cris drove into her one last time, a groan rumbling from his chest, as he gave himself over to ecstasy. He remained arched above her, the muscles in his arms shaking, before finally lowering himself onto her body.

"I love you, Amie." His whisper was raw with spent passion.

Amelia stroked her hands down Cris's back, feelings of love swelling within her heart.

She was complete.

Everything she'd ever wished for had come true. Her sisters were safe and their futures secure. In all of her childhood dreams, she'd never imagined love could be so powerful, so wonderful. Amelia hugged Cris to her, all of her emotions swelling at one incredible thought.

Her heart's dearest wishes had finally come true.

Epilogue

Dovedale, England
two months later

"So, tell me. What do you think of your wedding gift?" Aunt Patricia gestured toward the painting she'd presented to Amelia and Cris.

Amelia studied the painting, searching hopelessly for something positive to say about it.

Cris obviously felt no such compunction. "It's as awful as all the others, Aunt Patricia." He hugged his aunt. "We shall treasure it for all time."

"I knew you would," Aunt Patricia said with a laugh.

"What do you think of my fine gifts?" Hubert interrupted.

Amelia eyed the matching crowns Hubert had given to her and Cris. "They're unique, Uncle Hubert," she finally said.

"Try one on," he urged, picking up the bejeweled crown he'd had fashioned specifically for her.

Amelia looked to Cris for help, but he merely shrugged, leaving her to answer. "I'm afraid it might be a bit heavy for me. However, I believe Crispin would enjoy wearing his."

With a flourish Cris accepted the crown and placed it on his head. "What do you think, Amie? If I wear this back to our wedding celebration, do you think it will become the rage?"

"Perhaps. Why don't we try it and see?"

His eyes gleamed. "After you, of course."

"Clever, Merrick, very clever," she replied, grinning back.

"Sounds like a wonderful idea to me," Hubert said. "What do you think, Patsy?"

Aunt Patricia placed her hands on her hips. "What I think, Hubert, is that if you don't stop addressing me by that horrid name I'll have to start calling you Hubbie."

Hubert's eyes went wide for a moment before he burst into a roar of laughter, bending over from the force of his amusement. "Patsy and Hubbie. That sounds like a pair if ever I heard of one." He walked over to Patricia, offering her his arm. "Lady Patsy, will you do this merchant the honor of a dance?"

Aunt Patricia dipped into a curtsy before accepting his proffered arm. "It would be my pleasure, you odious man."

Hubert patted her hand as he led her from the room. "Ah, Patsy, you do know how to sweet talk a man, don't you?"

Amelia leaned against Cris, laughter weakening her legs. "Those two as a couple. Lord help us now." She looked up at her new husband. "You can take off that ridiculous crown now."

Cris shrugged, shifting it onto his head. "I'm getting accustomed to it, Amie. Don't you think I wear it well?"

"Shall we begin to call you King Crispin?"

"I believe Prince Cris will do just as well, don't you?"

"Most certainly, your highness," she said, dipping into a curtsy.

As she raised up into a standing position, Cris lifted one eyebrow, glaring down his nose at her. "Is that as low as you can curtsy? I believe my position commands you to bow to the floor."

Amelia twined her arms about his neck. "How about if I kiss you instead?"

Cris grinned. "That works as well."

Amelia lost herself in their kiss. They'd been married less than three hours ago in the small chapel in Dovedale and her heart thrilled at the knowledge that she was now Cris's wife in name and in love.

"Amie," Cris murmured. "My wife."

He tilted his head to trail his mouth over her neck . . . and proceeded to send the crown tumbling off his head. It landed with a loud crack, causing Amelia to spring out of Cris's arms. The two of them stood there, both breathing rapidly, both flushed with desire. They glanced down at the crown. One edge of it was dented.

Cris shook his head. "They just don't make crowns like they used to," he sighed.

Amelia laughed brightly at his quip as Cris bent

down and retrieved it. He placed it next to Amelia's crown, shifting it until the dent was in the back.

"There. I doubt if Hubert will even notice."

"My, you *are* in an optimistic mood today."

Cris pulled her into his arms, spinning her around the room. "It happens to be my wedding day. What else could I be?"

Her heart smiled at the sentiment. "What else indeed?"

Amelia melted into Cris, allowing her love for this man to soften every inch of her body.

"Here you both are! We've been looking all over." Deanna's exclamation was an unwelcome interruption. Amelia intended to simply ignore them and pray they went away. Tonight all she wanted was to enjoy her husband. Her sisters could sort out their troubles by themselves for one day.

Cris lifted his head long enough to mutter, "Go away, ladies."

As he began to lower his mouth again, intent on their kiss, Deanna interrupted louder this time. "This is serious, Cris. Camilla has decided she wants to marry Lord Appleton."

Cris's head jerked upward. *"Appleton?"* He glared at Camilla. "What do you want with that disreputable wastrel?"

"He is not!" Camilla insisted. "He's a fine gentleman and I'm desperately in love with him."

Cris released Amelia, turning toward her younger sister. "In love with him, are you? Tell me, Camilla, where does he live, what is his family like?"

"That sort of information doesn't matter one bit," she replied in a lofty voice. "Our souls communicate. We have no need for such trivial matters."

Deanna snorted. "What drivel."

Camilla glared at her sister. "You wouldn't understand."

"I'm afraid I don't understand either," Emma interrupted softly. "You've only met him twice. How much can you know about him?" She pointed toward Amelia and Cris. "Amie knew Cris for years and years before they wed. They knew each other so well that it was an easy match."

"Their way might not be the best way," Camilla stated firmly.

Amelia thought of all the heartache she'd experienced during her rocky courtship. Still, Emma had woven her romance with Cris into a saga of fairy-tale proportions. Amelia warmed inside at the thought. There was nothing at all wrong with fairy tales. After all, look at her. She'd eventually married the prince.

"You need to find your own way, Camilla," said Amelia, finally. "Still, it might be advisable if you can make sure that you will be able to speak with your husband. It's a bit difficult to depend on communication of the souls when you want to ask a tedious question like where to live."

"That is *not* important." Camilla crossed her arms and lifted her chin.

"Ah," Amelia said softly. "So it doesn't matter what happens to your piano? Nor would you mind giving up all your lovely clothes? Oh, and your piano lessons too?" She shrugged. "Perhaps not. After all, we lived for years in poverty. You are quite accustomed to it, aren't you, Camilla?"

Camilla's eyes grew wider with each word Amelia spoke. Her color drained at the questions. Amelia hid her smile. She knew quite well that she'd made her point. Camilla wouldn't be running off to marry anyone anytime soon.

Pleased with her gentle guidance, Amelia turned to her husband, "I believe they sounded a waltz."

Cris stepped forward, clasping Amelia's arm. "I believe this dance is mine."

She laid her hand over his. "I believe you are right."

They left the three youngest Ralston sisters bickering in the parlor and headed toward the ballroom.

Cris spun her onto the dance floor, next to Beatrice and Owen. Amelia clung to Cris as she smiled at her sister. When the other couple waltzed by, Amelia looked up at her husband. "Do you think they'll wed?"

"I'm not certain," Cris said briskly. "And I don't care."

Surprise overtook her. "But she's my sister."

"Amelia," Cris began. "This is my wedding day. I couldn't give a fig if one of your sisters ran away with the stable boy."

Amelia slanted a look at him. "Of course, Cris. That is why you took the time to speak with Camilla and let her know a match with Lord Appleton would not be acceptable."

"So, I made one effort and took a few minutes of our wedding day," he remarked. "I would not, however, be willing to give up one moment of our wedding night."

"Oh, then you have a grand plan for later this evening?" she murmured, sensual awareness spinning its alluring web within her.

"My darling Amelia, I have grand plans for you for the rest of your life."

His husky promise filled her with joy, as her golden dreams of youth became a star-filled future of bliss.

Amelia smiled up at her knight. "I'm counting on it." She swayed toward him, their bodies becoming one in movement. "Forever."

Cris kissed her sweetly, his eyes glowing with love. "And they lived happily ever after."

Amelia's laughter swirled around them as he spun her across the dance floor, weaving magic with their love.